THE PIANO TEACHER

You help me
to be brighter in the
morning!
Your CBS morning!

Please check out my first
published fiction story I wrote on a
dream I had 7 years ago...
more to come!

That's when you have time!...

Sincerely
Stephanie
Jacobs

THE PIANO TEACHER

STEPHANIE JACKS

Charleston, SC
www.PalmettoPublishing.com

The Piano Teacher
Copyright © 2022 by Stephanie Jacks

Cover art created by my firstborn grandson Kamai Jacks.

First Edition

Hardcover : 978-1-68515-917-7
Paperback: 978-1-68515-918-4
eBook: 978-1-68515-919-1

TABLE OF CONTENTS

THE MEET

I MET JOHN AT a Social event.

We loved John. John was intellectual, charming and full of wisdom and knowledge. You know the *important* wisdom, all about old school wealth and family lines… yea, he knew everything about everybody, well *"everybody that was somebody"* … But when John played the piano, something would happen to us, our Soul would feel somethin, somethin amazing that felt as if we just drank fine wine or had been touched by an Angel, it soothed our Soul and it sure felt good. John was *"old wealth"* in many ways, he was a blessing to our lives.

It was an exclusive Black tie affair in the Ballroom of the Ritz Carlton. Grand Pianos, beautiful gowns and who's who of the Philadelphia Social circle. The best champagne and Michelin Star Hors d'oeuvres, maybe with a slightly "privileged" feel.. but not as if we were snobs, we were here for a Charity fundraiser event, although we were certainly feeding our flesh in the meanwhile…

Whatever our reasons were for our various Social events, it felt great getting all dressed up in our black and white and getting the best of the "Arts," and of course, giving back to those less fortunate..

The Arts.. fine spirits, culinary designers and musical geniuses. That was what John was, a musical genius, very talented, able to reach souls.. I was very impressed with the way John played the piano. It was exactly what we needed.

It seems everyone's life has been challenged lately and that was across the board in all walks of life. The devil doesn't care who you are. What's this world coming to? Who knows, anyway, after experiencing what felt like ultimate pleasuring of the soul and feeling as if I needed a cigarette afterwards, I decided to introduce myself to this distinguished talented gentleman. Hello, my name is Stacia, I really enjoyed the piece you played, you got a cigarette, ha, I laughed with a flirtatious note.. I'm just kidding, but I loved the way you played that Piano.

Do you give Piano lessons? I asked as if I were joking. "Yes, as a matter of fact I do. I am a music teacher at the University, but I recently decided to take on a few students to give private lessons to. My time is very limited, so I can only choose the extreme few that are what I consider to be geniuses." Oh, that's great, I said. My grandson plays some, he has a unique talent. He's gifted, but his gift could really blossom with teachings from a master such as you... "I would love to meet him," said John. Really? I would greatly appreciate that, I said. I've been looking around for some professional lessons for him for some time now. With teachings such as yours he could really take off.

Over the next few months John and I became very good friends. John became a fixture in our home and we loved having him. He even got my husband and I to invest in a Baby Grand Piano. That beautiful White shiny Steinway absolutely set our top floor Condo Suite off. It was refurbished but still gorgeous. Besides, although we weren't poor, we wanted to instill the value of money in our grandchildren. That piano was a great investment, it played like a Grand Piano that was brand new for a lot less money. It was gorgeous and went well with the Vintage Ebony and Ivory floor tile in our Condo. John and that Grand Piano was an addition to our lives that felt Heaven sent. Life felt great and life was grand.

Our grandchildren would stay with us often and our home was filled with love. John loved children but never had any of his own. His wife had died many years earlier and although they didn't have any children of their own, their mission had been to reach and teach underprivileged children all over the country. That was another passion we shared, our mission to give the children within our reach access to all types of music and dance and indigenous foods. Expose them to the wonderful world of *Arts* and the education and background history of different cultures. Exposure to Arts, music and culture not only fine tunes a young mind to be able to learn better academically, but the Arts help us to express ourselves more clearly and give our minds a vivid imagination and a more creative direction in life. John and I shared these values and passions in life. The bottom line is that we ALL absolutely need the Arts in our lives to help grow our minds and become the best we can be in life. After all, it seems like life today is surely different from what we experienced as a child. Even though we didn't have cell phones or all the other technology, life was much richer...these poor kids today don't even know what they're missing. Humm...The world has certainly changed and with all the new and exciting things to make our lives better, the world certainly doesn't seem *no better.*

My husband Bryson is a little on the lazy side. He doesn't want to do much in life but sit in that damn chair and watch TV since he retired from the NFL. He mostly watches Sports these days, but he loves to occasionally watch those *Action Jack* flix like Rambo or Rocky. I get sick of that shit. I guess maybe he has a thing for Sylvester

Stallone. Anyway,.. Bryson was once the love of my life. He played Professional Football once upon a time and was the most handsome romantic gentleman I had ever met. He had dark deep eyes, but his eyes were very bright and sparkly. Bryson also had a smile that could be on a Colgate commercial. Just by looking at Bryson, you could see he was special, he had that *it* factor. He was going to be someone in life. He was always low key, but had an absolute zest for life. He had a lot more energy and was fun to be around, he was my best friend. Lately Bryson has become lazy and boring as hell and I just can't take his boring ass *no more*. John ended up pretty much becoming the husband/girlfriend I wish I had in my husband. Yea, I said it. Anyway to say the least he was a great addition to our family. Bryson didn't seem to mind too much, it was a way of letting his ass off the hook of all the things I had been nagging him about for years. The social events Bryson hated to go to, the Plays I wanted to see, the trips I wanted to take, hell, just the life I wanted to live. The life we should be living, just life… I love my husband but I had started to love John too…(not in the way a spouse loves) but in a way that was new to me. I thought John was God sent… Hm, it seems like Bryson started to love John as well.

The children Braya and Branson would stay with us through the weekdays to go to a Private school that was close to the city. Braya was a little angel, she had beautiful black wavy hair that looked like woven silk when she wore her little braided ponytails. And Branson was a gifted well rounded bright eyed kid who loved to learn and would light up like the morning sun when he would tell you all about something he found new and exciting. We loved that they were staying with us. Bryson of course wanted a little buddy to watch football with and teach him all about the game. And little Braya loved anything to do with the Arts, even though she was only 8 she had more fashion sense than most people I knew. I mean the girl knew how to shop and dress, she had a style of her own and knew and rocked her favorite designers. We all loved to eat, we had our favorite restaurants but we also could whip up some designer meals at home too. We wanted our grandchildren to be well rounded by exposing them to finer things in life but at the same time teaching them how to appreciate the simple things in life. Creating memories that are special and unique, like cooking and sharing meals and laughs together, those special times are the things that really matter at the end of the day…after all *"God gets mad when you don't notice the color purple"*…

The children loved John as well, they were always *playing hide and go seek* and other old school games. John had been giving Branson piano lessons and he was playing beautifully. It was like he had been playing for years,… he had an old soul. Although Braya loved the Arts and expressed some interest in Violins, she loved Ballets and fashion shows more. She maybe would tap on the Baby Grand pearly keyboard for a minute when she would walk past it but really wasn't interested in getting Piano lessons from John. But Branson on the other hand was becoming Grand, he stroked those keys like nobody's business and had developed a real feel for the theater. John said he felt Branson was almost ready to give his first performance. Wow, how exciting, we were so proud of what our first born grandson had accomplished in such a small amount of time. Although it was 10 years ago my daughter Andraya gave birth to him, it seemed like yesterday. We watched him look at us threw that gift of a veil over his vibrant blue eyes. We always knew Branson was special, but it took someone as talented as John to be able to show Branson how to bring out what was already instilled in him by God. "Yes!" John said. "He is ready to stroke these keys and turn these snooty bitches out! Let's book the Grand Ballroom and do some Invites!" John was very popular in the elite social circle of the "*Wealthy Philadelphians.*" He knew exactly what they wanted and he could give it to them. Mostly it was making some of these successful beautiful aging women feel spicy and spunky again and full of themselves…some of them a little phony if you ask me, but not all. But whatever, I was also successful but just didn't feel the need to act like it. I had my circle of friends that I grew up with since we were preschool age, also our parents and grandparents had grown up together, we were more like family than friends. I also had what I called business friends or associates, some of whom I have great relationships with and actually would consider them a friend. But I also have business dealing and am in the business circle with some folks I would never consider becoming "BFF"s with. But if we wanted to get the right exposure we knew the "who's who" of who should be on the VIP list. Everything had to be perfect. From the Caterer to the Décor to the Ambience. The talent was in the bag. My lil bigman Branson… I always knew he was special. Now it was our time to show him off. "This is only the beginning"… I can only imagine the heights he could reach, **God puts the right people in your life path at the right time,** I said to myself. It's all about timing and he is an **"on time God!"** Yes, The event planning was going perfectly. The Culinary designer had come up with some excellent cocktails and *two bite* combinations. Keeping in the "*Blacktie and White*" theme, he created a beautiful Espresso Martini with a perfect angelic froth topped with orange marmalade glazed fresh mint leave. It was beautiful. We paired it with a bite size crepe with turkey bacon glazed with spiced orange marmalade, gourmet chocolate shavings and a few crumbles of mascarpone cheese giving the palate something to explore. That was just one of several "drink and bites" we came up with. I also was in the Culinary field and although I hired the best Caterers around I would design my own menus and we would work together on execution of those food flavors and designs. The day had come. We were all so excited. Branson was calm, cool and collected playing a quick video game. Braya was focused on her fashionista debut. My daughter Andraya and her husband Mike were sipping some wine from our collection for special occasions and this certainly was a special day. Before you guys get toasted, I said, I would like to go over some minor details. Bryson was taking forever to get dressed. It was great to see him so excited, he seemed to be his old self lately. He and John actually went to Boyd Brothers to have some custom Black Tie suits made. Lately he and John had been hanging out a little. John could get Bryson to go out to lunch and shop, things that I could not get Bryson to do in years. The only thing Bryson wanted to do was watch TV in that chair. But lately he's been a little happier and motivated, the kids had noticed it too. The old Bryson was re-emerging… Wow, John had reached him in ways that I couldn't. That's okay I guess, as long as his ass gets out of that chair and puts some pep in his step, I'll take it as it comes. John finally showed up looking very handsome and dapper. You are always running late John, grab a glass of wine and go over some notes with Branson. " We have been going over lessons all week, Stacia," John said, "he will be fine." "The best thing he can do is relax and let his God given gift come naturally." John peeped in on Bryson, "you need any help there man?" John asked. "I'll be out in a minute," Bryson replied. Andrea and Mike were in the kitchen doing God knows what, and Braya was scrolling through her phone in her room. Branson was dressed and ready to go and the only one sitting in the living room prepared to go out the door. John sat on the sofa next to Branson and started playfully throwing the pillows at him. I couldn't believe how long Bryson was taking to get dressed so I started down the hall towards the bathroom and I noticed out of the corner of my eye John putting the throw cover from the sofa over he and Bransons' head. Something did not feel right to me. I pulled the cover from over both of them, Branson's pants were not fastened and a look of guilt was on both of their faces. What's going on here!? I said with a look of accusation on my face. "Nothing, what do you think is going on, Stacia?" I don't know but something doesn't feel right to me, I replied. Come in the room with me, Branson, I said. I took my grandson to the guest bedroom and asked him if John had done anything that made him feel uncomfortable in any way and his eyes started to tear up…his face said it all, John had done something to him, I thought. I looked at his pants unfastened and pulled up his shirt to see some scratches on his stomach, I was furious! Did John do this to you? I screamed! "No Mom Mom!" Branson yelled. "What are you talking about, stop pulling on my clothes!" Don't protect him! I said. Deep down inside I had always questioned Johns' sexuality but it was none of my business who or what he did in his personal life. But pedifile I don't do. I will kill without hesitation if I feel you're messing with one of my children. I was horrified. I immediately came out of the bathroom screaming at John, what have you been doing with my grandson John? I said, shaking and upset. I was raging with a range of emotions. My husband finally emerges from the bathroom confused and in shock yelling "what's going on here?" My daughter and son in law came running out of the kitchen towards us as I was approaching John. "It was completely innocent," John said, "I love him and would never hurt these children." Before I knew it I picked up my gold plated letter opener and started to jab John repeatedly. It happened so fast they were all pulling me off yelling this is not the way to handle this, please stop this! This is the way I handle it, I said, as I finally came to an eerie pause… As John laid on my black and white checkered marble floor in a pool of blood, we stared into each other's eyes. He whispered to me, "I will still always love you, please forgive me." I was devastated, what had I done to my friend!? I loved John! Oh my God, what have I done! Although John was laying in a pool of blood he was very much alive with a few puncture wounds I would say. Not that that wasn't serious but he should live I thought. Everyone was yelling and the house was in complete chaos. Just then John started to lose consciousness and out of his hand dropped a green tape dispenser he was holding.

Before I knew it Bryson and Mike had wrapped up Johns' body in the soft persian rug John and I found at an auction. Andraya was crying, cleaning up the blood off the floor, and Branson and Braya were eerily calm and numb. As I watched my daughter scrub the floor as if she just went insane, I was in a state of total disbelief as to what had just happened. This can't be real, I said to myself. We were just happy and excited, actually our happiest day in a very long time. Why did this have to happen? I'm confused, this can't be real, I kept repeating to myself. The room was spinning around and around, the walls were getting smaller. God! I need you now, I screamed! John couldn't be dead could he. I just lost my mind for a moment, I wanted to hurt him not kill him. Why were Bryson and Mike so quick to wrap up his body instead of calling the ambulance. Although I had "jabbed" him with the letter opener, I was willing to admit to what had happened and deal with the consequences, but he was alive... They had quickly carried his body to the back elevator that led to the parking garage and the back alley. Wait, I said in my head, let's get him to the hospital. Although I was saying that to myself, Johns' body was long gone... How could a day that began so brightly turn into an unimaginable dark day in a matter of moments. My best friend, my grandson, all of our lives had changed forever in an instant. There was a knock on the door. We all froze for a moment. Pull it together Stacia, I thought to myself. It felt as if I was waking from a coma as I looked around to make sure all evidence of any turmoil was cleaned up. I noticed my green tape dispenser and a few other items that must have dropped from Johns' pocket on the floor. I quickly grabbed them up, put them in a plastic bag and tied it up. Although Andraya had cleaned up the blood, I noticed the tape dispenser had blood on it. I threw the bag in the closet as I prepared myself to open the door. I straightened up my black dress and took a quick glance in the mirror, you got this Stacia, I said to myself. I peeked through the peephole and saw it was the neighbors from the lower floor. I partially opened the door so as not to let them see inside. "Are you guys on your way to the event?" The neighbor asked. "I know it's early but we wanted to see if we can go together with you guys." I'm actually waiting for Bryson and Mike to return from their Starbucks run, we will see you there, I said with a fake smile. "Oh ok," the neighbor's wife said, "I saw John getting on the elevator earlier on his way up, rushing and running late to give Branson a brush up on his lessons I imagine." Oh no, I said, we had not heard from John since early this morning and told him we would just go straight to the Ballroom and meet up with him there. Maybe he started to come up the elevator but he never made it to our door. Well anyway, we will be on our way in the next few minutes, we will see you there, I said. I assured them we would move quickly to ensure my grandson's timely performance as I anxiously started to close the door. I turned around and looked at my family, we all had sadness in our eyes, we needed to freshen ourselves up and gather our composure. *"The show must go on."* That was what John would have said. A little Visine in the eyes and fresh makeup goes a long way. And so does a little Johnny Walker Black. Where the hell are Bryson and Mike, I said to myself. Oh, I thought, I better get that bag out the closet. I looked at the bag in my hand, opened the window that leads to the back alley and dropped the bag out of the window without any thought. Oh shute, I thought, what am I doing? I looked down and saw that the bag had dropped right in the bed of a decorative small pick up truck with an "FMX" logo on the side of it. FMX, I thought, what the hell is that? Just then Bryson and Mike walked in the door with looks of disbelief and exhaustion on their faces. You guys have to clean up, we have to get over to the ballroom. I turned to see the little truck pulling off with that bag in the back. Hopefully they would just think it was trash someone put in the truck and wouldn't look inside the bag. As Bryson and Mike cleaned up themselves, I sat on the bed next to Branson, looked into his eyes and we both started to cry. I could not express any of my feelings because there were so many,… and I did not want to make Branson talk about anything right now, we had a show to do. He would have to bury what he had just witnessed for now. Do you still want to do this Branson?, I asked. "Yes Mum mom," he replied. We will deal with all of this later, when we have time to digest all of this. Now look, I said, we have to put on the biggest performance of our lives and it starts right now. Let's pull ourselves together, (surfacely anyway) and give these folks something to talk about. Are you sure that you still want to do this Branson? I asked. "Yes," replied Branson. Ok, the car is waiting out front for us. As we walked down what seemed to be an extra long corridor, I could see the Doorman James waiting for us at the end of the hallway. He was smiling as usual. "Go get em champ," James said as he touched Bransons' shoulder as he always did, but this time my grandson and I both seemed to pause as James patted my grandson on his shoulder. We never noticed his touch before, it always seemed so innocent. But this time we noticed and we both knew life would never be the same and it would just be the beginning of life that had lost all innocence… "By the way," James said, "where's John?" We all looked as we got into the limousine. I replied, he left a little earlier. "Oh," said James, "he must have left when I was on break." Yea, I said, see you when we get back, we won't be too long, Branson isn't feeling too well, ***but the show must go on…***

THE BALLROOM SCENE

AS WE ENTERED THE ballroom, my grandson Bransons' eyes lit up as people started to applaud just at our arrival. One thing John had taught us all is that with this group of *Social Elites*, *"you had to know how to fake it"* (Wow, I can see John in my head and hear him, almost smell him saying that to me…,John's presence was overwhelming me, almost as if his spirit was haunting my soul…

Branson sat at the Piano, bowed his head and began playing. Wow, we all thought. Is that our baby? I said to my daughter. Look at the beautiful talent God has given him, his performance is amazing, brilliant and full of passion…(I could feel all of his emotions through his playing) My husband, daughter and son in law were full of emotions as well, as was Braya. We were overwhelmed in every sense of the way, wow, how could everything so right go so wrong. But as a glass put threw a fire, look at the beauty that had emerged from it….

The Ballroom was filled to see our new rising star. The crowd erupted into a roaring applause as Branson closed out his performance. And as he stood and bowed, they followed with cheers and a standing ovation. *Glory to God*, we were so proud at the moment, so

emotional, so everything… "Where the hell is John?", people started
to ask. "How could he miss his prodigys' performance?" Some of the
guests started to ask. People were starting to take notice that John
was nowhere to be found. Normally he would be buzzing around
hosting and entertaining the crowd, but John's presence was definitely
missed which started to create a buzz of its own. Bryson stared at
me in my eyes, he started to tear up and so did I. Andraya and Mike
looked over at us and I could tell they were also back in that horrible
moment that had taken place only hours ago. But we had to put on a
show as well. We acted as if we were concerned, but made up a story
about John having an emergency of sorts at his home, some busted
water main pipes or something, but we were sure he would be here
as soon as he could…," so we explained anyway… Well anyway, the
party went on. Drinks were flowing, Butler service with beautiful
hor'dourves and folks having a good time conversing, gossiping and
getting their grooves on. We were ready to get out of there. "We are
going to excuse ourselves a little early," we announced, Branson is
starting to feel under the weather. I could see Brayas' eyes roll in the
corner of my eye. She had amazingly seemed unscathed by this whole
crazy whirlwind of a day we just had. You never know with kids these
days, she has been surfing social media all day, so God only knows
how all this drama and trauma is really affecting her and when it will
manifest. But we had learned a lot from John and before our exit we
were sure to make plans with some influential people for upcoming
events for our new rising star. "He's on his way to being one of the
greats," everyone was saying. We smiled and waved goodbye as we
walked into the elevator and out into the lobby. We might as well
take a walk instead of *The Car*. A walk always helped me to think
and sort through any problems I may be having but I never had
a problem like this before…this was a monster. As we exited the

building and stepped into the bright city lights, we felt eerily calm by this gorgeous sexy city. I always did love this city, especially at night, but John taught us how to love it even more… What do we do now without John? Where do we go from here? Why didn't they listen to me and call the police while John was still breathing? Why did they have to suffrocrate him? All these questions and more were swirling around my head like a tornado. I wish I could turn back the clock. I could have prevented this, prevention was always the key. An ounce of prevention is worth a pound of cure, my favorite saying, but I hadn't prevented *this* and we were all in some very deep shit.

BACK TO THE SCENE
OF THE CRIME

AS WE APPROACHED THE Phoenix building, we could see James, the doormans welcoming face, begin to open the door. "Thank you James," we said. It's so refreshing to see a familiar face, it's similar to putting on that comfortable robe you like to change into after a long day, familiar and comforting. Although I was not sure if any of us would ever feel comfortable in that once so loving condo again. We all were walking as if we were going to the plank to be beheaded. Not sure how we would feel once we stepped back into that place. Would we break down and lose it, or should we just not go back into this door and that horrible memory right now. Maybe we should just get a hotel room or drive out to the Burbs, but really, who feels like driving...

THE MOVE

ALTHOUGH I LOVED THE city, I thought it was a good idea to go stay in our home in the country for a while. The condo was a constant reminder of that nite, when I stared at what I once considered my grand beautiful dream floor, was now a reminder of a nightmare. Flashbacks of John's body laying in a pool of blood on our floor and of us staring into each other's eyes. "I love you, please forgive me," I kept hearing his voice over and over in my head. We were trying to hold on and express our love with our eyes for what seemed like a trip into the obisque. I could see John falling or being pulled into another world, a world unknown, I could see him slipping into the cosmic... We needed to clear our heads, listen to the birds sing upon the Sunrise, take a walk along the lake, sit on our wrap-around porch and listen to crickets.... The suburbs were also home and it felt safe. A TV and a chair was all that mattered to Bryson, it didn't really matter where that TV and chair was. He seemed to go back to his old pre John self after John was gone. Although he would go out for long drives, something he didnt do in the city. The children loved the Lakehouse. It was really refreshing. Children are quite resilient, they seemed like nothing had ever happened. But I'm sure it was buried somewhere in them. I didn't want to make them talk about it until they were ready but burying it couldn't be good, it could only manifest into something not so good in the future. Branson wanted to take a break from playing the piano for a few, he just wanted to go back to being a "normal" kid. He already knew some of the kids in the area, there was a bike trail close and he started hanging out with some local kids his age. I was happy to see him having fun and making new friends. It was summer and that was what summer was about. Braya thought the countryside was too slow for her. She couldn't dress in her chic little outfits. A tank top and cutoffs was all that was needed in the countryside. Just nature, trees and crickets, no one really cared about designer duds, well they still cared on Tik Tok I guess, but at least she got a chance to wear those brilliant colors of lip gloss she loved so much. I spent a lot of time in my garden during the summers, I loved growing fresh vegetables and herbs and having the children help to prepare them. Nice fresh salads, fish and veggies on the grill was all we needed, and some watermelon and Rita's Water Ice with the whip cream on it. It made us all feel closer to nature, closer to God, maybe we were trying to get God's forgiveness, but would he forgive us and would that night catch up to us…was it only a matter of time?

THE CALL

WE GOT A CALL from the police stating that the University called them to report that John had not shown up for classes and or called anyone and that was highly unusual for John. We expressed that we had not heard anything either and that we had concerns as well. We agreed to come to the police station to give any leads that we could, being that John was always at our house and the last time anyone saw John was at our "Phoenix Condo" around early afternoon the day of our grandson's recietel. The police station is right next door, and there are steps in our corridor leading down to the Suburban train station. Although the police station is there, there are known to be robberies and other crazy situations sometimes.

On the way down the hall, I am thinking of what we will say about the last time John came to our Condo, I'm wondering if they have video surveillance of the hallways. When we got to the Station, the police told us of recent purchases with John's credit cards. My husband and I looked at each other as if to say, *how could that be?* They said they would pull surveillance cameras from the places the cards had been used at. We thanked them for trying to locate John and told them we would let them know if we hear anything from him. We both looked at each other as we walked down what seemed to be a long hallway back out of that station.

LIFE IN THE SUBURBS

A LITTLE TIME WENT by since we heard anything from the police. Life in the country was just what we needed to try to pull our lives back together. Branson had made new friends and had become close to one of the kids named Cameron. The 4th of July was approaching fast and a barbecue by the Lakeside was an annual tradition of ours that we always looked forward to. One of the neighbors had the most spectacular fireworks. We would roast a pig for the occasion and I would make my special Caribbean Rice and Beans dish. And of course good ole "*Nathan Franks*" and Hamburgs and Corn on the grill. In the past we would invite some of our friends from the city. But I just don't feel like that right now. Being questioned about whether or not we had heard from John, or talking about anything with those gossiping folks I was not up for. Not right now anyway...

THE 4TH OF JULY

THE 4TH IS HERE! It felt good to get the yard all festive with flags and summertime table sets. Bryson got out his old fishing gear early in the morning, Mike and Andraya brought over Mike's brother Ron and his wife Angie. Angie always made her famous Apple Peach Cobbler. It went so well with Bryson's traditional homemade Vanilla Bean Ice cream and lets not forget about Andraya's Grilled Watermelon Salad and her Watermelon jello shots to get us nice. Some of the other families that had homes by the lake would come over and we would sashay over to their yard as well to see what they had cooking. The Donato family lived in Florida Christmas time through Graduation time, but they would come home to their lakeside house in PA just in time for the annual 4th of July celebration. They always had the Crabfest thing going on and plenty of craft and tap beer to go with it. The husband was into new home Construction, the wife stayed at home but had a Real Estate license. They were the liveliest festive couple we knew, always about having a good time. Their kids were about the same age as Branson and Braya, so the kids loved to see each other every summer. Between the other families Branson and Braya had plenty of kids to have fun with. And the adults played horseshoes, cards and other fun games of their own.

The day was beautiful, hot but not too hot. Steamy enough to sit poolside and sip frozen Martinis. We were having a great time. Andrea called herself DJing and she actually was doing a great job. We danced, sang, ate, drank and even smoked a lil tree and ate and drank some more... "*Summertime*", Jazzy Jeff and Fresh Prince and Frankie Beverly and Maze "*Before I let go*" the official summertime kickoff songs that always made us even happier. We were really having one of the best times we had in a while. Dusk was starting to set and we knew it was almost time for the fireworks show to begin. Branson's friend Cameron had come back early from their family reunion cookout and came over to watch the fireworks. Cameron lived a little further up the road so I told him to call his parents and make sure they knew where he was. Cameron, tell your parents they are welcome to come over to join us and watch the fireworks. They may want to have a drink or two, we would love to finally meet them. "Ok Miss Stacia, they said they would love to, and they're on their way, " said Cameron. "My Uncle is going to drive them over." Oh, Ok, great! Let me shake some more Limoncello Martinis.

Bryson, I yelled, Camerons' parents are going to come by to join us and watch the fireworks! "Oh ok," Bryson said. "There's plenty more food and beer out there." The Donato's were laughing heartily as always, they sounded like 18 people with just the husband, wife and the two kids. I laughed to myself. "Miss Stacia, my parents are here, " Cameron said. Ok, I'm in the kitchen, I will be right there to greet them. Hi, it's great to meet you, I'm Stacia and this is my husband Bryson.. "Hi Stacia, nice to meet you too, and thanks for inviting us over, I'm Mary," said Cameron's mother with a cheerful attitude. "And I'm Ken," said Camerons' father. Well, I'm going to grab Bryson's homemade Ice cream out of the deep freezer and shake the Martini's, but yall can go out on the deck to meet the rest of the family and neighbors. "Oh ok, my brother in law is parking his truck," said Cameron's mother Mary. Oh ok, I will let him park right next to Mike and Andraya's SUV, I said as I started out the door. Just as I went outside feeling a little tipsy directing Cam's Uncle where to park with the Martini shaker still in my hand, my smiles turned to shock as I witnessed the unpleasant surprise of the little pick up truck with the "FMX" logo wrap on it. Awe shit, I dropped the shaker, it couldn't be...

"Uncle Peter hurry up," said Cameron. Oh my God, this can't be the truck, could it? Does this man know who we are? So many things started swirling around in my head. There goes my damn buzz. Fuck the Martinis, Im gonna need something stronger, some shots, I thought to myself.

"Hello, I'm Peter Cooney, I'm Kenny's brother." Oh, nice to meet you, everyone is outback and the fireworks are about to start." I said. The freaking fireworks are really about to start I thought, what the fuck is going on here. As that sneaky looking hillbilly man started out the sliding door to the deck, I couldn't help to get this feeling that made my hair stand up on my newly waxed pussy. I quickly poured a half a rocks glass of Vodka and immediately started to slam it down. I'm coming with the Martinis, I said, running like Edith Bunker. Oh my God, I'm not sure what to do or think...

FIREWORKS

JUST AS I STEPPED out back to pour the drinks, *Boom*,... the beautiful blast of colors erupted in the sky. *Wow,...* we all stopped to stare at the electrifying firework display. The Johnsons always showed off and had more fireworks than the professional ones. Out of the corner of my eye I could see that Uncle Peter guy checking out the surroundings. He seemed a little creepy to me and looked like he needed a good scrubbing. We were all doing our oohs and ahhs with each blast. Maybe it's just a coincidence, I thought to myself. Maybe he just threw the bag away in the trash. But even if that were so, he wouldn't have known where the bag came from and it was just trash anyway... But I just keep seeing that green tape dispenser over again in my head. I'm just tripping, I thought, everything is ok. I'm just so glad to finally see Branson having a good time. Branson seemed to be happy again, as if his innocence had been restored. I was happy to see him smile and laugh again, smiling from the heart. I hadn't seen that smile since that day....

As the fireworks ended, the party started to spark back up. Drinks and weed were flowing, music was pumping and we had some good shit going on. The kids were throwing the football and running around. Life felt good. Yeah, it was summertime, complete with humidity and crickets. I love me some Summertime by the countryside.. The barbecues lasted till wee hours of the night. We were usually pretty plastered by then. Camerons Uncle Peter only drank a few beers. Even though he was staying with his brother and sister in law only up the road, he said he was the driver, and was worrying more about eating food like he was starving and staring down all the women's bras. I told him to make some plates to take with him. All the kids got worn out and went into the basement to watch some movies, so I said they should just stay overnight.

The neighbors staggered over to their yards, Andraya and Mike went upstairs to their room and Ron and Angie went upstairs to the guest room. I walked Camerons' parents and Uncle out to that truck. That truck,.. oh my god, I can't believe that truck is actually here on our property away from the city alley where I first saw it. This is kind of crazy. But anyway, we had a good time and the night was finally coming to an end. We said our goodbyes and I told them that I would have Cam call them when he gets up in the morning. I had never told my husband about that bag or that truck. Nor had I ever asked them what they did with John's body. I didn't want to know what they did with the body. I was trying so hard to put that God awful memory out of my mind. For whatever reason, Bryson and I had gotten closer after that horrible ordeal. I guess it made us form some new bond in a crazy eerie way. Or maybe under the circumstances, we just had to become closer.

We started cleaning up and Bryson said, "what's this?" What is it Hun, I replied. Just as I looked over to my shock and horror there it was,... the freaking green tape dispenser.. It still had pieces of tape stuck to the side,..with dried blood still stuck in the pieces of tape. Get the fuck out of here. It cant be...What the fuck...who put this here!? Did they know and seek us out!? What do they know!? Oh my God!...

THE KNOW

THE ANXIETY KNOCKED OUR buzz and good mood rite out the door. I needed a damn drink or something, quick, fast and in a hurry. Bryson was amazingly calm, too calm. I was starting to panic, but men sometimes are just naturally more calm than women or just don't want to show their true feelings. Andraya, I called upstairs, are you still up? "Yes Mommy," Andraya said as she peaked her head out the bedroom door. Come down here for a minute, I said. I stood at the bottom of the steps anxiously waiting for Andraya to walk down the stairs. As she always does, Andraya started down the steps as if she were walking the plank to some ungodly place. What the hell, I wanted to quarterback this thing with her so I had to put up with her stinkin spoiled attitude for a minute. Watching her sashay down the stairs with her pink, pom pom 3 inch heel slippers irritated me for a second. Bitch just get down here, I thought to myself. "What is it Mommy?" Andraya asked as if she was irritated. I need to take a puff of that weed Andraya, I said. "Is that what you called me downstairs for Mommy?" No Andraya, but the weed will help what I'm about to say. You wouldn't guess what just freakin happened Draya. "What Mommy?" she said as she pulled a sandwich baggie of "Indigo" out of her leopard robe pocket and started to roll up a conehead. Do you remember the little things that were left on the floor of the Condo the night that shit happened with John?" "Little things like what Mommy?" Draya said. Well, just a few things left behind after Bryson and Mike wrapped Johns' body up. Draya looked at me as if I were crazy. Anyway girl, I said as I anxiously awaited for her to finish rolling that damn joint and light it up. There was a green tape dispenser in John's hand when that crazy shit happened. I picked it up off the floor with a few other things after we cleaned up and put it in a little trash bag, I noticed it had a little blood on it. I dropped the bag of trash out of the window without thinking and it landed in a small truck with some logo on the side of it. "And?" Andraya said, somewhat tired and annoyed. "What does this all mean at this ungodly hour in the morning Mom?" How about after all this freaking time, somebody just put that tape dispenser, dried blood and all on the table tonight. Bryson just discovered it as we were cleaning up. "Oh shit Mommy," Draya said as she finished licking and sealing the joint. Oh shit is rite Draya, I said and give me that damn joint. I need to light it up right now. "Well who do you think put it there Mommy?." I don't know Draya, I think it was probably that damn creepy looking Uncle Peter dude with that little truck with that "FX" logo on it. When I dropped the bag out of the window, it had the nerve to fall into the back of a truck that looked exactly like the truck that Uncle Peter guy is driving. I couldn't wait to get that long ass drag of smoke into my lungs and head as I slowly exhaled. This is some shit, I said, and your damn Dad has the nerve to be so calm and cool about it. But really, I never did tell him about that trash bag and the truck it fell into. "So what are we gonna do?" Andraya asked as she took what seemed to be a two minute drag that almost completely finished the damn joint. Damn girl, hurry up and roll another one I said as I shuffled through the fridge looking for a beer and whatever else I could find. We have to quarterback this shit, let me think. And what the fuck is Bryson doing out back...

Bryson, I yelled out back, are you out here? "Yes, Stacia, just cleaning up a little. I'll be there in a few minutes. Let that shit go until the Sun comes up. Just come in the house. "Ok Hun, just getting this trash together, I'll be there," said Bryson. It's dark and still outside, the dark before the light seems to be extra dark and extra quiet and still. It's a different world in the wee hours of the morning before daylight, a little too quiet if you ask me. I appreciate the quiet, although I await the Sunrise to grant me permission to start my new day and thoughts,... even though the new day starts a second after midnight...

TIME TO CALL NEPHEW DANNY

WE GOT ABOUT AN hour of sleep before it was dawn and I heard the birds singing. I got it, I thought, I'm going to call Nephew Danny! My nephew Danny...my sister Tonya's son. Although I sometimes don't get along with my sister and her ghetto ass ways, my nephew Danny has always had a special place in my heart. Danny was always a little grown man, he was born that way. He was always smart and wise beyond his years. Even as a baby, he would look at you as if you were crazy if you tried to speak "baby talk" to him. I knew better since the day he was born. I said Hey "Little King," whoever and whatever you want to be in this world, I'm Aunt Stacia and I'm here to support you. I am very blessed to meet you and I'm looking forward to walking with you on our journeys. And ever since day one we had a mutual divine respect for one another. Another precious soul that knew where he just came from, knew what we were made of and knew somewhat of what we were up against...life.

Draya, let's call Danny and get him to find out what's up with that creepy Uncle Peter guy. I think it had to be him that put that green tape dispenser on the table. That bag fell into his truck and he must have seen something. Maybe he saw Mike and Bryson carrying out the body…the body, oh my god, that night that horrible night, trying to put that awful night out of my mind… John…I sure miss John. I wish I could go back and change what happened that day, but I can't change the past.

Draya, did you call Danny? I ask anxiously as I'm shuffling through the fridge to get round 2 of this interrupted party started. Let's do steaks and eggs with that Hollandaise sauce and fresh made salsa on the side. I'm going to have a Mimosa or two, do you want one? "Yes Mommy, I want one, '' said Draya. '' Mike and Daddy are already on the deck playing chess, they probably want a Mimosa too." Bryson and Mike, would you guys like a Mimosa? "Sure," said Mike. "Mine as well," said Bryson. The morning feels nice and calm, still.. It had been a light shower right before dawn, Mike and Bryson had wiped off the chairs and were enjoying the peaceful morning before the day began. The early morning smells like a beautiful summer dew, a refreshing smell, it should be a candle…maybe it is.

Turn on the grill Bryson, I yelled from the kitchen. The steaks are seasoned and ready to go as soon as that grill gets going. I'll make you and Mike's eggs Sunny side so you guys can have that yolk gravy you all love so much. "I want my eggs scrambled Mommy," said Draya. "And you mine as well make enough for the kids now and get that out the way." Now you know those kids are going to want fresh eggs Draya, I replied. They are used to everything fresh out of the pan. I spoiled those kids but at least they have food standards, I said with a smile. Matter of fact, let those kids sleep. They were up all night anyway. We can eat and get in a mid morning nap before they get up and start driving us all crazy. I'll make them some pancakes, eggs, bacon and sausage when they get up. That will make them full and lazy. Maybe then they will chill and watch Netflix or something and be quiet for a while, hopefully.. Bryson, did you turn on the grill? I said for the second time. "Don't interrupt our Chess game Woman," Bryson said. "Yea, he is getting ready to get his butt beat by you and me," laughed Mike, "he better concentrate." If yall want to eat these steaks your ass will get up and turn on the grill Bryson. "Yes Dear," said Bryson. Draya, you know Danny gets up and out before the crack of Dawn, call him and give him a heads up on what's going on. "Ok Mommy," said Draya. Tell him to come over anyway and have a Ribeye and a Sunny egg. Danny loves his juicy medium Ribeye steak with a Sunny egg with the egg fried crisp on the bottom. The egg has just enough yolk to make that steak juice a gravy. We all loved our steaks that way, except Draya and my sister Tonya. They want their steak well done with scramble eggs with cheese, and ketchup drizzled across the steak and the eggs. They sure have that in common, and a few other traits. I guess you can say they have a special bond in some ways, the same way that her son Danny and I have a special bond,..family..

The grill is hot, steaks are on, and I'm shuffling through the fridge to see what else from yesterday we can put on the table. Oh, some of that carribean rice dish with the seafood on it is still left. I'll put that on a serving plate too. That dish will go perfectly with the steaks and it's a lot of the fruit salad from the neighbors left also. I'll put that on the table too, but I better save some for the kids when they get up. Bryson and Mike, can you leave that damn game alone for a minute and sit at this beautiful colorful table Draya and I put together and eat.. "Yes Dear, it looks like a table fit for Kings," said Bryson. And Queens!, I said with an eye rolling snap. Would you like to say Grace, Bryson? "Yes Dear," said Bryson. "Heavenly Father, please Bless this food we have prepared to eat, We thank you Heavenly Father for this New Day, this beautiful food and our presence with you and each other, please make this food pure and nourishing to our bodies and our souls,... Amen." " Get the beers out the cooler Mike," Bryson said as he started to dive into the food. "I need those bubbles for a good burp and digestion." "Yeah, nothing like a nice cold beer to compliment some steak and eggs," said Mike. "You sure can hook up some food Ma, this feels like good living."

Right on time and a pleasure to see, here he is my nephew Danny pulling up in his big Red Caddy. He is always fresh as if he just got out of an oasis shower, and as usual has his slides on. Always energetic and full of life. He was larger than life. You had to smile when you saw him pulling up. His car was always clean, shining and detailed, and smelled magnificent too. Smelling like a man with a plan, to a tee, he was him. But overall Danny was a simple guy, a good guy. He had a girlfriend or two from time to time, but his wife was his Queen. She was number one and what she wanted she got. Although she never had to want too much for anything because Danny provided her with all that she needed and more. They also had a baby girl three years old named Princess.

Danny loves his family and his wife just loves that man. He would always be there as soon as you called him, you could always count on him. Danny was also very streetwise, he was a natural born Hustler. A survivor but has a heart of gold and is very protective of his family. He and Andraya grew up more like brother and sister than cousins. He owns a Home Improvement business as well as a few other businesses and has his hand in a few night clubs of different levels . "Auntie, Draya," Danny yelled as he approached the yard. He could be heard across the lake, his voice was large, larger than him actually. His voice was so hearty, it seemed to create ripples in the still lake waters. "What's going on!" said Danny. Hey Nephew! I replied, I'm so happy to see my favorite nephew, my one and only nephew and the best nephew I could ever have been blessed with! We ran to each other embracing before we even touched. We would always give the most heartfelt hugs there were, long bear hugs, hugs that made you feel inner joy... it's a shame my sister and I couldn't hug like that...maybe that was my way of hugging her as well, holding on just a little while longer. My one and only sister...Tonya.

"Hey Cousin!" said Draya as she was bear hugged and lifted off her feet by her beloved cousin. "How you been Darling," said cousin Danny as he looked her in her eyes. "I've been a blessed cousin," replied Draya. "What's up Unc!" "What's up Mike!" " I see yall got that Chess game going already this morning." "I'm not going to interrupt y'all right now. I'll get back to yall on that Bru Love in a minute," said Danny. "Yea, I'm killing him this morning, this game will be over in a minute," laughed Bryson. "Yea, I must have drank too much last night, that's why he's getting me," said Mike. "I guess I'll have another Mimosa." Are you having one Danny?, Mike said as he got up to give Danny a hearty Bru shake and hug. "Nah Bru, Ima just take the orange juice right now, it's early." Danny said. "I have to keep on point, I have a few more things to do today. Then I'll kick back some later." " I got ya," said Mike. '' You always have something happening and going on." "Yea, you know I got to be making my moves and keep things happening," laughed Danny who was as serious as bankruptcy. "Where's the little ones Draya?" "They are all downstairs in the basement asleep," said Draya. '' And I want to let them stay that way for a minute to have some peace before the storm this morning." "Grandma don't play any games with nobody," said Danny. Hey, what I tell you about that Grandma stuff. I'm Mum

Mom for now until I figure something else out. They sometimes call me GG or just plain Mom when they forget. "Awrite Auntie," Danny said as he laughed. "You still look young anyway Auntie, you still look like a teenager." Thank you my nephew, you always make Auntie feel so good. You're just in time I just made your plate as well, sit down and eat. You missed Bryson's Blessing but I know you'll bow your head and give your thanks to our Lord. "I sure will Auntie, we know we're blessed and you know before anything else I will give thanks to the Man above." "Yes, let's tear this steak and eggs down while they're still hot and juicy," said Bryson. "Then we'll get back to the Chess board." "You have time for a game Danny?" "Of course Unc," said Danny. "I'm here now, let's do this as soon as we finish our grub." " I heard that," said Mike. "I'm a little tired of getting beat this morning, I'm going to take a little rest and get my strength back so I can wear your bull out a little later." "Yea rite, '' laughed Bryson. "You better take a week's vacation and maybe you will get enough mind games back to beat me." "That's OK Babe, come on and let's play some Checkers!," said Draya. "Checkers," laughed Danny and Bryson, "yall mine as well break out the Trouble game." " That's all he's good for anyway," said Bryson. "All that's deep Unc," said Danny as they all rubbed that last piece of steak thru that yolk gravy on their plates at the same time. "Yum, this is so good Auntie, you always know how to make our taste buds happy and our bellies feel nice." "Thanks Auntie, everything was good as always." "Are you ready to get that game going Unc?" "Sure am, Danny, be over there at the Chess table in a minute," said Bryson.

"I'm sorry to do this to you Unc, but CheckMate," Danny said with a respectful smile. "I'm gonna hollar at Ma n Sis a minute," said Danny as he stood up and gave Bryson a Bru Unc Hug. "Ok Man, I'm coming in for a minute too, '' Bryson said, "I need a midmorning movie and a nap." "I heard that Unc," said Danny. "Ma", Sis", as he sometimes affectionately calls us, "where yall at?" "Oh shute, y'all are really in here playing a Trouble game from way back," laughed Danny. Yes we are, I told him, I always play Trouble with the kids, we love this game. Oh shute, I have three men home and I need to pop a four to win, pop, four! I won! Yay! I shouted. "Okay Auntie, what's going on with this dude yall talking about?" Well Nephew, it's kind of a long crazy story...so crazy that I don't even know where to start. So crazy that I am getting anxiety just at the thought of reliving that whole thing. Maybe I'll just let Draya tell you the story, as much as she can anyway. It's a lot, a whole lot but yall can go down by the lake and talk about it. "OK Ma, we gonna get you straight, you know I got you no matter what, always, you know that." Thanks Baby, I know you'll take care of us, we take care of each other, no matter what, we look out for each other, we family… although your Mom and I sometimes don't see eye to eye, we still will always love and protect each other. We still are sisters. "I know Auntie, yall both stubborn, but deep down inside yall are alot alike, yall will be alright," Danny said with a smile. "Yall will get it together eventually." I hope so Danny, I miss my little sister…

DANNY'S ON IT!

"**WELL, AS ALWAYS AUNTIE** Mommy, the food was bangin and as always I loved y'all's company," Danny said. "I'll get on that for you Auntie and get back to you in a minute." Ok thanks my nephew I knew you had my back. As we gave Danny hugs on his way out, we were all smiles and love. We love that man, he was the real deal, die hard and loyal. They don't make them like that any more...but we may have a few lil good guys in the making. Just then the kids came up from the basement hungry and lazy. "Awwe!" "Did we miss the food?" asked Branson and Braya. "No," both Draya and I said at the same time. There is the fruit salad in the downstairs fridge and do y'all want pancakes or French Toast? "We want both pancakes and French Toast," said Branson, Braya and all the other kids that spent the night. Well it's five of yall in total, get out the Hefty paper plates, you still might need to double the plates to be able to hold this mini feast. "Give me some love, young soldiers!" Danny said with meaning as he's shaking hands and giving hugs to his young cousins. " What yall been up too?" "Going to school?" "Getting good grades?" "That's good, good, learn all yall can and always listen to yall Momma's and Big Momma, cool?" Danny said as he handed them each a $20 dollar bill, that was Danny, kool as shit or shall I say kool as a Summer breeze under a willow tree…

Of course Danny being Danny he was already on the case. He spotted that little Logo wrapped truck parked in front of this raggedy strip club on the Hick side of town. Danny had checked that Bar/Clubhouse out a few times before looking to see what's over there. "Always know what's going on around town and beyond ," Danny would always say. But I'm the one who always told him that when he was growing up. We always kept it cool with the Clicks from the other parts of town. We were respectful and real, but we were taught to keep the streets in the streets, you can kick it here and there with other folks from other parts of town but keep it Sunday Monday, in other words keep people out of your business and stay out of other people's business, period.

"Danny's inner mind world….."

…"let me see what this Hick is up to. Oh shit, These folks are all up in here (DMX rocking in the background) what…I see ya… I see ya, nice healthy Big ass broads over here, Hey Ma, you looking fabulous, strippers going up n down the pole under the blue light, like the Devil under the Blue Moon light blue…steamy in here…Im liking this set up though, hm, I'm gonna steal a few of these Hotties for my club…where this dude go, oh shit he over there fuckin wit some young ass chocolate, he know whats up, hum, new found respect for this dude.. Oh shit he like them Bad ass girlz, bad in all kind of ways, he better had that money though fuckin wit these kind of hoes..well let me get out of here.. I see what's up a little with him now, I will definitely be back though, I see a few

little Hotties I'm going to holler at,... oh yea, I will be back, let me get back over here to my own shit though, I need to see what's going on at my own clubs and get on some asses.

WHAT'S UP WITH BRYSON LATELY!

BRYSON!.....BRYSON! THIS MAN IS always on the move lately all of the sudden.

Matter of fact he's been dressing a little sharper lately. Hum... Draya did your father say where he was going? Draya knows when I address Bryson as *"your father,"* she knows I'm feeling an attitude coming on with that Man. And he forgot his cell phone again,..hum. Anyway, I guess his ass did need to get out and start to do things. He sat in that chair with a grip on those controls way too long. At least here out in the Country he goes to visit his brother sometimes. That's a good thing. When we were in the City, his ass barely wanted to go out the door,... that is until John came along. John got Bryson to do all kinds of things I couldn't get Bryson to do for years. John...I sure miss John. I miss the talks we used to have about everything. I miss the laughs we would have. I missed his positive vibe that everything would be okay, "it will be alright, Stacia" is what he would always say and it would end up being alright in the end just like he said. "God has your back, it's all in his time and his terms..." John used to say. Wow, I wish John was here, oh my God John... What really happened? Did I jump to a conclusion? Branson has not wanted to talk about that night since it happened and I don't want to push him right now. It all happened so fast. Stacia what have you done! My bad ass temper and my quick to judgment attitude has always been something I wish I had more control over. Now my best friend is gone... gone forever..

"Mommy, your Sister is on the phone for you," Draya said as she handed me her phone with this look on her face. Um, ok, Hey Tonya, what's going on? "Nothing all like that." "How come I wasn't invited to the Cookout?" asked Tonya with an attitude. You know we have a cookout every 4th of July Tonya, you could have just come over. Why do I need to personally invite you every time? "Because you be acting funny sometimes Stacia, anyway you could have at least made me a plate and sent it with Danny." Oh, I'm sorry Tonya. I'm making some Crab Cakes, Corn Fritters and Slaw later, I'm going to fry some Jumbo Shrimp too. I'll tell Danny to bring you a plate, he's supposed to be stopping back over later. "Ok Stae Stae, that sounds good, put a few beers in the bag too." "And can you put me a mixed drink in a jar and send it over too?" Damn Tonya, there you go, I have a Strawberry Lemonade with some Grey Goose. "Ooh, that sounds good too." "Do you have some tree?" Well damn Ghetto Princess, what the hell else do you want, a new car with a driver? "Well Sis, now that you mentioned it..ha, ha, you can send me a new friend over, you know one with some dollars." "I know you have some rich snobby friends in the City, hook a Sister up." Yea rite Tonya, I'm going to need to find one myself soon if Bryson doesn't get his ass together. "Yea rite Stacia, you've been complaining about Bryson for years, he might be lazy, but at least his ass doesn't cheat on you. He's always at home in the chair with the controls in his hands. He's a good man

Stae. He's just a little boring and predictable. I'm the one that needs a good man, I'm tired of these no good, good for nothing men that I seem to attract. If only I was smart and had class like you, maybe I can hook up with a man like Bryson," said Tonya with a sarcastic tone. There you go Tonya, you get men that act just like you act, and on that note I'll talk to you later. I'll send everything over in a few hours when Danny stops by. "Thanks Stae, even though we don't always get along, you will always hook a Sister up. That's my big Sis… Love you." Love you too Tonya and bye Tonya! Sisterly love, wanting to pull each other's hair and call each other names sometimes but we will be damned if we let somebody else treat either one of us badly. Or the other sister is sure to come to protect and kick ass if need be. That's how we were raised by our Mom and Grandma, to look out for each other no matter what, even if we don't get along ourselves. Keep our loyalty in our circle, blood first.

Finally he shows up. Bryson! Where have you been? I was starting to get nervous. Did you go over to your brother's house? I called his phone but he is just as bad as you are when it comes to cell phones. "Stacia I told you I was going over Kenny's to watch the game." "You don't need to check up on me like I'm a child, I know my way home, Woman." Oh know you didn't! Excuse me for asking my husband his whereabouts. I wasn't checking up on you Bryson, I was just concerned, you usually don't go out and stay that long. But okay, the next time I won't check and make sure you're still alive, I said to him with a snip. Next time take your damn phone with you just in case you want to let someone know where you're at. "Ok Woman, I'm going downstairs in the basement to watch TV down there." Oh ok then, rolling my eyes at him, I'll be upstairs watching my shows. I made some Crab cakes, Fried Shrimp, Corn Fritters and Slaw if you want some, Danny is stopping by to pick up a plate for Tonya.

Draya and Mike went out and the kids are staying at the neighbors tonight. "That sounds good Stacia, maybe I'll get some later." Did this Man just say he will get some later to my Crabby Patties. Whatever, I'm going to have a nice Cocktail and tear this plate down and watch my shows. It's my TV night. I only watch TV on Tuesday and Wednesday nights and maybe a Lifetime movie or two on Sunday afternoon. Other than that it's the damn news, sick of the news, but in today's times we need to know what's going on or at least what they're reporting...

"Hey Stacia, Danny is here." Okay Babe, tell him I'll be right down. "Hey Auntie, my Mom told me to pick up her big order," Danny said laughing. "She is a mess." Yes she is, I made you and your wife a plate too. "Thanks Auntie," said Danny. "I checked out that dude for you a little yesterday, I saw that truck you told me about at this strip joint club. He was in there fooling around with some gold digging girls. They were some cute little hottie girls too. He better have some deep pockets fooling with those types of girls. He didn't look the type at first look but looks can be deceiving sometimes. I'll swing by there another time and check things out a little deeper. I gotcha Auntie, give me a little more time and I will have all the info on this guy and see where he is coming from. I'll find out what he knows and if he was at yall house tryin to make a come up on yall." Thanks, my nephew, I feel better already knowing that you're on the case. "Damn, all this for my Mother?" asked Danny. Yes it is Danny. "Thanks for all the Love Auntie, Michelle aka Wifey always loves your plates," Danny said while kissing me on my cheek with a mighty hug. "Are Draya and Mike out for the night?" Not sure Danny. They went down to the city tonight. They might stay at the Condo. I haven't been there since the incident and really I'm not ready to go there right now. "Answer me this Auntie, did that Piano teacher dude really do something to little man Branson?" asked Danny. Now I'm not so sure Danny, I'm not so sure about a few things. When I have quiet time, scenes keep passing in my head and I'm trying to remember little things about that night and things prior to that night and piece things together. I still don't know what Bryson and Mike did with the body. "Oh shute Auntie,.. well we need to get to the bottom of a few things here." "Ima get out of here Auntie before this food gets cold, see you later Auntie." Yea Baby, see ya later. I'm going back upstairs, you know it's my TV nite...

GIRLZ GIRLZ GIRLZ

DANNY— (THINKING TO HIMSELF) *"Had to steal a few lil hotties from that club. They weren't treating them girls right over there anyway. Ima give em a lil more money and dress em up real nice and sweet, turn dem into my lil money making stars, Ima have all the High Rollers over here spending dat dough. Killing two birds wit one stone wit taking that pretty brown model looking girl, she looks like a girl that attracts the High Roller dudes too. Let's see what she got going on wit that dude Auntie wants me to check out. I might have to hit that myself, I always did love me a nice tall babe.*

DANNY'S GRAND OPENING

NO, I'M NOT GOING to any strip club, Draya, I don't care who's going to be there. I love my nephew and will do anything for him, but strip clubs I don't do even if a few celebrities are going to perform. I'm just too old and I do not go to strip clubs. "Tonya is going," said Draya. That's even more reason for me not to go. She's used to acting all wild and crazy, I'm not. "Come on Mom, please, we are always asking Danny for favors, let's show him our support." "I think Mary J. is supposed to be there!" What you talkin bout Draya! I love me some Mary! Well, you're right, ok I'll go, but just for Mary, then I am leaving. "He will have us sitting up in a booth anyway Mommy, no one can really see us up there," said Draya. Do we have to sit in there with my Sister? "Well Mommy, that is your one and only sister, Tonya, Danny's mom and this is a big night for him." Well ok, as long as I'm in and out before the strip shit takes place. I don't feel like all of that. "Maybe you should stay and learn something Mommy." "Daddy probably would love it if yall spiced things up a little." I'm sure he and Kenny will come with their old selves drooling over those young girls. Like I said Draya, I'm out before any of that even starts. "He has a great chef in the back," said Draya. You mean they serve food at strip clubs? "Well people have to eat Mommy," said Draya sarcastically. Oh ok Draya, I'm going to get dressed. What kind of outfit should I wear to a strip club? "Not that Ballroom attire Mommy, get a little sexy for a change," said Draya. Whatever, Draya. I really didn't feel like this shit at first, but I'm just doing this for Danny. And of course, now that I know that Mary might even be anywhere near there, I'm going! But anyway, I have to show Danny some support in his business ventures even if a Strip club is not something I'm a fan of. "Well, it's a Nightclub, Mommy, and Danny has all kinds of businesses." I do know that, Draya, I said.

Damn, Masseratis, Bentleys, and all kinds of cars at this place. I'm so proud of Danny, he's starting to do more business in the City and everywhere. The City, I sure miss the City. I don't miss those snooty uppity bitches though. I know they are talking about us like we are murderers and low lifes, they can kiss my ass. I hope I don't bump into any of them. Well, I'm only here for a few anyway and I'm going in the side entrance straight to one of the VIP booths to watch the opening performance and taking my old ass back home to the suburbs and going to bed. Hey Danny, I'm so happy and proud of your business success. You're looking like a movie star yourself, nephew. "Thanks Auntie and Sis, I'm going to have the Chef send you some horderves sample plates and send up some Champagne." "Ma on her way, she's always late, she's on CP time," laughed Danny. "Unc and Mike are gonna come later when the real party starts." Whatever nephew, I'm showing my support and taking my butt home. Draya who's that tall girl over there that keeps staring? "I don't know Mommy." She sure keeps staring, I hope that's not anyone that your father might know. "Alright Mommy, don't start, she is probably looking because she sees us going in the VIP section and thinks we are important." We are important, Draya. Oh wow, is that her?! Is that Mary J.?! Damn, my nephew is doing good to get *"The Queen"* to stop by! Everyone is looking good, I'm loving it!... Oh wow, I thought, what would John say about this, I said to myself with a smile. Could I have got John to even come to an event like this? If it wasn't for what happened I probably wouldn't have come to an event like this myself. I would have been with those phony people in the Society circle. Oh here she comes late as usual, Tonya, it's about time you got here, I said enthusiastically waiting for Mary to come on stage. I'm leaving as soon as Mary does her song. "Well I might stay for a while after the performances and learn a little somethin from the strippers, Stae," said Tonya. "You might want to see how these girls work these poles, I have a new found respect for some of these strippers," said Tonya. "That tall one keeps staring." I said the same thing to Draya. "That necklace she got on looks familiar, almost like the one Mom used to have that Daddy gave her when they renewed their vows, right before the accident," said Tonya. "Where is that necklace Stae?" asked Tonya. "I thought you put it in a safety box." "That necklace was so expensive, how many carrots was that again Stae?" More than you can comprehend Tonya. "See, that's the shit I be talkin about, putting me down all the time," said Tonya. Anyway Tonya, I put it in a box and only Bryson, Draya and I have the key. "Whatever Stae." Oh shute, here Mary comes out of a Giant glittering sky cage, that's my Girl!!! Mary! Mary! Mary!"

OH SHUTE,.. MARY!!!

"YOU REMIND ME!" YES Mary, we are on our feet happy and singing along with her! Tonya and I forgot about all the egos and dumb shit. We were just happy and jamming, damn life felt good! The power of music and nostalgia…how it can take us back in time or to another place. A good place where love is flowing and we don't want the nite to end and go back to reality…but which is reality, I guess it all is… the devil is a liar. And the dancers are the shit too!

The performance was great but was for VIP's only. There's a whole lot of money in this Mother. Some real money is flowing in this club. Yes, I also could smell that money. Mama always said to me, "Stacia girl, you sure can smell money." "That's a gift in itself if you use it wisely." The food was also great. Yeah, my nephew had the Chef really take good care of us. He sent us all kinds of tasty bites. I'm going to steal some of those ideas and make them at home. Hell, I'm going to have to borrow that Chef the next time I entertain. We stayed and partied for a while. I didn't want to interrupt or end this good time I was having, especially with my lil Sister. Watching her smile and having a look of inner peace and light and laughter warmed my heart. I wish I could see that look forever. At least I will with some photos. We sure took a lot of selfies tonight. It actually brought back memories of our childhood when life was rich, life was good and life had character… I wish we could bring back those days as well, but until then, this was good. A taste of what once was, as good as it gets right now, it was a good nite.

Mike ended up showing up all alone. Where's Bryson? I asked with raised brows. "I went by the house to pick him up and he said he would come later," said Mike. What, that's bullshit, he really was just coming with us to give Danny support and see Mary perform. He usually doesn't like all this hyped ass nite club scene. So he's gonna come later and do what? Get a private dance or something? I mean what. Well anyway, that means his ass should still be there when I get home. And I don't know why he would be coming this late, but yall have this VIP spot for the rest of the night. The Horderves are great, and bottle service is flowing. You missed the best thing about the nite, **Queen Mary's** presence. We all love Mary, I want to listen to some more of her songs when I get home. Well, anyway, enjoy the rest of the night and stay safe. "What do you mean the rest of the night?" Draya said with an attitude. "Mike's ass is not staying here that much longer either." "I learned a lot of hot little lessons about pole dancing, dirty dancing and then some tonite. And I'm going to lay it all on your ass as soon as we get home Big Daddy," Draya said teasingly while looking at Mike like he was a Ribeye steak.

I hope nobody slipped you one of those pills that make you horny Draya, I said. Are yall going to stay in the city tonight? Y'all can have y'all damn privacy there. Bryson and I will probably put the TV on and drink another glass of wine and fall asleep. "You better use those little lessons on Daddy tonight Mom and spruce things up a little. You two are not that old, do something different for a change." Whatever Draya, at this point we are getting stuck in our ways. It works for us right now, but I guess our lives could use a little spice of something. Speaking of spice, I'm going to go back to the kitchen and holler at that Chef for a second and get some of those tasty horderves to go.

Um Tonya, that Chef is looking alright back there. Ima have to stop over here early from time to time before too much is jumping off and holler at that Chef. "Yea," said Tonya. "Danny books a lot of Business meetings throughout the week in the early part of the day, then they close for a few hours to get ready for the nightclub scene." "Let me see what else you got in that bag, Stace." No Tonya, you should have come back there with me and got some appetizers yourself. These are mine for when I get home and watch TV. "You are selfish, Stacia," said Tonya. I know you are not calling anybody selfish, after all your shit and I'm always looking out for everyone on the food tip but damn it's not that many appetizers in the bag, Tonya. I can tear these up in no time. I sent you the Crabby patties yesterday, did you eat them all? "Girl, they were good, I tore them up that same night," said Tonya. Did Draya go back inside the club, Tonya? Where is the Limo? There are so many people out here. Wow, this line goes all the way around the club. Lots of nice ass cars too. Lots of Ballers and High Rollers here tonight. That's a good thing, spend that money y'all and make that money Nephew.

Oh Tonya, here comes our Limo. Draya better bring her ass on, I'm ready to go. I'm ready to take off these shoes and this tight ass dress. "Stacia, let's pour some Lemoncello shots from the little mini bar in the Limo." Here comes Draya, I'll pour her a shot too. I guess I'm tired too, I've been running around all day," said Tonya. Draya, are you going to the City tonight? "Wow Mommy, are you putting us out of the Lake house?" "You know we're still in our Summer holiday mode." "Let me call Mike and see if he wants to stay in the City tonight," said Draya. Hurry up Draya and let the Driver know what you're going to do. "Ok, I'm calling him now," said Draya. "Babe, do you wanna stay in the City?" "We mine as well, ok, I will get dropped off by the Limo, see you when you come and don't be too much longer." "Oh, and also get me some Horderves to go." "Dammmmn Girl, come on, how am I going to ask for a Doggie bag at the Strip Club, now come on," said Mike. "Please Babe, Ima call Danny now and ask him to tell the Chef," said Draya. "Don't forget to bring it to me, I feel like a nice late night snack." "Ok Draya," said Mike. "See ya soon Babe, I love you," said Draya. "I love you too," said Mike. "I will be there soon." "Damn, everybody is getting some take home goodies but me," said Tonya, "that's not fair." And Danny is gonna be in that Club all night and then some. Yea, but Michelle will make that Man lay down and sleep when he gets in. She looks after that Man. Although she never goes to any of the Clubs and/or Grand openings, she's very supportive of his businesses and looks after the books, she ain't no dummy. She's just a homebody and she doesn't like crowds and Club atmosphere, but she will go on vacations and local outings with family and friends. She's laid back and quiet, the opposite of Danny, that's why it works for them so well. I like that about her.

THE LIMO RIDE

"ARE YOU LADIES ALL ready to go?" asked the Limo Driver. "Where to first?" "I'm going to 16th & Arch," says Draya. "Oh, the Phoenix?" "Ok, yes Mam, I will have you there in a few minutes," says the Driver. A tap on the window came at the last minute. "Thanks again for coming, my favorite ladies," said Danny. "Oh and here Ma, a lil bag from the Chef." "Oh, praise God, my baby looked out for me, see there Stacia." Don't start Tonya. Just then, something in my head clicked. Oh no, I thought, we are going back there, to that place, that place that I tried to bury, temporarily, so I thought, it came back quick, fast and in a hurry. I didn't know I was going to be sacked like this tonight, I didn't see it coming,...Limo, Driver, My Condo, it's all coming on me too fast at once, now I would have to confront what I thought I was hiding from. Ready or not, here it comes, face it and deal with it or crumble and destruct… One thing Stacia, you have never been a punk, so don't start now...Hello Hell, I'm coming back for a minute to get myself out of here… only for a minute, but this time I come with Armor..Courage and Strength,... Please God...take the wheel…

THE RIDE BACK HOME

AS WE PULLED UP in front of the Phoenix, my heart started to race, I poured another shot. Hey James, how have you been? Long time no see. "Hey stranger," said James the Doorman, "I miss you Miss Lady." "Hi Andraya, let me get the door," said James as the Driver started to get out of the car. See ya later Baby girl, give me a kiss, I love you. "Yes Mommy girl," said Tonya. "Have a great night." I'll be back later in the week James. "Ok see ya then," said James. "It was good seeing you." "I see Bryson from time to time." Oh really, hum…I thought, Bryson didn't tell me he's been coming to the City...

"Where to next?" said the Limo Driver. We'll take my Sister home first, her address is… "Ok, relax and enjoy the ride ladies." "We sure will," said Tonya. As soon as we got on I-76, my mind started to calm down. Brysons' ass better be there when I get there, shit, it's too late to be going to some club at this point for his old ass. "You know Stacia, I'm just thinking, that really did look like Ma's necklace that the tall girl was wearing," said Tonya. That necklace is in the safety box at the bank Tonya. That did look like Ma's necklace, but maybe that girl has one just like it, it can't be Ma's necklace though, how would she have gotten it. Anyway, I'm going to rest my eyes for a second, Tonya. "Ok Stacia, maybe you should stop by the bank and make sure it's still there, I'm just saying, it won't hurt to check it out," said Tonya. Yea, awrite, I said sarcastically. I'm just thinking about Bryson and him doing things that are uncharacteristic of him. I started thinking about things in my head. I wonder if his ass is cheating? Maybe I have gotten too comfortable with him..maybe I take him for granted...We seem ok...actually we seem closer since that John situation… Well, all but our sex life, it's pretty much non-existent… Is it me? I lost my sex drive a lil ways back. Funny, I actually don't remember the exact time or reason, it just got lost somewhere,...Bryson seems to be ok with it, he's getting old himself...but we do have intimacy...I guess... We Okay...We good… That Man loves my ass and I love that Man... no matter what goes on, or what doesn't go on. He might be boring but he gets me, hell, he even smiles when the "Golden Girls" song comes on...it's the calm TV we put on when we turn off the lights. Sometimes we watch it but a lot of times it's just on, background light noise…"*thank you for being a friend*"...that's what Bryson and I were right now...Friends...can't wait to get home to him, put some jammies on and heat up these lil snacks...maybe I should take Draya's advice and spice things up a lil...Bryson probably wouldn't know how to take it… I was so busy talking to myself in my mind that I didn't notice that we were already at Tonya's house. See ya Sister, I said as we pulled up in front of her house. I'll call you when I get in. "Okay, love you," said Tonya. Love you too, I said.

WHERE THE HELL IS BRYSON!

HEY SIS, DO YOU know that Man is not here and he's not answering his phone. "Oh shute Stacia, did you talk to Mike?" ask Tonya. I called Mike and he said he is on his way out of the club and hasn't seen Bryson. "Hm Stace, I keep thinking about that tall girl at the club who kept staring at us and had that damn necklace on that looks like Ma's," said Tonya. Well, something definitely is not right, this is unlike Bryson. He is probably going to come in here and tell me some lie about being at Danny's club or he fell asleep on his brother's reclining chair or something. All I know is he better answer his phone. If I knew his ass was going to start acting like this, I would have put a tracker on his phone. "Not good ole Bryson, I have never seen Bryson act like this either, I can't imagine Bryson cheating on you Stacia," said Tonya. Sounding as if she was narrating a soap opera. I hope not Tonya, but where is he? "He might have just driven over there to the club Stacia to show Danny some support, Mike may have just missed him," said Tonya. Well, I'm starting to miss him too, Tonya,... I want my husband, I said pouting. "So now he's your *husband* Stace, any other time he's just Bryson or *dat Negro* when you get mad at him. He'll be home soon Stacia, just give him some time. Relax and put on Golden Girls and eat all the hor'dourves. By that time you'll probably hear from him," said Tonya. I hope so, Tonya, I'm warming up the food as we speak. We had a really good time tonight. "Yes, like old times, I really had fun," said Tonya. "We have to get back to that *Sisterly* fun we used to have before you started hanging out with those snobs," said Tonya sarcastically. Now there you go Tonya. But I know what you mean, we sisters need to stick together, at the end of the day we will be the ones that will have each other's back when the going gets rough, no matter what...and I love you no matter what. "I love you too Stacia,... now have a good night regardless of where Brysons ass is at." Yes, you're right about that Sis,... Nite Nite baby Sister. "Nit Nite big Sister."

DON'T LET ME FIND OUT

BRYSON'S ASS DID BEAT the Sun in, but barely. Bryson! Where were you at and why didn't you answer your phone? "I went by Kennys to see if he wanted to go with me to Danny's club. I got there late, stayed a while and came home, what's the big deal?" said Bryson. After I stared at him with visions of hitting him upside his head, I replied the big deal is you seem to be disappearing alot lately,... are you having an affair Bryson? "No, I am not having an affair, Stacia. I have been bored being in the house all the time lately and I just wanted to start doing something a little different. You know, mix it up a little, just get out of the house a little bit." Yea right Bryson,doing something different my ass. Don't let me find out something is going on with you and some bitch, it won't be pretty Bryson, don't play with me. "Stacia, I'm not doing anything with anyone, don't you trust me?" I always trusted you Bryson, but lately something just doesn't feel right, but what's done in the dark will come out in the light...eventually. I don't have to go looking for it, it will reveal

itself, at some point anyway.. Anyway, now that you finally decided
to bring your ass home, I'm going back to sleep.

I wake up to find I am in this bed alone once again. Damn, what
the hell Bryson, you're already up and out?, I thought. What's that
smell, Weed and Bacon? Since when did Bryson start smoking weed?
Bryson! I said just as Bryson almost jumped out of his skin. Oh, did
I startle you?, I asked like a detective. I saw him abruptly hanging
up his phone and I abruptly asked, who are you all smiley with on
that phone Bryson?... "That was Kenny, Stace, we were talking about
some of the things that went on last night at Danny's club." "It was
very entertaining to say the least." Yea, I bet, who is that real tall girl
that kept staring at me last night riding that damn pole? "How am I
supposed to know Stacia, I wasn't there when you were there." Well
I'm sure you saw her when you were *so-called* there last night, Bryson.
Actually she had on a necklace that looked like Mommy's. You know
the expensive necklace that Daddy gave her? "No, I didn't notice
that Stacia. Of all the people there, I don't know how you expect me
to know who you're talking about, especially about some necklace.
With all them big asses and big titties sliding up and down poles,
celebrities and high rollers and all kinds of people all over the place
and I'm supposed to notice one particular *Tall girl* with an expensive
necklace," said Bryson. "How dumb does that sound Stacia?" Dumb
my ass Bryson, all I have to say is don't let me find out. Anyway, I will
be going to the Condo tomorrow. James the Doorman told me you
have been spending some time in the Condo lately Bryson, why didn't
you tell me you've been going into the City? "Do I have to tell you
everything, Woman?" asked Bryson. No, it just seems that at some
point you would have told me that you've been at the Condo. Well
anyway, I needed to check the mail and just check on the Condo in
general. It's only been a little over a month since we left the Condo

to come to the lake house as we do every year by the way, it's just that we left a little earlier this year because of the situation. "What situation is that, Stacia?" What the hell do you mean Bryson, you know damn well what situation I am talking about. "Oh, that situation," said Bryson. Anyway Bryson, I have to go into the City a few times this week to take care of some things, so that's where I will be if you're looking for me, my husband, I said sarcastically. I'm not like you in that respect Bryson, I will tell you where I'm going. "There you go Stacia, making a big deal out of nothing, at first you say I'm boring and don't ever leave my chair and the minute I leave the house a few times I'm doing something wrong." "But ok, thank you for telling me in advance where you will be my wife." "I appreciate that so I won't worry about where you are." "By the way, how long are Draya and Mike going to be at the Condo?" asked Bryson. "And when are they going home?" "It almost seems like they have no home at this point," said Bryson. You know every year they stay at the Lakehouse with us over the 4th of July and then some, anyway I love having the kids around, they keep me busy and keep me company. Especially since we don't seem to do too much together anymore. Besides that, you know that their house is still under renovations.

Anyway,...what happened to us Bryson? Did we just get too used to each other like my old comfortable robe? We used to desire each other, we had a spark in each other's eyes every time we saw each other. We would lust for each other, make love anywhere and everywhere. Remember when Draya was little and she would want to sleep in the bed with us and we would put her on the floor for a minute and call ourselves slipping it in from the back quietly and the shit would get too good and we would have to move a little more than we wanted to and the next thing you know we heard this *"Mom, Dad,* what's that noise," and we would say, nothing we are just stretching, go back to sleep. We would get it in whatever chance we got, sitting on your lap watching TV, my pussy was wet and throbbing just anticipating your dick on it's way in there. But now my pussy doesn't even know what wet is unless I'm peeing and I haven't felt that dick hard while you're holding me from the back in so long, I forgot you had a dick. Hell Bryson, I don't even know what sex is anymore. I have not thought about it at all, not even when I'm watching Lifetime. I watch romance movies with absolutely no emotion at all. What is going on with us,... what's going on with me,... what's going on with you? I lost track and how do we get back on track at this point Bryson? "I don't know Stace, I just don't know," said Bryson. "You know I still love you, I guess we are just at a place where we are just comfortable." "We are just cruising I guess, but we are ok, everything is ok, Stace," Bryson said as he gave me a kiss on my forehead and a brotherly hug...Damn.

BACK TO THE CITY

WELL, AFTER THAT CONVERSATION with Bryson, I felt like I needed a renewal, a revitalization of some sort with myself. I need to get back to my exercise routine and back to a schedule of something. I had lounged around enough. The kids were still in summer vacation mode doing their things. Braya had started to get into making her own lip glosses in different colors and flavors, and Branson was skateboarding but started rapping a little. Well, whatever made them happy made me happy. We have to let them be and explore what they want to explore in their young lives. I had to get back to me, actually reinvent me. I was at a crossroad, although I had dabbled in the Culinary road, the Investment world, I knew it was much more inside of me that I had not yet tapped into. *"Made by God so I must be special"*... I know I am special. God didn't give me a whole lot of talent just to waste it trying to please everyone in my life but myself...and God. Anyway, God will let me know of my next move... and I will listen and hear God...and obey God. God knows what's best for my life, after all, he created me for a purpose and that purpose will give me the most fulfillment and joy that I could ever get from money or a man or whatever flesh feeding thing I could do in life. But I sure do feel like a little something flesh pleasing right now from somewhere Dear Lord...

Riding into the City on a Sunny weekday morning riding past boathouse row and listening to Jill Scotts' "**Golden**" gave me some new energy. I got a little spark here, yes, I'm feeling good. I think I'm going to stop by and see Nephew Danny at the club before it opens up for the business lunch crowd. I want to see what that Chef got cooking. I love food. I think I'll stop by the Condo first. I hope Draya and Mike left the place neat and clean, they know how I am about that. Hey James! It's so good to see you this morning! How's it going this morning so far? "Well it's going great now that I see you Ms. Lady!" said James. "You are looking good and chipper this morning Miss Stacia, I guess chilling out at the Lakehouse has given you a nice rest and rejuvenation, you look great!" said James. Thank you James! I needed that James and you're looking good yourself, I said with a somewhat flirtatious vibe. Alright now, don't start any stuff here James, I said joking and blushing. Do you know if my daughter is still here or did they finally decide to go home for a few? "They left early this morning Ms. Stacia." Oh ok, I didn't hear from her yet this morning and you know the kids are always with me, you mineswell say they are my kids. "Yes, I know," said James. "Those kids love their Mum Mom, and that little Braya is a little business woman in the making just like her Grandmother," said James. Yes she is, I said. "Hey, is Branson still playing the piano?" asked James. Well James, I am just letting him be a kid right now, he's enjoying summer fun at the lakehouse with some friends and skateboarding and starting to rap a little, I said laughing. "Rapping?" Asked James. Yes, rapping James, but it's all good, whatever the kids feel like doing rite now, it's all good. As long as it doesn't hurt anyone it's all good for them to explore. "Yes, your rite Ms.Stacia, it's been great talking to you this morning, I miss our morning talks," said James. "It was great seeing you and I can't wait until you come back home"…said James. "By the way, have you talked to John lately?" asked James. Oh shit I thought, why did I know that question would come up sooner or later. No, I said. He does that disappearing thing sometimes. He's probably up Martha's vineyard or something, he gets that way sometimes. I probably will hear from him towards the end of summer, I said as I started high tailing it away from that conversation. See ya later James.

As I started down the corridor, waving and smiling at all the familiar faces, I did not feel like stopping and talking to anyone. I just smiled, waved and kept it moving. I was on a mission. As I entered that Condo I didn't know quite how to feel, I felt a lot of feelings at the same time and I also felt numb. Thank God Draya and Mike had everything clean and in order. As I approached Bryson's desk in the study, that letter opener brought a quick flashback of that night across my head. I had visions of that night. I tried to shake it off. *Shake that shit off Stacia*, I said to myself, but eventually you're gonna have to dig that shit back up in order to bury it for good. *Fight your way through it*, is what I kept telling myself. I kept telling myself that, coaching myself, *you will have victory*. I kept telling myself, *be strong but let God. He will resolve this issue and you will come out unscathed and victorious, just let God*…. I know this but at the same time I knew I had a long road ahead. I needed a healing bad, a deep healing, a healing from some things I didn't even know I needed to heal from. What the hell, since when does Bryson have the desk drawers all locked up. I wanted to look at the mail, and while I was at it, get the key to the safety deposit box at the bank to put Tonya's mind at ease about Ma's damn necklace. Anyway, let me call Bryson and see if this key is in the house somewhere. Bryson!, why is this desk all locked up and where is the key? "Stacia, I just locked it up so Mike and Draya don't be messing with the mail and paperwork and things," said Bryson. "You know how Draya likes to be nosey and open mail and be all in our business sometimes," said Bryson. Well where is the key Bryson. "I have the key with me, Stacia." Well I did say I was coming to the Condo to check mail and do paperwork Bryson. Why the hell wouldn't you have said that or given me the key? " I just forgot Woman, that's all." Stop calling me Woman all the time Bryson, it's getting annoying. Well now that I can't accomplish anything here I guess I'll stop by Danny's club a minute and talk to him for a few. "What are you going over there and bugging Danny about Stacia?," asked Bryson. So what now Bryson, I'm not allowed to stop by my nephew's club? "I didn't say that, Stacia, but you know he's probably busy right now," said Bryson. Well, I'm on my way over there just for a minute, then I will be back home to the lakehouse a little later, love you Bryson. "Love you too Stacia."

As I approached Danny's club I felt a good feeling. As if I was on to something I wanted to be a part of or something. Whatever the feeling was, it was a happy feeling. Hey Nephew, what's up I said as we embraced into a jolly hug. "Hey Auntie, Danny said, my boy back there in the kitchen was just talking about you." Talking about me? I said as I raised my eyebrows. "Nothing bad Auntie, he just said you knew what you were talking about in this kitchen that's all." "I told him you could throw down with food and have been in the restaurant and hospitality world yourself," said Danny. Oh, ok, well let me go back there a minute and see what he got cooking, I said. He's a little cute anyway, I said jokingly... "Alright there Auntie, don't have Unc coming up in here acting up now," said Danny. Whatever about Bryson Nephew, I said. "Oh shute Auntie, it's like that?" Yes, it's like that right now Nephew, I said with a cat smile. By the way, did you see Bryson the night of your Grand opening Nephew? "I'm not sure Auntie, there was so much going on and so many people, but I didn't see him come into the VIP spot I had set up for yall," said Danny. Oh ok. Hey Chef, what you got going on back here today? "Hey Mommy, I was just talking about you," "You know they say there are no coincidences right…," said the Chef. Yea, that's what I hear Chef, I said. So what is your name anyway, I ask with a sly eye… "Oh, we never really officially met," said the Chef. "I'm Gustave, Gus for short." "And you are Auntie Stacia, ha ha, that's what your nephew calls you affectionately.." Well you can just call me Stace, I said with a smile, and I like your accent, are you from some island? "I am from Trinidad & Tobago," Chef said. Oh ok, I said with a smile. "But although I am Trinidadian Creole I cook all kinds of different foods from a lot of different cultures." " My specialty is infusing different cultures and flavors." "I think of myself as a Food Stylist, I love to create," said Chef. Oh ok, Chef Gus, I like to create all kinds of things myself. I would love to create a few dishes with you sometimes…I said flirting. It actually felt good to flirt, I hadn't even felt flirtatious in a long while. I hadn't seen anyone that I felt like flirting with. But my Mother always told me, *"never stop flirting, it keeps you young."*

Anyway, it's so good to talk to someone that has something with them if you know what I mean Chef. I'm going to go out front and talk to Danny for a minute and then I'm going back to the suburbs for now. But I will definitely catch up with you later. "Ok Mommy, nice to see you too." "I look forward to seeing you again soon and maybe we can create some nice new flavors if you have time," Chef Gus said with a sexy smile. Nephew, that Chef is gonna stop playing with me back there, I mess around and leave Bryson's ass for him,

I said with an ornery smile. "Stop Auntie," said Danny. "You know I'm not having no Man running no game on my Auntie." Who said he is the one running game, Danny, I said with an ornery cat laugh. Well anyway Nephew, Auntie is just messing with him right now, you know Your Unc and I got a little comfortable and boring lately, I guess we are just getting old, I sighed. "Nah, y'all are not old Auntie, you and Unc just been together so long you just need to get back into yall groove." "Maybe you two should take a trip or a Cruise or something. I know this Travel Agent I could hook you up with, I'll give you her name later," said Danny. Ok, thanks Nephew, a trip does sound good right about now. I'll talk to Bryson about it later. Anyway Danny, did you find out any more about that Peter Cooney guy? "No Auntie, I haven't had the chance lately with the Club opening and all." "But I'm sure I will bump into him soon." "Especially since I stole a few strippers from that club he hangs out at." Well, let me know Danny, I'm going back to the Lake house. I guess I will be back in the City later in the week, Thursday or Friday. "Ok, see you then Auntie," Danny said while giving me a big bear hug. "Love ya Auntie." Love you too Nephew, I said as I watched the Strippers do their practice routines. Hm I thought, that does look *hot* actually *hot* and *sexy* and damn that has to be a great workout too. Good for the Abs, Butt ,Legs, Arms and Cardio,..just good for you all around. That can be my new workout routine if I knew how, wonder if I could get lessons. Danny would laugh at me if I asked him about lessons. Well, Bryson would surely appreciate it or maybe he wouldn't even notice. But it would make me feel a little better about myself and give my self esteem a little boost. I surely need that, I have not been feeling the best about myself lately….You know what Danny, I'm going to have myself a little Cocktail and chill here for a second before I get back on that road again if you don't mind. I'm going to look at a few of my emails and texts. It's no use rushing back to the Lakehouse rite now, I'm going to check on these kids real quick though before I have this drink. I sure wish I had the skills and energy those girls have. " Auntie," Danny laughed, "you could do that, you're still young." I wish I could Danny. I'm going to sit here and watch them for a minute, maybe I could learn something, I said sarcastically.

As I sat there listening to the music and sitting back in the dark sexy ambience of the club, I was really feeling pretty good in the middle of the day, too good actually. It feels like a sin or something. Im feeling no stress, no pain, no feeling like I had to be doing something, no running a million errands, no housework or grocery shopping, although I do sometimes get off on shopping for some sexy colorful food,... no doing a hundred loads of laundry, no taking care of everyone else's shit,... just relaxing, exhaling and being me... Wow,..God please tell me this is ok, and that this is not a sin,..thank you Dear Lord…Thank you. I could get used to this.

"Hello," I heard a voice say. I looked up to see the *Tall Girl* standing there with a confident smile. Hi, I said looking at her as if to say, at last we meet face to face, what's up. " I'm Nubia," she said with an African accent. I'm Stacia, Danny's Aunt, it's good to finally be officially introduced. "I just wanted to introduce myself to you. I have seen you around lately and I like to introduce myself to people that I think are Hot," said the Tall Girl. Hot!? I said with a laugh. Thank you Momma, I said blushing. As the Tall Girl walked away with a confident strive like a Black Panther Queen, I thought to myself, hum, she got it going on. No wonder Tonya seems obsessed with her. I don't really think Bryson is messing with her, number one, she would be too much for his ass and the other number one is, she is not having no middle aged man that would sit on a reclining chair all day. Anyway, she sure has grace and confidence about her. That made me think about my own confidence and self esteem… although I at times felt as if I had poise and self confidence, I am coming to realize that my confidence is not what it used to be. Or did I think I had it before, but was covering up something I had inside of me all along. Maybe something I was not so confident about, something I experienced growing up, or actually some things I experienced growing up that made me feel I needed to wear a *Mask*..but never really realizing I had a *Mask* on. Not a full mask anyway, because I do know where I come from, a good stock and a child of God. But I think I need to work on some things and go deep inside. Maybe even relive some shit a little, and learn from it. What was meant for my harm can turn into Gold. We have some work to do, Stacia, I said to myself, so let's get this party started….

I might as well have another drink, Handsome, I said to the Bartender. That drink was really good and it made me feel nice over here. What is the name of that drink and what is your name? "Haaa, thank you, I'm glad you like that drink, it's called '*Take me there*', and my name is Ben." Well Ben, please *"take me there"* once again. Two is my limit and I don't usually drink in the middle of the day, Ben, but this atmosphere makes me feel like I'm on a mini vacay or something. I hope you guys don't have me hanging in this Club all the time and turning me out, I said laughing. "You good Ma," said Ben. "Just do you and don't let nobody take you from you." You said a mouthful there Ben…. Thanks I said, I'm Stacia, Danny's Aunt. You just might start to see me around here a little more Ben. "Well, it's a pleasure to meet you Stacia and I look forward to seeing you around," said Ben. Damn I said to myself, I'm feeling better already here. Who can give me pole lessons around here Ben? I asked as if I were joking but I was as serious as a cat in the alley. "I will ask around

Stace, if you don't mind me calling you that," said Bartender Ben. No, actually that is what my sister, Danny's mom, calls me. And my parents used to call me that too. "Use to call you that?" Ben asked. Yea, used to, I said with a half faded smile, they both died in a car accident years ago. "Oh, I'm so sorry, said Ben. "I don't want to take your good mood away". You didn't Ben, it's all good, I talk to them all the time anyway. I'll be talking to them a little later about some things. It's all good..and they actually talk back sometimes in their own way. "I know the feeling Stace, it looks like we have some things in common and can have some great conversations sometime in the near future." Sounds good to me Ben, and I'll look forward to enjoying some unique cocktails and conversations. I'm going to go over there and sit at that sexy booth with the exotic beads and let this drink *take me there*. I said flirting again. Looks like you found something New New Stace, I thought to myself.

Let me call Draya and make sure she is on her way to the Lake-house and check on those kids. No telling where Bryson might sneak off too while I'm gone. Here you go again Stacia, I said to myself, stop all the worrying and enjoy the moment while you're here. This music sure sounds good. "Auntie, are you still here chillin?" said Danny. Yes I am, my Nephew, and having a good time too, almost as good of a time as when it was full of people, but you know I like an intimate crowd even better. "Yea, I know what you mean Auntie, I have some investors upstairs, I just came downstairs to give the Chef an order of lunch for them." "Does Chef know you're still here?" Not sure Danny, I said, I've been chatting with your bartender Ben a little and finally got introduced to that Tall girl. "Oh, you've been busy down here Auntie," Danny said laughing. I'm going to take this order back to the Chef and make sure he knows you're still here." Ok Nephew, I said, let me take this call, it's your mom. "Aww shute Auntie, don't have her come here in the middle of the day, y'all will end up here all day and get all fired up." That's okay if we get fired up in the middle of the day Nephew as long as we have a ride home, you know I don't drive after 2 drinks. "I know that's right," said Danny.

Hey Tonya, what's up? "Hey Sis, where are you at?" At your son's club sucking down a few drinks and flirting with that Chef, um, and the Bartender is hot too. He has a nice Cocktail selection. I'm drinking one now called *Take me there*, and I'm going there too! I said laughing. "Oh shute!" said Tonya. "I should come there!" Come on then! I said getting a party started. We can call an Uber or something and leave our cars here if we get fired up. "Sounds like a plan," said Tonya. "Give me about 45 mins and I'll be there." You better hurry up because I'm already a few drinks ahead of you and I'm getting hungry. "Ok, I'm already dressed and was heading out the door anyway, see you in a minute." Ok, Tonya, drive safe and don't speed.

"Heyyyy Stace," Tonya said as she came in bopping to the music. Let me catch up to your ass, Sis, order two of them damn "*Take me there's*" for me." Tonya you are so crazy, I feel a session coming on and I'm a little scared, I said laughing. " As long as we feed this alcohol we'll be okay, let me see the Menu," said Tonya. "This menu looks good, the Chef has some good sounding dishes on here, these Voodoo fries sure sound good, short rib, crawfish, jalapeno, scallions and cheese with a special voodoo sauce. Damn and a Mini Bam Burger sounds good, Blackened Gator with Trinity pepper slaw and Creole Mustard, I think I'm going to order that. What are you going to have, Stace?" I think I'm going to have the Jambalaya Salad, but I want to taste some of your fries, I said. I really want to get Pole dance lessons but that's not happening today. Do you want to get Pole dance lessons with me Tonya? "Pole dance lessons Stace?" Tonya said laughing. "Who are you going to be dancing on a pole for Stacia, Bryson's tired ass?"

Tonya said laughing with a sarcastic tone. Whatever Tonya, I said like Charlie Brown, it will be good exercise and will help me boost my self esteem. "Self esteem?" asked Tonya with a new found stare. "Since when do you have a self esteem problem Stace? You are one of the most confident people I know. If anybody had a problem with self esteem it was me. Mom and Dad were always so proud of you. They talked about you all the time with everyone, but they thought of me as being in need of help," said Tonya. "I felt they thought I wasn't too smart and I couldn't be successful at anything." Oh my God Tonya, you were Mom and Dad's favorite, you were the cute child. I had to be smart, they thought, because I wasn't going to be successful in getting a good husband. Both of us looked at each other and smiled and grinned. All this time we had a jealousy towards each other that we never communicated to each other. I could remember how as a child, I used to get teased at school for being dark skinned, although I was just average brown skinned. I used to have a crush on a cute boy when I was 12 years old, his name was Reggie Brown. He didn't like me because he thought my 10 year old sister Tonya was cuter because she was light skinned. I was so crushed, it made me have a complex about my complexion ever since. I never told anyone. I just pretended as if I hated him because he acted too immature. I could picture it in my mind like it was yesterday... "Stace, are you over there daydreaming again?" Tonya asked. Just thinking about some childhood memories Tonya. "Yeah, I think about our childhood too. We had great parents and a very rich childhood, not necessarily money rich, although we weren't that poor either, we just had a lot of people in our lives that were full of character." "Larger than life people and the adults were in our daily lives." "We had our Aunts and Uncles, neighborhood Moms and Dads and just regular everyday people that had a big presence in our lives and we had good old fashioned fun," said Tonya. Yea, remember the Cookouts and Holidays were so much fun. All of the family would get together and the Aunts and Uncle dressed like movie stars. They seemed like movie stars to us. We would form a car train and visit everyone's house on Christmas to see each other's Christmas Decorations and gifts they got, I said. "Yeah," said Tonya. "The good ole days were so much richer than these days, I kind of feel sorry for the kids of today...

Oh, anyway Tonya the Bartender is coming with our drinks. His name is Ben and he is fine, and I don't see a ring, I said with a cat smile. "Stace, there you go looking up and down a man from his head to his feet." "While we're on the subject, how big are those feet?" laughed Tonya with a cat smile. Check it out for yourself, I said. Hey Ben, this is my sister Tonya, Danny's mom. "It's a pleasure to meet you Tonya," said Ben. "Good looks obviously run in the family and I can't believe you have a grown son. "You must have had him when you were 10 years old," Ben said with a polite well spoken sexy voice. "Thank you Ben," said Tonya blushing. "You are going to have me here all the time when you're working," laughed Tonya. "I look forward to it," said Ben. "Are you ladies going to be ordering some food?" Yes we are, I'm going to have the Jambalaya salad with the Creole mustard dressing. "And you Tonya?" asked Ben. "I'm going to have the Voodoo fries and a mini Bam burger." "Awrite," said the Bartender. "I will put the food order in. Would you like our Lemon, honey and Fresh mint water with your food?" "Yes we would," we both said at the same time. "Enjoy your drinks and each other's company in the meantime Ladies." "We sure will," we both said simultaneously again and laughed. "He sure is cute, Stace, how old do you think he is?" I don't know Tonya, about 30 something. But you know your son would have a fit, I said. "Well, I'm not saying I want to marry him, Stace, but maybe a hot steamy shower together would be all I need to jump start me again," laughed Tonya. Um Um, Tonya, well I'm checking out that Chef back there, he is sexy and there's something else about him I'm feeling. "Oh, you talking about me Stace, Bryson would have a fit." "And anyway, you know you are not going to cheat on Bryson," said Tonya. Whatever about Bryson, his ass might be cheating on me. By the way the Tall girl is here and she came up to me and introduced herself, her name is Nubia, she is African. I don't think she would even be interested in Bryson with his lazy ass. Oh, look Tonya, there she goes practicing on the pole now. "I still am feeling some kind of way about her, Stace, it's something shaky with her," Tonya said, side eyeing Tall girl. We will soon find out what's going on between her and that Peter Cooney guy, they might be trying to set us up about John. "Oh shit Stace, I hope that situation doesn't come back to haunt yall, I sure don't want you going to jail, not my sister." I don't want to go to jail either Tonya, that's why I have to see what he is up to and what he knows about that night of Branson's Piano concert. "Yea, it will all work out for the good somehow, Stace," said Tonya. "God has his Angels of protection over us, and you know Mom and Dad are watching over us." Yes they are Tonya, I miss them so much. "I miss them too, Stace, but I'm glad we still have each other. I love you Sister." I love you too, baby Sister.

"Here are your Voodoo fries and Bam Burger, Miss Tonya, and Your Jambalaya Salad, Miss Stacia," said Ben. "And here are your Lemon Honey Fresh Mint Waters, would you like anything else ladies?" asked Ben. Just then I saw Tonya's eyes light up. No, I think we are good for now Ben. "This food looks and smells so good, Stace," said Tonya. "Let's say our grace." "Heavenly Father, please Bless this food and the hands that made it, Amen." Yea, you got that right, I want to caress those Chef's hands all up and down my body. "Oh no you didn't Miss Stacia, we are both being ornery Sis," said Tonya grinning like a chessy cat, and I'm loving it. Damn these blackened shrimp, chicken and sausage are good, nice big fresh shrimp, how is your food Tonya? "This Bam Burger is really good, they probably blended this with a little pork sausage," said Tonya. "And the Blackened taste with Creole mango mustard and pepper slaw go well together. It has a little sweetness in the mustard. Give me your bread plate so I can put some fries on it for you," said Tonya. You don't have to tell me twice, I was getting ready to ask you for some anyway, I said. We were eating our food and making noises like it was good sex or something. We love some good food. Good food was always that magic that would always bring us together when we weren't feeling each other that much for a moment. Good food and good laughs about anything and everything would make us forget about the argument we just had 15 minutes ago. That came from our home life, Mommy and Daddy both were good home cooks. They would cook together in the kitchen and drink some wine and laugh and listen to some good music and dance while they were cooking. That's what made me want to go into the hospitality business. Watching them enjoying each other's company while doing something they both loved, made me love to make people's special times enjoyable unforgettable moments.

"Damn I got a good stomach now, Stace," said Tonya. "It's time for a couple of shots." Shots!? I said. Are we going to start on shots now, I said with a terrified look. " Yes, let's do some of those Lemonchello shots like we had on the opening night," said Tonya. I'm going to the bar and let Ben know to give us two shots a piece and flirt with him a little while I'm over there." Ok Sis, don't let Danny see you flirting with him, you're going to mess with that man's job. "Don't worry Stace, I'm not going to get him in any kind of trouble," said Tonya.

It was pure Candy shop action in this club. Some of the Investors came down on the floor looking good, sharp and buffed with their nice suits on. They were checking out the scenes before the club opened, wrapping things up and making power moves with upscale spirits in hand. "Oh shute Stace, we picked a good time to hang out here," said Tonya. "'It's just a few of us grown and sexy ass important people, hanging out and gettin it in for a minute," said Tonya. As the day turned to evening, Tonya was working one end of the bar and I was working the other end. We were in our glory with these nice looking men. I was also checking out the Dancers and learning some things. I'm going to get my ass on a pole when all these men aren't here. I am not trying to embarrass myself. Shit, I might get my ass on a pole in the basement at home. As the drinks kept flowing, we were feeling more and more free..shit we were feeling good. Tonya and I even smoked a little weed in a Hookah, damn we were feeling it. Before we knew it the damn club was packed and we were on the dance floor wiling out. We were dancing and flirting with a little of every kind, young and old, hot and not, black, white and in between and even a few hot sexy chicks. Hell, it didn't matter what, we were wild and free. At this point, actually downright drunk. We were drunk enough to potentially get into some bad shit. Shit, drunk enough to go into some VIP rooms and do some lap dancing. Oh damn Tonya, where is nephew? "I'm not sure, Stace." "He must be over checking on one of his other clubs, I didn't see him leave," said Tonya. He probably left while we were up there being bad in some shit we might be sorry for later. Just like in our younger days,we were being feisty and bad. Well hell, we are still young,...Well, we are not old anyway.

Oh shit, I must have dozed off for a minute. How the hell did I get up here in this private dance room? I feel like shit. Where the hell is Tonya? What the funk, 30 missed calls? 5am? Where the hell did the time go? It was just 7:30pm. Shit, where is my sister? Tonya, Tonya, I called down the hall. Where the hell is she? Let me call her phone. "Hey you, bad Mommy, you finally woke up," said the Chef. What the hell happened and how did I get up here? I ask the Chef, still half drunk and confused. "Well," said Chef, " I thought you needed some assistance after you swung on the pole and fell." Oh shit, no I didn't do that. "Yes you did Mommy, but it's all good, I was watching out for you." I saw you going for it, so I went over and started a little dance move with you so you kind of fell into my arms, but I had you, don't worry, nobody really noticed." So where is my Sister? I asked frantically. "Don't worry Ma," said Chef. "I got Ben to drive her home, he lives out that way." "Danny knows about it." "I called and told him what was going on." "He called Ben and told him to make sure she got in the house safe and to lock the doors and make sure she was safe," said Chef. "He was handling business at the other club and went home from there," said Chef. Well since I'm already still half fired up, I might as well catch it back up with a light beer and another hit off that damn weed. Since I'm already in trouble with Bryson, I might as well make it good. Damn, Bryson called ten times, Draya called ten times and the kids called 10 times. I guess I better call one of them back and let them know we are ok. Where the hell are my shoes? "I put your shoes over there next to the chair, you took them off when you were trying to give me a private dance and fell into my lap," said Chef. Oh my God Chef, I don't remember any of that, I am so embarrassed. I don't even want to ask what else I did, I said as I kept staring at my phone. I can't believe I lost track of time like that. I have a million missed calls. Can you please excuse me while I return a few calls? I asked. "Yes, no problem, get your phone calls out and just relax, you are here safe with me," said the Chef. Ok, I said, sounding like a teenage girl. I sure liked the sound of his confidence and it made me feel very secure. It felt like I had some kind of blanket around me, soft and warm but strong and protective. Damn, I like the way he makes me feel. Different from the way Bryson makes me feel. I also feel comfortable with Bryson but like an old pair of slippers. Bryson makes me comfortable, but does not necessarily make me feel like a sexy woman..

Tonya, I said with a sigh of relief as I heard her half still high voice, are you okay? "Yeah girl, I feel like I'm still kind of drunk, laying here with no clothes on," said Tonya. Oh shute, are you there by yourself? I asked. "Yeah I am, but I'm not sure if my ass feels a little wet from me peeing and not wiping good or playing with my new toy. How the hell did I get here Stace and where the hell are you, and where the hell is my damn truck?" I'm still at the club. "What!" Tonya said. "How the hell are you still at the club?." I'm not really sure yet Tonya, all I know is I woke up in a private dance room, but the Chef was watching out for us. Thankfully, he said he called Danny to make sure it was okay for Ben to take you home and make sure you got in the house safely. "You mean Ben drove me home, Stace?" asked Tonya. "I don't remember how the hell I got home, this is crazy Stace." Yea it is Tonya, I said as I sparked up a joint. "Are you smoking Stace?" Yea Tonya, I'm already feeling buzzed so why not level it out. Chef went downstairs to get me a lite beer. You probably need to have one too and just chill in bed and go back to sleep for a few. "Yea I will, I had like over 20 missed calls," said Tonya. Yeah I know, I had over 30 missed calls. I better call Bryson and let him know I'm safe. I'm going to tell him both you and I came upstairs at your house to sleep some of the alcohol off. So make sure you stick with the story Tonya. I'm going to drink this light beer and go back to sleep, I will talk to you later. I'm so glad we are both okay. "Me too Stace."

Shit, I think I should just text Draya and let her know to tell Bryson that I am over Tonya's house, we got drunk and fell asleep. That's my story and I'm sticking to it. I will see them in the morning, although it's morning already, but technically, it's still a little dark. In any case, I will see them a little later. Tonya and I are okay, that's basically all they need to know. Fuck Bryson anyway, payback is a bitch. Draya can let him know I'm safe and accounted for. That's that and let me live in the moment. Actually a good moment, quite a few good moments I shall say… Damn Stace, didn't we do the thing last night, didn't we. Still doing the thing right now girl… "How ya feeling Ms. Lady?" asked the Chef while he handed me a 7 ounce Heineken lite, a small mineral water and a mini BLT. "This will help to keep you from feeling bad." "You need some protein, tomato and a piece of bread to help you out." "I also put a lemon in that beer but take your time on that." "Also there is a toothbrush and other toiletries in the powder room over there," said Chef. "Lay back and get some rest," said the Chef as he put a plush throw cover on me that felt so comfortable. "I'm going downstairs to prep some things for today, my Sous Chef should be here soon." Thanks again Gus for looking after us, I said while I was glazing in his eyes. I feel like a damn ornery ass teenager that did some stupid shit. But thank you for looking out for me and my Sister, I really appreciate it. "Awwe Mommy, don't worry about it, I loved to see beautiful Black Sisters hanging out and enjoying themselves and each other, the pleasure was all mine." "Now relax and go back to sleep for a minute, I got you." And I did just that, just like that…

THE MORNING AFTER

THE SUN IS UP, I can feel it. Although you would never know it in this windowless relaxing ambiance in this club. As relaxing as it is, it's time to be out and about. Brushing my teeth while looking in the mirror, I had to smile at myself just thinking about the good and crazy time we just had last night. My sister and I haven't had one of those wild times in a long time. It sure was fun but crazy. That's okay, we survived and then some. Brush this hair and pull it back in a ponytail Stacia and put the good ole Cocoa Butter Vaseline on the face. You still look good in the natural state girl. You always said to yourself *you wake up like this.* Let me go downstairs in this kitchen and thank the Chef again for him watching out for us. Good morning Chef, how are you this morning? "I'm feeling blessed, Miss Lady," said the Chef. Well Chef, I guess technically we already saw each other this morning only a few hours ago but now it's daylight. Anyway Chef, I see you have everything already going this morning, everything looks so good and fresh. "Yes, Good Morning Stacia, *You* are looking very fresh and naturally beautiful this morning." Thank you, I said blushing but looking in his eyes. I feel pretty good despite the fact that we drank entirely too much last night. I owe that to you with the BLT and also the mineral water you gave me with that little lite beer I wanted so much. I didn't even drink but a sip of that beer to put me back to sleep for a few hours, the mineral water felt so much better going down. "That's okay Stace, you were enjoying yourself." "Are you heading back to your place out in the Suburbs?" Eventually Gus, but right now I'm on my way to my Condo here in the City. I haven't been going there in a few months but I all of the sudden tapped into some new found strength in myself. "Okay Mommy, that's what I'm talking about." I can see that you are a phenomenal woman, full of inner beauty and God given gifts and purpose." "Too bad you are taken…I can see that there is a lot more inside of you that has yet to be discovered and brought to the surface. "I can tell you have a lot of exceptional beauty on the inside just as well as on the outside." "I'm glad to see that you have renewed strength, Stacia, you always had it, you just needed to rest and let God set the stage for you." Well thank you for saying that Gus, it makes me feel good and encouraged to hear someone say that to me, thank you. "You don't need to thank me for acknowledging what I see in front of me, it's my pleasure to even spend this time with you." There was a moment of silence that seemed to say a lot. "You better get going, Stacia, I don't want to hold you up any longer." A moment more of that same unsilent silence… Yes, I'm going to get going and let you do your thing Chef, can a "*Taken*" woman get a hug? I said with a flirtatious smile. "You sure can Mommy," said Chef. As we gave each other a nice warm embrace, I felt warm, safe and overall carefored. As our bodies parted from that hug, we both undeniably felt something. We smiled and gave each other a quick glance into each other's eyes and turned away not to let each other know how either of us felt, although we both knew, it was undeniable...

On my way to the Condo, I kept having flashbacks of Gus's eyes. They were deep dark sparkly eyes, I could see **him** when I looked into his eyes, gentle and warm, he had a depth to him, a depth I'd like to explore, undeniably...

Hello, I greeted as I answered my phone. Hey good morning Bryson, I said with a cheesy grin on my face. Yeah, I know, Tonya and I started out by having a few drinks at Danny's club after I talked to you but the next thing we knew we had one too many and Danny had someone drive us to Tonya's house. We ended up having a good girls sisterly night, had a few more drinks and passed out. But we did have a good time where we bonded and reconnected. We had some good revelations about how each other felt about our childhood and our sibling rivalries. We had some really good, well needed conversations about what we felt were our truths. How our parents treated us differently for the reasons that were real to each of us and we started a much needed healing. I'm so glad Tonya and I were able to have that night, Bryson. Anyway Bryson, I don't know why you should have anything to say about me not coming home being how your ass seems to disappear lately. "I don't disappear, woman, I don't know what you're talking about," said Bryson. "I came home late one night when your nephew had a grand opening at his club, showing him some support and getting out of the chair, just like you are always bitching about and now I disappear." "So are you on your way home Stacia?" asked Bryson. No, I'm going to go to the Condo for a minute or two, I said with some sense of strength. "Oh ok, you feel you are ready to spend some time in the Condo now Stace?" asked Bryson. Yes Bryson, I all of the sudden now have a new found sense of empowerment. I have to face these demons head on, that's the only way I can move on with my life. "Ok Stacia, I'll be here in my chair as usual," said Bryson. "The kids are outside with their friends, and Draya and Mike are upstairs. I will see you when you get here, drive safe, I love you." Love you too Bryson, see you later.

GETTING MY GROOVE BACK

HEY JAMES, GOOD TO see you again. "Hey Miss Stacia, Good morning and good to see you too." "You are looking great as usual Miss Stacia." Thank you James, and I'm feeling great too. I'm going to be here for a little while today James. I was doing the Lake house thing like we do every summer but I'm ready to come back to my City home soon. Although I love the relaxation of the lake house, I miss the City. "Well the City is here when you're ready to come back," said James. "Enjoy your day Miss Stacia."

I had a different strut as I'm walking to the elevator today, not trying to run and hide from anyone. Actually, quite the contrary. I am seeking the slight bit of info from any nosey neighbor that would give me some insight of just what is going on with Bryson. Also, I want to know what the gossip is about John's disappearance. The bottom line is I need to find out some things here and take control of this situation.

Opening the door to the Condo doesn't seem as dramatic as it once felt. Although memories hit me as soon as I walked in and looked at my Black and White floor and that Piano,...that Piano, the start of it all, maybe or maybe not... Anyway, I felt that I could breathe and go back to the moment that traumatized myself and my family. I paused and listened, listening to the sounds in my mind. I hear laughter, Piano playing, the sounds of my Branson and Braya playfully bickering with one another. The sounds of Draya and Mike in the kitchen, opening wine and whispering sex talk to one another they think no one hears. The sound of the TV that Bryson is always watching,..the sound of John when he comes through the door with his larger than life theatrical entrance, sounds of good times, many good times we had in this beautiful scenic Condo. The sounds of life that once lived in this Condo, the sounds of life that are hopefully to come.

Let me turn on some music and get my ass in the shower. Thank God for soap and water as I say every single time I bathe. Precious Lord, I thank you. Something about the shower, I hear God when I'm in the shower. I hear myself when I'm in the shower. I get revelation when I'm in the shower. I love the shower, but don't get jealous Clawfoot deep tub, I love you too. When I just want to relax, feel sensual and think of nothing but the moment.

Comfy clothes are on, order some food and start getting this place in order. I think I will order something from one of John and I's favorite spots, a good ole cheesesteak with cheese wiz and crab fries. Hm, while I'm waiting on this food, let me see if I can get into this desk drawer to see what Bryson's ass got in here. Mail, mail and more mail, mail is a job all of its own. Travel agent card, Real estate agent card...huh? Why does Bryson have all these cards like he's going to do any traveling or investing. His ass doesn't even know how to do business without me handling everything. I'll call these people later and see if he's been in contact with them. *Buzz,* I jump, it's just the front desk letting me know the delivery man is here. Hi, you can let them up please, I'm starving. tell them. "Hey Miss Stacia," the food delivery guy said. Hey Tony, long time no see. I sure miss you guys even though I'm watching my Carbs and my figure, I said laughing. "I got your favorite Miss Stacia, Cheesesteak with a little American cheese, fried onions, hot sauce, and Cheese wiz and Cherry peppers on the side and of course your favorite Crab fries with extra lump crabmeat, nice and hot and crisp." Oh damn Tony, just hand me that bag, I can't wait to tear this food down. I probably will go straight to sleep after I eat it, terrible but I will exercise tomorrow, I said laughing. Here you go, I said, handing him an extra tip. "Thanks Miss Stacia, you always take good care of us." "I didn't see you but your husband had a delivery a few weeks back." "He ordered your special and his Chicken cheesesteak with his ketchup and cherry hot peppers on the side with chips like he always gets," said Tony. " I was a little surprised, I know you always usually do the ordering for you guys, but anyway, I'm going to let you eat before the food gets cold. It was great seeing you again, enjoy and have a great day." Well, it was good seeing you Tony. Thank you for delivering this slammin food yourself, and you have a great day too Tony!

Damn that shit was good! Oh shute, it's already 2:15 in the afternoon, naptime. Hold up, what did Tony say? Bryson ordering our cheesesteaks? Huh, when did Bryson bring me my favorite cheesesteak my way, or should I say the way John and I usually get our cheesesteaks. He never orders anything. I know Bryson is not turning that girl on to my favorite food spots. His ass must be cheating and that shit must be good to him because he has lost his damn mind or maybe he's trying to find his mind, either way he's going to make me hurt his ass. And then the Travel agent card and Real Estate Agent card. Oh no, no, I know his ass aint! Let me call Draya and see if she and Mike have noticed anything going on here at the Condo with Bryson. But then again those two are so busy fucking all the time, they probably didn't notice shit or she would have said something. Well at least somebody is getting fucked, cause it sure ain't me...Hum, well all that might change here in a minute, I'm sure feeling Chef Gus over there... Let me get my ass back home and get some housework done. Cinderella is on her way...Tired of being Cinderella, I have been everyone's servant since I was a little girl, it's time to make a change.

BACK ON MY CITY LOVE VIBE

AFTER BEING IN THE house watching food shows all week, I feel like creating some new recipes. Bryson, I'm running to the Italian market, I'll be back shortly. "You are running to the City in all this rain, Stacia?" You know I love the rain Bryson, as long as it's not storming, I don't mind being out in the rain, it's actually soothing to me. "Ok, Stacia, I'll be here when you get back," said Bryson. Hum, his ass sure is sticking at home a little more lately since that night I didn't come home. He also probably detects that I saw those cards and things at the Condo, that's alright Bryson, I'm prepping my ass too. I've been doing my pilates and I am thinking about having those pole lessons. I don't want to have them at Danny's club though, I don't want the Chef to see me looking crazy nor do I want that Tall girl to see me looking as if I was desperate to get my man's attention back. I'll google some places on the internet and have Tonya go with me, it will be fun.

This rain is steady but sexy at the same time, something about the rain that makes me feel a little something something. I always did have a thing for the rain. I have all these new recipe ideas in my head I want to try. I might as well stop by the Reading Terminal also. I like some of the fresh produce stands and the meat and seafood stands. I guess I should stop at *"Beck's Cajun Food"* while I'm there, Bryson and the kids will be happy about that. Thank God I bought a few Cold and Hot bags. Those Prawns were looking extra fresh today, I sure wasn't going to pass those up. Hum, they say never go food shopping hungry. Anyway, I'm starving as usual and it's lunchtime. This Beck's line is always so busy at this time of day, people everywhere, let me just stand back and look at this menu. I'll do a few samples as usual, I know they sometimes get sick of me asking to taste the same things all the time. They love me anyway.. I have too many bags in my hand to sit here and eat. I will order a few things and wait until I get back home to eat. Damn, there goes my diet. I'm going to order some Gator Gumbo, Shrimp and Crawfish Etouffee and I guess I should get at least 4 Trainwreck sandwiches. And I will get some Mac and Cheese bites with the Bacon on it for Braya and Branson. We all like Beck 's at the house. I'm going to need to order damn near the whole pan of the Bread pudding with the Bourbon sauce, we all love that too. Shit, my damn hands are going to be full walking back to the car, good thing I didn't park too far away. "Stacia," I heard someone say. I started looking all around in this crowd of people only to see a familiar smile that immediately caught my eye. Hey Chef, I said with a hearty reply, what are you doing out of the kitchen at this time of the day? "This is my day off Stacia, I see our taste buds are in the same universe today," said Chef. Yes, I said, I am feeling extra greedy now just looking at this menu board. "I see you have your hands full, girl, let me help you carry some of those bags to your car." I sure would appreciate the help, Chef Gus, but I can wait until you order your food. "No Stace, I can order when

I come back, or better yet, do you have time to come back in for a moment and share a lunch with me?" ask the Chef. Well, I guess I can since I have this food in the Cold and Hot bags. I can spare a moment or two before I head back home. "Great," said Chef. "I'm glad I bumped into you today." Me too, Chef, I said like a purring Cat. "I love rainy days," said the Chef. Oh my God Gus, I love the rain too! I said with excitement, I think it's sexy. "Yea, funny you should say that Stacia, I always thought rain is sexy too," said Gus.

As we entered back into the Reading Terminal wet with a little rain on our faces, clothes and body, we both blushed and laughed as we started to wipe our faces with napkins. Who needs an umbrella to protect us from God's magical and enlightening showers, we both thought in our minds as it was apparent on our faces and gitty smiles. "I am going to take a few things back to the house as well," said Gus. "I have a taste for the Jambalaya and also the Blackened Catfish Po Boy today." "Would you like to share some Snapper Turtle Soup to warm up our wet bodies, Stacia?" asked Gus. Yes I would. I haven't had any of that in a while. Let's also get some of the Fried Mac and Cheese bites with the Gumbo and the Bacon on top, I said with an ornery laugh. "Oh shute Mommy, that does sound good too," said Chef with a sexy subtle laugh. Let's have a sweet ending with some Beignets, I said being bad. "Well," said Chef. "I do like sweet end-ings," Chef said being bad too. "I am surely with you on all of that Stace." We both smiled at each other constantly with each bite and the great conversations we had. We both really enjoyed our lunch together, actually we just enjoyed being together..

As the Chef walked me back to my car in the drizzling sexy rain, we both felt like we wanted to walk and talk some more. Maybe we should be walking off those Fried Mac and Cheese balls we just de-voured, I thought to myself. Anyway, walking in this rain with this sexy ass Man was the best use of my God given time right now. It was perfect. I didn't want it to end. I know I'm wrong but... Where do you live Gus?, I asked as if I was really saying something else. I live about 5 blocks down, Stacia, why do you ask that, do you want to see where I live?" asked Gus with the same look on his face. Yea, I said, I want to see what your apartment looks like, how you have it decorated, see a little more depth of the Chef who is so inspiring to me. "Am I inspiring to you, Stace?" Gus asked, with a look of child-like innocence on his face. Yes, you are Gus, you have brought back a spark in me that I forgot I had. I came to the City today because I all of a sudden had a new found passion in food," I said with excitement. A flood of new recipes came pouring in my mind since I have been hanging out in the kitchen at the club with you lately, I revealed to Gus with an inner look of myself. "Wow Stace," said Gus, "that makes me feel so good to hear." As we kept walking block after block in the misty rain, something made me feel like touching this mans' hand. He must have had the same thought because just then I felt Gus take my hand...what the hell are you doing, Stace, I thought to myself. But anyway, I sighed and exhaled, this must be heaven...

Boom! A clash of Thunder followed by some webs of nature's beautiful fireworks of lightning started a new and different feel to the morning relaxing rain we felt just moments ago. The rain became more intense as Gus and I both started to make a run for it. Splashing in the puddles and laughing all the way like children having innocent fun on a summer day. We noticed the usual City foot traffic as if it were moving in slow motion as we were running. At the same time, Businessmen and Women in suits with umbrellas heading into Restaurants and Cafes to have lunch and escape the rain that day, also noticed our light hearted run and enjoyment of the moment.

As we approached a building that I somehow sense that this is where Gus lives, he started to pull a key fob out of his pocket. Just then a couple that was leaving the building held the door open for us as they smiled and greeted Gus by name. "Thank you guys for holding the door open," Gus said. "No problem," said the other residents. "We see you guys have your hands full and caught the weather without an umbrella." "Yes, the rain was just a light mist until about a block and a half ago," laughed Gus as we entered the Corridor. "Be careful out there." We will, thanks man," said the Resident. "Yea, and thanks again for holding the door for us and you guys have a beautiful rainy day, said Gus. "You two have a great day as well," said the couple.

While I was standing behind Gus' dripping wet body as he pushed the button for the elevator, holding all those bags, I couldn't help but notice his strong back and shoulders in that soaking wet tee shirt. Just stop, Stacia, I thought to myself, you are a married woman. But then again, why is my married ass standing behind this sexy wet man about to enter his apartment. Hum, Stace, what are you doing girl... Whatever I or we were doing, it happened very spontaneously. This was not planned. I came to the City to get some groceries and lunch for my family today and go back home. But bumping into Gus today was not a coincidence, this was something more, this had to be destiny..

I have the bags babe, I said before I realized I had just called him Babe. He turned around and gave me a quick eye to eye glance as he handed me one bag and the elevator door opened. We both got kind of quiet in the elevator ride that felt more like a warehouse rather than an apartment building. The elevator door opened up to a dark mysterious area that showed the outside elements. I took an inner deep breath as he guided me towards some unique vintage huge double doors. He swiped a sensor and the doors opened like something from a

"Bond" movie. I looked around and wondered what the hell we were stepping into. Once the doors opened, to my complete amazement the mysterious dark warehouse area in an instant turned into the most Chic upscale loft I have ever seen, straight out of a magazine. It was full of beautiful and unique artwork everywhere. My eyes were all over the place. Damn Chef, this place is hot, I love it! As we headed towards the kitchen area to relieve our hands of the bags, it felt as if we were going into an Art Museum. I was overwhelmed as I looked all around. Wow, who did the renovations? And the decor? This was a masterpiece and the Giant windows exposing the lightning across the City skyline was a spectacular scene. As I stood in the kitchen area and looked around this incredible loft with beautiful art work everywhere, I couldn't wait to start to explore. "Thank you Mommy," said Gus. " I did a lot of the renovations myself with the help of a few of my buddies. The rest I do here and there, and I pick up Artwork at different countries I visit from time to time. You can put that bag right here on the counter, I will get us some hand towels. Make yourself comfortable Mommy, there are a couple of bathrooms in this place, pick one and I will get you some dry clothes to put on and put your wet clothes in the dryer."

Heard Chef! I said playfully at Gus' military style orders. Do you mine if I kind of take a look at some of your beautiful artwork? "No I don't mind at all Ms. Lady," Gus said with a playful sexy accent as he handed me a hand towel, white T-shirt and Chef pants. "I feel all wet and sweaty." "I have to shower and freshen up, take your time looking around," said Gus. Ok, I will find my way to one of your other bathrooms, I laughed. Looking around I noticed a few pictures of Gus in different places with different people, a few of them were women. Hm, I wonder if this is his girlfriend in this picture or maybe it could be a relative. Don't be nosey Stace, this is not your man, I said to myself. **Boom**, a loud clash of Thunder shook the whole loft, followed by some pretty impressive streaks of lightning. Then the power went out. I better get out of these wet clothes and get my clothes dry so I can head back home, I thought, as I peeped around the darkened loft for a bathroom. Oops, I opened the wrong door, (or should I say the right door) and caught a glimpse of Chefs' reddish bronze buff and firm well endowed body. I hurried and pulled the door shut, and said I'm sorry for opening the wrong door. "Don't worry about it," laughed Gus, "it's another bathroom on the other side toward the left." Ok, I'll find it, I said somewhat embarrassed. This bathroom is very nice, it has a nice *feng shui* feel to it. The storm is getting worse, I might as well wait until it stops to head back anyway. With each *Boom of Thunder* the energy in the loft seems to light up, but not just with the lightning. My heart is starting to beat faster, my body and mind is starting to feel sensual just by being in the moment. My pussy is starting to pulsate and feel all wet and warm inside. I feel like going back in that bathroom and getting in that damn shower right with him, but how do I know that he would even want that... All I know is that right now, at this moment, I do want that. And while I'm in his bathroom with all my clothes off, feeling full of dangerous passion in this storm, I'm willing to take the chance. The Thunder is starting to rumble a little longer and softer, I can hear the rain against the window, I only have this hand towel to walk through the hallway with. Knock Knock,.. Gus, I want to come in there with you..I said.

Before I knew it I opened the glass door to that incredible Cave like shower and found myself engaged in a passionate kiss with Gus. You started something for sure now, no turning back Stace, I thought to myself for a hot moment. There were multiple shower heads spraying all over our bodies. But the huge Waterfall Rain showerhead that lit up in blue, seemed to electrify the bronze color in our skin. The blue water drops running down our faces felt like we were actually in the Rainforest under a misty real live waterfall. We were kissing and licking each other all over. It was like there was no one else in our world but us on a Blue lagoon,.. just me and him. I felt that rock hard dick against my body and I wanted it in me as soon as possible. But I wanted this feeling to last, I wanted to take it slow, I wanted it so badly, we both did, it was only a matter of time until this would happen. And this was the perfect day. The perfect moment. This was no accident or coincidence that we bumped into each other on this perfect rainy day, it was the perfect time, this was meant to happen… ***Rumble Rumble***, the Thunder seemed to purr, like a lion, and it made me feel like a Lioness. I was taking what I wanted for the first time in a long time. Kissing down his muscular chest, going down his six pack tight abs and licking across his sexy belly button felt so damn good. The water pulsating all over our backs from the wall mounted shower heads felt like mini massages on top of the other massages we had going on. He pulled my head back up, looked at me in my eyes and we looked into each other's souls. There was no need for words, our looks and actions said it all. And despite the fact I was doing something I never thought I would do, this was something more than just lust, I felt this man was…my soul mate…

Boom, Boom, Boom, the clashes of Thunder were so loud it seemed as if we were in a volcano eruption. He started to kiss me softly on my face and down my neck. He kissed all around my breast and gently sucked on my nipples. He kneeled down as if he were proposing and started kissing and licking my long awaited inviting wet pussy. I sighed, it felt too damn good. He suddenly picked me up and thrust himself into me against the wall of the shower. Oh shit, oh shit,oh shit,that damn dick felt so good going in and in and in and out just a little deeper with each thrust. I felt so warm inside, like I was coming a thousand times, showering his dick with my love juices, I was all wet inside and out. His back, his body and his thrust was so damn strong and good. He felt like a strong damn man, fucking the hell out of me, making love to me, pleasing me and somehow protecting me all at the same damn time. What I didn't know I was missing. I was missing out on alot. So much rhythm, our bodies fit together and were in perfect rhythm. I started to softly bite his shoulder, I had too. Holding on to the back of his neck, my face just rested on his shoulder. This man was fucking the shit out of me and I haven't felt this good in forever... or maybe never. All I know is that I wanted this feeling to last forever...

It lasted long enough as we moved to the shower bench and then down to the shower floor. I rode him from the front and he rode me from the back. Then he turned me back around to the front, stared at me for a moment and pushed me back against the shower wall. He put himself back in me softly and just let that nice diamond rock hard dick just sit in my pussy, I felt like crying... and I felt his raw emotion all up in me, like I had just taken in his spirit..and then we both started to whimper and shake and go hard like a belly dancer on a spin, round and round and harder and harder. Then we both exploded at the same time, at the same time of the thunder, wet and warm all up inside, we shook, we embraced, we held onto each other tightly. Then he picked me up and layed on the shower bench with me on top of him. He held me, he kissed me, he ran his fingers through my hair, pulling my hair back while looking at me in my face. We laid there with the shower water raining on us and we both shook some more and sighed with pleasure. I wanted this moment to last forever...but I know it wouldn't.

The Thunder seemed to pick back up in intensity, I looked in his face, smiled and said, we better get out of this shower Gus. "Yeah, we don't want to get struck by lightning in the shower," joked Gus. "Let's wash each other and get out of here." Gus had beautiful smelling natural homemade body baths and candles. The coffee coconut vanilla bean body wash made me feel like eating Gus. Washing each other was just as sexy and meaningful as that ultimate sex we just had. We laughed and started to talk about food and spice influenced body washes we would love to create. Leave it to two culinary junkies to want even our soaps to have flavor. "Let's get out of this shower before we start this all over again," said Gus. "I could go a few more times if you let me." I just turned around and looked at Gus' sexy ass body and that sexy dick and replied, yeah I could too...

Before I knew it we were putting our body butter on in Gus's bedroom and Gus had given me another fresh white tee shirt and some comfy shorts. The electricity had only gone out for a little while, so the dryer was back on drying my clothes that were wet from the rain. "Let me put the shea butter on your back and give you a mini massage Mommy," said Gus. "You can use the relaxation." You are always taking care of everyone else, Stace." "Just take this time to relax in the moment, especially until these storms pass." Ok Babe, I said, this time I felt right calling him Babe... My phone must be dead in my pocketbook, I thought to myself, usually by now my phone would be ringing off the hook with the kids, Draya and Bryson calling. Oh well, I'll make up some story and deal with them later. It's still only a little past 2 o'clock, but it seems like I had been in another universe and had been gone for neons,.. As Gus massaged my back with that tropical smelling body butter, my wet pussy started getting wet again. I want some more babe, I whispered to Gus. Just then I felt that warm hard dick glide in from the back softly and gently, damn, this man feels good. He laid on the back of me softly and gently started moving that dick up in my super wet pussy. I didn't even want to move. I knew I would come in a second, damn this shit feels too good. Um, this is better than any massage I ever had. He's massaging my back and grinding his ass all up in me hard and soft at the same time. Damn, before I knew it, we was all up in some good ass sex again. Let's make it last, let's please make it last just a few moments longer. Umm, we are coming again, coming over and over, again. This time he just collapsed laying on the back of me... it felt good. I felt comfort being wrapped up inside of him. It's 2:45 in the afternoon and we both need naps, but this is my usual nap time anyway...this feels heaven sent...although this was surely a sin.

After about an hour's nap, the sky was starting to clear of the intense darkness but still had an overcast of a relaxing gray. " I have some nice wines, I'll pour us a glass of this light sparkling Rose' and get us a few light snacks," said Gus. Sounds good to me babe, I said smiling. Gus and I chatted and snacked and laughed and connected,... Yea, we just started something. Shit Stacia, I thought, what are you going to do? Well Gus, I said as I smiled and looked into his eyes as I kissed his full lips gently. I had the best day that I can remember ever having before in my life. Thank you for bumping into me today Gus. Even though we started something that I'm not sure how it's going to turn out, it felt right to me and I have no regrets, I said to Gus looking deeply into his eyes. I didn't want to ever feel this vulnerable to anyone and I'm not sure where this feeling came from all of the sudden, I thought to myself. I didn't ask for this or go looking for this, it just came into existence. This was no coincidence I thought to myself, but I didn't want to put all of my feelings out there to Gus, not just yet anyway. I think I should be heading back to my car, I said. "I can either walk you back to your car or drive you back to your car, whichever you would like, Stace," said Gus. Gus and I both looked at each other like yea rite.. Weak at the knees is an understatement rite now… "I'll get the car," said Gus.

As I stood outside of Gus' building I noticed the sky was getting lighter to signal to me that the rendezvous of the day was coming to an end. The Sun would come out and back to reality I must go… The food has been in the car since noon, it was now after 4pm, I can explain 4 hours to Bryson. My story is after I left the Reading Terminal, it started storming and I went to the Condo to wait out the storm. Whatever,… What I need to focus more on is what just happened between Gus and I, before I even go home to Bryson.

Here he comes, my sexy ass Boo… Gus pulls up in his Baby Blue freshly restored TR6 with a silver drop top and new reupholster white leather seats and a brand new wood grain and leather steering wheel. Before I could take the scene all in and give him the compliment he deserves right now, Gus puts his flashers on and jumps out the car to open the passenger car door for me. He is a perfect gentleman. Thank you Babe, I said while looking at him, trying to *see* the inner him, and see who this man really is. Well, I thought to myself, you have about a 7 minute ride back to your car, so this time spent with this man today is officially over and it will be either a precious memory or a start of life to come. You have a lot to think about, but don't think about it too hard. God will guide you through this decision. Just marinate on it and live for the moment. You already made the choices you made today, and even though you committed one of the ultimate sins of the Lord's Commandments today, you still are forgiven, you still are human, you still have needs and there are no coincidences…

"How do you feel over there girl"? asked Gus as he glanced over at me with that sexy eyebrow look. I'm fine over here Chef, I said looking back with a sexy look of my own. I'm sure glad I had those hot and cold bags. I put an ice pack in the bag with the fresh shrimp and seafood. As far as the Hot food, it will hold up well in the hot bag. "I was asking more about how you feel about what just happened, Stace," said Gus. "I don't want to put any extra pressure on you, but I don't just do things like this, Stace. I have had feelings for you since the first time we started talking to one another and looked each other in the eyes in the kitchen at the club. I knew this would happen between us. This is deeper than either one of us knew, we didn't choose this, don't beat yourself up about this," said Gus. "I will not put any pressure on you Stace, I will give you your space, you let me know what you want to do, I will be here"… " I will give you the time you need to see the path you want to take." "I will say this though Mommy, today is one of the most precious moments that I ever had in my life. I will replay this day over and over again in my mind until I see you again." "You are very special to me and it all happened so fast I don't know what hit me." I looked at Gus and felt so secure in his passenger seat, that I really didn't want to get out of his car. Thank you Gus, I said as we pulled up in back of my car. I really enjoyed this day. We both laughed and said, of course we enjoyed this day, it was something straight out of a sexy ass xrated Lifetime movie or even better. But was it just physical? Was I looking to fill a void or was it the real thing… This is what only time and God can tell.

Let me get my little bad ass home to this man and these kids. I hope this food is alright. It should be, I wasn't there that long, or was I, or was we… Shit, I'm probably going to have a stupid ass look on my face when I get home. Maybe I should stop at the Condo, have a beer and take another shower in my Bath and Body Works girly wash to get this reminder of a *oh my God what have I just done smell* off of me. Although my body smells so good and the day was so beautiful, I really don't want to wash this smell off of me. From shopping, to the rain, to lunch with the Chef, to running in the rain, to that spectacular view of the City and the lightning show, and to the most incredible love making I ever have experienced...it was one of the best days of my life...did I just say that..?...yea, I think you did, Stacia.

Freakin ass traffic, why is it that every time you are in a hurry, there is more traffic and slow ass drivers everywhere in front of you? I'll just stop in here real quick and get my ass right back on this road. Hey James, I don't have time to talk to him right now, I have to keep it moving. I hate to be rude but I am "Heying" everyone with my respectful sincere smile with a look of I got to keep it moving look all the way up the elevator.

Grab a beer, get in the shower and hit this road back. Wait.. do I smell John? Maybe I'm just imagining things right now. Anyway I need to get this food home asap. Thank God for the thermal bags and the ice packs, but still, over 4 hours is pushing it. Bryson will have something smart to say about me being gone so long. Whatever, I had the time of my life today. I started something new and exciting but I need to take in what just happened and decide what to do. It may be time for Bryson and I to separate. I'm just so confused right now. In a way I feel guilty. Even though I've been questioning Bryson about him having an affair, I would have never thought I would have done something like this with another man. I don't even know if I'm going to be able to look Bryson in his face. Get it together Stacia, men do this shit all the time and lie about it to your face like it ain't shit. Go in that house floating on cloud nine, put these groceries away and tell everybody to help themselves to the Beck's.

BACK TO HOME LIFE

"WHERE HAVE YOU BEEN all this time, Stacia?" asked Bryson. In the City Bryson, just where I said I was going. I took my time and waited out the storm. I was also at the Condo for a little while. It was strange, I thought I smelled this bodywash John used to use. Bryson got quiet for a second and had a dumb look on his face. Perfect, I spotted a little weakness so I used that to get a little cockiness of my own going. I told him to get his Beck's and help the kids with theirs. I'm going upstairs and lay down for a while and watch the news, I told Bryson. As soon as I got in my bedroom, I shut the door and stretched across the bed, f---the news. I'm going to turn anything on and daydream about the afternoon Gus and I just spent. All I know is my body is floating like I'm walking on air and my mind is in a zone of some kind. I just got zapped by that beautiful lightning I saw all afternoon while Gus and I were together. It was something magnetic, something in the cosmos, something that I can't explain.

"Mum mum, are you still sleeping?" I heard Braya say. I was just taking a lil nap Braya, I was tired from running around in the city all day in the rain. What time is it? "Mum mum you were sleeping for a while, it's 10 oclock," said Braya. What? 10 o'clock, oh my God, I was sleeping hard. It felt like I just dozed off and I've been sleeping for almost 5 hours. Well, I guess I must have needed the sleep, Braya. Did you enjoy the Becks Mac and Cheese balls and the Trainwreck sandwiches I bought for y'all? "Yes Mum Mum, Pop Pop made our plates, then we ate the bread pudding and Pop Pop put a little ice cream and whip cream on it for us, everything was really good." I'm glad you all enjoyed it baby, where is Branson? "Branson is in his room playing a video game, my Mommy and Daddy are in Atlantic City and Pop Pop left after we ate our bread pudding and ice cream." What time did Bryson leave Braya? "Pop pop left after he watched the lottery numbers come out." Well the PA daily lottery number comes on at 7 o'clock, so he hasn't come back since 7 o'clock? "No, it's just us here, Mum mum, do you want me to turn Golden Girls on?" Braya asked. You can turn on whatever you want to watch little Mommy, I'm going to go downstairs and get a small piece of that bread pudding and the whiskey sauce. I'm just going to put some whipped cream on it and skip the ice cream tonight. "Mum mum, I miss the City, can we stay at the Condo for a few days?" Well Braya, I'm sure you remember what happened the night of Bransons' piano concert. "Yes I do Mum mom." We never really had an in-depth conversation about what happened that night, but I think we should have a conversation with you and Branson about that night and how it has affected you guys and how we are going to heal from that. "Is Mr John dead Mum mum?" asked Braya with a look of reluctant fear on her face. That's the thing Braya, I'm not really sure where Mr John is right now. The thing that I do know is what I did was really impulsive and down right wrong. I really truly didn't mean to hurt Mr John. I really had grown to love and trust Mr John. I was so hurt by what I thought he was doing, and I am so protective over you children. I acted like a lioness protecting her cubs. It was a motherly instinct, but that does not excuse my behavior. Human beings are not animals though, we have more intellect than animals and we have the minds to make choices and rational decisions. But how I reacted that day was not a good choice or a rational decision. I reacted without thinking and most of the time those types of decisions will never end well. I am so sorry that you saw me act like that Braya. That is not who I am, and that is not who we are as a family. I jabbed him with the letter opener in his shoulder and arm, it all happened so fast and the next thing you know Bryson and your father took John out of there and we haven't heard from John since. I wish I could talk to John right now and discuss what happened and why it happened. I was so hurt by John because I loved John so much as a friend. I felt betrayed by John but it's no excuse for what I did. I hurt someone I loved very much and I will pay some kind of consequence for that in one way or the other Braya, that's how life works. "Everything will be okay, I love you Mum mum," said Braya. "I don't want anything bad to happen to my Mum mom." "You are the best Mum mom ever, and God and Mr John will forgive you." Awe, thank you Mommy girl, I said with inner joy, I love you so much and I always want to be here for you and Branson, and oh, your Mommy too! I said laughing. Well, I guess I need to talk to Branson about this too when he's ready to talk about it. "Branson acts like nothing really bothers him Mum mum, he's a typical boy keeping everything on the inside." You are wise beyond your years Braya, I said. Those boys grow into men and still act the same way, but we need to get them to start to communicate with themselves, first about their true feelings and then communicate those feelings to the people they care about in life. Then, the world between Man and Woman would be a much better place. "You are so smart Mum mum," said Braya. No Mum mom is not that smart, but smarter than some though, I laughed. I'm just learning lessons from life and asking God to reveal those lessons and what am I to learn from my life experiences. Whether they are good experiences or bad experiences or just regular days, we are here to learn from our experiences. Got it Mommy girl? I ask my little Angel in training. "Yes Mum Mom, I got you."

BACK TO CONDO LIFE

I WAS MISSING THE Condo just as much as the kids were. Draya and Mike have been staying at the Condo here and there. There isn't too much that bothers those two as long as they're together and getting something or the other on. And it seems Bryson's ass has been going back and forth to the City a little more lately than I knew about. But anyway, here we are, Branson, Braya and myself back staying at the Condo, for a few days to start anyway. Then soon, we will transition back to the City as always by the start of school. "Mum Mom, I want to eat at Dolce *Carini Pizza* on Chestnut Street," said Branson. Oh, that does sound good. I'm going off my low carb diet here for a minute or two. "I miss the City Mum Mum, we mine as well walk over there and eat inside the pizza shop," said Branson. Okay Bran the Man, I said endearingly, sounds like a good idea. I was glad to see how the kids just maturely flowed back into the city vibe. They enjoyed the hustle and bustle of City life. Although slower life in the suburbs feels more intimate sometimes. I can hear God talking in the leaves blowing on the trees in the suburbs. The birds singing at

4:15 am sounds like heaven and nature music. The majestic hills and valleys of green grass and beautiful trees look like a painted portrait. Less noise and congestion of honking car horns and buses, that is for now anyway. Everywhere you look they are building more and more housing developments in the suburbs and taking away precious land and nature, and the deers have nowhere to go. The world seems to be getting more crowded here lately, I guess.

While walking down the street with the kids, we felt the need to look in some stores. We love stores. Something about shopping makes you feel good. We're not happy unless we come in the door with bags in our hands. Maybe it's some kind of issue or feeling we're trying to obtain I guess, but anyway, I do love bargains. I started to reminisce about the Chef and our rainy day. I haven't heard from him since that day. Although it was only a little over a week ago, I would have thought he would have maybe sent me a text or something. But then again, what happened was just something that just happened on a whim. We never really communicated on a regular basis before, outside of Danny's club anyway, so why would I expect that he would start now,.. I guess I was just expecting something. Maybe I should send him a text...hum, I think I will when we get back to the Condo.

"Mum mum, like always, we have all these bags and have to walk all the way back to the Condo carrying them," said Braya. Well you knew we were going to buy something Braya, how can we walk past stores without buying something, I said as Branson rolled his eyes at me with a smile. "I just got one pair of sneakers Mum mum," said Branson. "I'm not trying to carry a lot of bags." But thank you Mum mum for buying my sneakers." "Although I was going to pay for them myself," said Branson. The next time you can pay for mine too since you're the big Baller rite now, my handsome grandson. How many lawns do you have now on your lawn care roster, dude? I said jokingly to Branson. "Mum mum, we have six lawns now," said Branson. "I cut and trimmed the front with the mower Pop pop got me, and my friend Cameron's Dad let him use the ride mower to do the back of the houses." Speaking of Cameron, have you seen his creepy looking Uncle Peter around the Lake House lately? I asked Branson with an automatic eyebrow raise.

"Well I didn't see him but I saw that truck that he drives with that FX logo on it parked on the street near the Condo," said Branson. Near the Condo? I asked with the eyebrow raise going up even further. "Yea, come to think about it, I saw that truck there earlier today but nobody was in it at first. Then a Tall lady came and got in the passenger side of the truck," said Branson. Then what happened? I asked. "I don't know," said Branson, "I went back into the building." Hm, I wonder why they were here. Well he obviously comes here for some reason. That truck was parked in the alley the day that happened with John. He must have some connection with someone in the building. I have to find out who that is.

Darn this pizza is good! "It sure is Mum mum!" both kids said at the same time. "The chicken and fries are good and crisp too!" said Branson. Yes they are, I'm so glad we are walking back so I feel a little less guilty about eating all of this tasty but fattening food. "Yeah Mum mom, it's going to derail all your hard work getting your body back in shape," said Braya. I'll call your Aunt Tonya to work out in the gym with me tomorrow. The only thing about that is she is going to want to go to lunch afterwards and so will I to tell you the truth. Let's start to head back to the Condo. I want to stop at DiBruno brothers to get some cold cuts and cheese. "Don't get too much Mum mum, who's going to carry all that?" said Branson, "you know how you start picking up too many things." I know my little

GrandMan, a combination of my grandson and my man. I will try to contain myself this time. Let's start walking back up the block.

Oh my God, I know that is not Gus over there with some woman. I hope that is his sister or something. My heart is starting to beat fast and I'm actually feeling jealous. Maybe I should act as if I don't see him or maybe I should go up to him and say Hello and introduce myself to his friend or whoever she is. I just want to turn around and walk out of this store, my heart is starting to sink. Hey Gus, I said to him trying to conceal the look of hurt that my heart was feeling. "Hi Stacia, so we meet again in a grocery store," said Gus with a look of surprise on his face. Yes we do. Hi my name is Stacia, I said to the suspect. She looked at me with this sly smirk on her face that I just wanted to smack right off her face. "Hi, my name is Tessa," she said. It was a warm summer evening in the City but Gus looked as if he was sweating in a jungle. "I haven't seen you around the club lately," said Gus. No, I've been home in the suburbs for the last week or so, but I'm staying back at my Condo here in the City for a few days with my two grandchildren. "Oh cute grandkids," said that Tessa chick with a sense of sarcasm. Maybe I'll see you around the club sometime Chef, it was good seeing you. "Yes, it was good seeing you as well, Stacia," said Gus. The nerve of his ass, I haven't heard from him since that rainy day and I have the nerve to bump into him with some chick. I'm so mad right now I forgot what I came to DiBruno brothers for. I'm ready to go, I said to the kids. "I thought you were getting lunch meat and cheese so we can have sandwiches tomorrow," said Branson. I suddenly got a headache, I'm just ready to go back to the Condo. "Ok well let's go then," said Braya. "Mum mum, who was that guy you were talking to?" asked Braya. He's the Chef at Danny's new Club. "Oh ok," said Braya. What does oh ok mean Braya? I asked as we were shuffling fast down the block. "I just asked, that's all Mum mom." "Are you ok Mum mom?" "Your whole mood changed," said Branson. I'm ok, maybe I just got tired after eating all that heavy food. Let's watch a movie when we get back. "Oh yea, let's check out Netflix and see what's on there," said Braya. "And Branson doesn't get to pick the movie tonight either."

I was trying to watch a movie with the kids, but all I could think of was Gus and who was that woman he was with. I wanted to call him or at least text him, but I have no right to question him when I have a husband. But the fact still does remain that I can't think straight right now. I must have more feelings than I know for Gus. What about your husband Stacia? I asked myself. What are your feelings for him right now? Do you still love your husband? Of course I love Bryson, but am I in love with Bryson? That's the true question and how long has it been since I didn't know the answer to that question? I really feel crazy now. I have to open a bottle of wine. "Did you like the ending of the movie?" asked Braya. It was okay Braya but I'm getting tired. I'm going to my room to lay down. You two can watch your shows that you like. Did your mom call? "Yes, she said her and daddy are staying in AC another few nights." Well I hope they can finally go back home to their house after that. I love your Mom and Dad, but they kind of wore out their welcome the last month or so. "Okay Mum mum, nite nite," said Braya. Nite Nite guys, I love you, I said smiling at their cute innocent looking faces, but you two will never wear out your welcome. You guys are always welcomed to be with Mum mom wherever I'm at. Okay? "I know that we're your favorite and only grandchildren," said Braya. Yes you are. I love my daughter but I have more fun with you guys, I said sincerely. I usually stay up later with them but all I felt like doing tonight was laying on the bed and hugging my pillow. Let me call Tonya and ask her to come meet me for lunch tomorrow. I'm not even sure if I want to work out tomorrow morning.... or maybe I should, that's even more reason for me to work out extra hard.

"Good morning Guys," Tonya says loudly as she comes sashaying in the Condo. "Good morning Aunt Tonya," said both Branson and Braya. "Are we working out this morning Sis?" asked Tonya. Yes, I said, I need to work these monkeys off my back. "Oh shit, the monkeys are piling on the back again Sis?" "I thought we were starting to learn how to relax again," said Tonya. Yea I was, but I have something new that kind of popped up that I was going to tell you about. "Kind of popped up?" asked Tonya. Yes, something sure did pop up in the last few weeks. "Oh my Goodness," said Tonya. "Should we save this situation until we are in front of some drinks?" asked Tonya jokingly. I don't know if I can hold it in that long Tonya. "Oh well, let's hit this gym," said Tonya. Okay you guys, I will see you in a few hours. There are some French Toast sticks in the freezer and all kinds of snacks in the cabinet. I will call you when we get to the restaurant and see what you want to eat. "Ok Mum mom," said the kids.

"So Sis, what is going on?" Did you find out more about that weird man with the little truck and the Tall girl?" No Tonya, not really, not yet anyway. I haven't talked to you in a few weeks. At the beginning of last week, I went to the Reading market to get some fresh seafood and produce. It was that day it was all rainy. "Yea, I remember that day it was all rainy, the Bartender actually called me and ended up stopping by," said Tonya. Oh yea bitch, I said with a meow, you didn't tell me about that one either, I said with new found excitement. "What do you mean either?" asked Tonya. Well, I said either because I had an encounter too. "An encounter with who?" ask Tonya. With Gus the Chef, I said. "Oh shit," Tonya said as she rode the exercise bike faster and faster. "Well what happened?" asked Tonya. Well, I bumped into him standing in line at Becks. We ended up splitting a lunch and he helped me put my groceries in the car. Then, the next thing I know we are walking in the rain to his apartment. "How the hell did you end up going to his apartment with your married ass Stacia?" asked Tonya. See, that's probably why I didn't say anything at first Tonya, I'm already feeling guilty and confused. "Why are you feeling guilty, Stace?" "I know you didn't Stace," said Tonya with a look of conviction on her face. It just happened, Tonya. "What do you mean it just happened?" ask Tonya. "You knew what could happen if you went to his apartment, especially since you've been having vibes with him." What do you mean by vibes Tonya? "You know you two have been flirting a lot and the last thing you should have done was to go to his apartment with just you and him." "I don't even know if I want to know the details." You sure you don't want to hear the details, Tonya? The shit was hot and juicy as hell. I can't stop thinking about it. "Let's finish this workout and tell me this story over some drinks and food," said Tonya. "I think we are going to need it."

"You mean you busted in on him in the bathroom and started fucking him?" asked Tonya sucking down a Cosmo. Yea, basically, but between that built sexy ass body and that sexy Cave looking shower and that blue rain forest shower head misting all over our bodies, it was just calling me… And the whole day, from lunch, to us walking in the rain, running and laughing in the rain, our conversations, the lightning and the thunder, everything about that day seemed mean-ingful and special. It wasn't a coincidence that we bumped into each other that day, you know Mom always said there are no coincidences. "Yea but who set you up, God or the Devil?" said Tonya with an ah ha moment. Well Tonya, although it was a sin against my marriage, just being around Gus makes me believe in myself again. He lifts me up and supports me in my dreams and goals. Gus makes me feel alive and brings out my best self. Me and Bryson's relationship has hit a dead end. We haven't had sex in over a year. When I'm around Bryson my zest for life is not there. I feel like I'm not growing, he's not growing, we are just waking up each day and existing. That's no way to live. He and I have to sit down and have a serious talk about what direction we want to go in our relationship, and what we are going to do in our marriage. I'm not going to have an affair with someone while being married. "Looks like you already are having an affair while being married, Sis," said Tonya. Well, I'm not going to continue on with this though, not until I know whether or not Bryson and I are at least going to separate. And to top it all off, I had the nerve to see the Chef with some girl at Di Bruno brothers. "Some girl?" "Did he say who she was?" No he didn't. I saw him and went up to him and surprised him and introduced myself to the girl. She said her name was Tessa and he looked surprised to see me and never formally introduced her. "You should stop by the Club and see him, ask him who that was and what his intentions are." "Was it just one of them things, or does he think that there can be something more with you two?" "If so, you are definitely going to need to talk to Bryson about either fixing your marriage or going your separate ways," said Tonya. "I wouldn't want to see things get even crazier than it did a few months ago." Yea your right Tonya. I don't even know if Gus is in a relationship. If he is, it can't be much if he had me in his apartment. I didn't see any clothes or anything of a woman there. I did see some pictures, but it kind of looked like pictures with family members. But before I make plans for a new man, I need to know if he feels the same way that I do, the way I think I feel anyway...

Well I'm going on and on about my shit, what about yours Tonya? "Oh for number one Sis, I'm not married, so my shit is nowhere near as complex and as sinful as your shit." "But, me and the Bartender have been kicking it some lately." "I know he is young and all, but he is mature, has confidence in himself and makes me feel confident in myself." "He makes me laugh and not take everything so seriously." "Right now we are just good friends with benefits." But it is working for us right now so I'll take it." "I'm not going into details about the sex like I would have done in the past." "Although I will say you read that right when you said he had big feet," Tonya said purring like a cat. Oh shute Tonya, I want details. But before we get into that let me call these kids and see what they want to eat.

Are yall going back to the Lakehouse with me or home with your parents? "We would rather stay here for a little while longer Mum mom," said the kids. Well, I'm going back to the Lakehouse tomorrow. I have some things to do there. "Mrs. Jackson from the 5th floor invited us to come over to her place tonight with her grandkids, she wants you to come down too." I don't feel like going to nobody's house and sitting and gossiping. Well, on the other hand, she does always have something good to eat and makes the tastiest little cocktails, but I still don't feel like it. "Well Mum mum, you can just go over for a few minutes and Branson and I will stay and play some video games for a while," said Braya. Yea, maybe I will go down there for a minute and do nothing. Doing nothing every once in a while is good for your peace of mind. What time did she say to come over? "She said anytime after 5," said Braya. Ok, I will walk you guys down there and go inside with you, chat for a moment and then I have to come back up to the Condo and take care of a couple of things. Just call me when you are ready to come back upstairs. "You mean you're not going to gossip and have a cocktail?" asked Braya with a side eye. Well maybe one little chat, chew and chug session, but that's it. I have things to do.

Come on so I can get back, I said in a rush. Hey Ellen, how have you been? Haven't seen you all summer. "Hey Stacia," it's great to see you. "Hey Branson and Braya, how are you guys?." "Hello Mrs Jackson, we are doing good," said Branson and Braya, sounding like Stepford twins. "You two can go back to the bedrooms where Nolan and Noel are," said Ellen. "They will be so glad to see you two, they have been asking for you all summer." "In a minute it will be time to go back to school." Yes Ellen, I know, I'm not sure if the kids will still be going to that expensive Private school next year though. "Yea, I know what you mean Stacia," said Ellen. "It is expensive but I want them to get the best education I can give them." "Also, I like when the children stay with me throughout the week, it keeps me company since Walt passed," said Mrs. Jackson. Yea, how long has it been Ellen? "It's been 2 years and it seems like just yesterday when Walt got sick and died, I miss my Walt," said Mrs. Jackson. I know you do Ellen...I know you do.

Well what do you have to snack on today, Ellen? I know you always have something good cooking. "I made a Taco Lasagna with a lime crema sauce and some Key lime pie cheesecake and some Key lime pie Margaritas." Oh, that sounds great and actually right on time for a happy hour! We are going to have to get you a new friend Ellen. You are still young, girl, all you have to do is invite him up here for one of your great dishes and cocktails and you can do a little cocktailing of your own girl, I said with an ornery laugh trying to lighten up her outlook. "Well, you know I've been going up to the Hamptons a few times this summer and I have been chatting with a handsome Professor," said Ellen with a mature girlish smile. Oh ok Ellen, that's what I'm talking about, live your life girl. "You know I've seen Bryson up there a few times." "Are you guys buying a house in the Hamptons?" asked Ellen. I was so busy enjoying the food, I was on a delayed reaction and didn't really know how to respond on such short notice. What I really wanted to say was ***What the F---***

you talkin bout Willis. But I didn't want to give her anything more to gossip about. So I kept it cool and said yea, we had talked about selling the Lake house and buying something in the Hamptons for years now. "Oh ok, I think I saw him talking to your friend John one time I was there, it was a few weeks ago," said Ellen. I'm sorry, I didn't hear you, did you say you saw Bryson talking to John in the Hamptons a few weeks ago? I asked with the bottom of the glass turned way up in my face. Here my heart goes again pounding out of my chest, I needed that Tequila straight and make it a double, quick. I tried to smile and play it off but I was in total shock, disbelief and every other emotion that I couldn't describe right now, and it was hard to keep my emotions in check in front of Ellen. Bryson didn't tell me that he bumped into John in the Hamptons Ellen. I have to ask him about that when I talk to him later this evening. What kind of Tequila is that, Ellen, do you mind if we just take a shot? "This is Petron, and of course we can take a shot Stacia, it's Friday but any reason will do," Ellen said laughing.

Well Ellen, it's been nice chatting with you. I really hate to eat, drink and run, but I really have to take care of a few things. Can I put this piece of Taco Lasagna in a container? "Yes sure, I always have extra containers just for that." "The children will be fine here for a while," said Ellen. "I know Nolan and Noel are going to ask if Branson and Braya can spend the night." "It's okay with me if it's okay with you," said Ellen. It's fine, we were going back to the Lake house tomorrow anyway but the kids want to stay here in the City. "They can stay over the weekend and have fun, the children really miss each other," said Ellen smiling. That will be okay with me and I'm sure Andraya and Mike will be fine with it too. Thank you for inviting us over Ellen, we always enjoy your hospitality. I have to go back upstairs to my Condo and do a few things, but first I want to go back in the room to tell Branson and Braya goodnight and I love them. Miss Ellen says you two can spend the weekend. "Are you going back to the Lake House in the morning Mum mum?" ask Braya. I will probably be going there in the morning Braya, but I will be back here at the Condo by tomorrow evening. I will be right upstairs, so just call me if you need anything or you want to come back home. "Okay, we love you Mum mom, '' said the kids.

As I got on the elevator heading back up to our Top floor Condo, I started to feel really anxious. Oh my God, I thought to myself, I don't even know who the f--- to call first. This shit is incredible and crazy as hell. What the f--- is going on! How the hell is John alive and well and talking to Brysons' ass in the Hamptons! Calm yourself down Stacia and don't have a heart attack! I said to myself. Breathe deeply,.. breathe four in and four out! Calmly Stacia, ok Stacia get it together, get it together! This is some shit! Oh my goodness, let me call Draya! Oh damn, she didn't pick up. Let me call Tonya! Tonya, you wouldn't believe this shit! I was at Ellen Jacksons' place downstairs and she told me that she saw Bryson in the Hamptons a couple of times. She said she saw Bryson talking to,... you're not going to believe this shit, but she said Bryson was talking to JOHN!!! "Say what Stacia?!" "I know you just didn't say JOHN!" Yes I did say JOHN!!! Ellen said she saw Bryson with a Real Estate agent and she thought we were buying a house in the Hamptons. I played if off like Bryson and I had been looking to buy a home in the Hamptons for a while. Actually Bryson and I did talk about selling the Lake house and buying something in the Hamptons a few years back, but we hadn't talked about that in years. But anyway, this is freaking crazy on all accounts. I don't know where to start, I feel like I'm going to explode and go crazy. What the fuck is going on.. "Calm yourself down first Stace," said Tonya, being unusually calm. "Let's figure out where to start here," said Tonya. "So number one, we have to see why Bryson was in the Hamptons looking around at houses without letting you know about it." "B, we have to see why in the hell Bryson would have seen JOHN of all the crazy shit in the world and not tell you and everybody else as soon as he saw him." "3, where the fuck has JOHN been for the last few months and why hasn't anyone seen or heard from him up until now?" "Did she say whether or not she talked to John herself?" Was she positive it was John?" asked Tonya. No, she didn't say she talked to John and I didn't ask. I was so shocked I could barely keep a straight face. What do you think I should do first Tonya? "I'm not even sure myself, Stacia." "I might need to marinate on this one for a minute," said Tonya. "Shit, let's just call Danny and put him on this, he'll figure out how to get to the bottom of this," said Tonya. Yea, are you going to call him or am I? "You call him and let him know what she told you and see what he comes up with." Ok Tonya, let me call him. "But I don't think you should confront Bryson right now until you see what he's up to," said Tonya. "The fact that he didn't mention John means that something real fishy and crazy is going on." "I can't even believe this shit Stacia." "This is some Lifetime movie shit." I know Tonya, I'm over here pacing like crazy, thank God Branson and Braya are staying at Ellens for the weekend. I couldn't even hide how crazy I feel right now. Oh, that's Draya calling back on the other line, I will keep you posted on everything. Love you Sis. "Love you too Sis," said Tonya, "but the good thing in all this Stacia is that it looks like John is alive and well and you didn't kill John's ass after all."... Yea, but how mad I am right now, I just might kill Brysons' ass and John's ass again.

Hey Draya, I was on the other line with Tonya. "Hey Mommy, I see you called, is everything ok with the kids?" "Yea, everything is okay with the kids, they are downstairs at Ellen Jackson's place with her two grandchildren. She asked if they could stay the weekend with Nolan and Noel, I told her it was okay since you two are still in Atlantic City. "Yea, we are still here at the Tropicana, but we will be coming back tomorrow morning." Okay, where are you coming back to? I asked with a look on my face that I was glad I wasn't talking to her in person. "I guess we were going back to the Lake house for now Mommy." "Our house is still under renovation, but the Contractor said they will be done by next week." Oh ok, anyway Draya, something crazy is going on with your father. "What's going on with Daddy?" Well, while I was downstairs on a Sip and Chew with Ellen, she matter of factly told me that she had been in the Hamptons lately and saw Bryson there looking at some homes with a Real Estate agent. "What?" "Are you guys still thinking about selling the Lake house and buying a place in the Hamptons?" ask Draya. We talked about that a few years ago, but we haven't really talked about it recently. "So why would he just be there alone or without you looking for a place?" "Do you think that he is trying to surprise you or something?" asked Draya. "I'm not sure what's going on Draya. Ellen said she saw Bryson talking to John. "To WHO?!" She said she saw Bryson talking to John in the Hamptons a week or so ago. "Say WHAT Mommy!"

THE QUARTERBACK

THANK YOU DEAR GOD for allowing me to sleep last night, although Bryson kept calling. It seems like he senses that I know something. Thank you Dear Lord for calming my mind and heart down. I did a lot of thinking last night. I did a lot of Soul searching. I know that I am not in complete control of the things that happen in my life. But I do have some choices, and can at least *choose* the path that I want to go down, although it most certainly will be twist and turns along the way . Although I won't be sure of the encounters I have along the way, I do know that as long as I put God first, HE will guide me in the direction HE has instored for me and I will make the best of it and pray for guidance.

Maybe Bryson is just looking for a new place for us. Maybe he thinks this will bring us closer. Maybe he just needed to take some time for himself and look at homes in the Hamptons. We used to always talk about buying a house there. Maybe Ellen was mistaken. But there is no mistaking John for someone else, John is one of a kind. What actually happened when they took John out of the Condo wrapped in my soft persian rug that evening? Why did Bryson keep everything a secret from me about what they did with John? Did I just assume John was dead? Was John alive and going to have me prosecuted for attacking him? Was Bryson protecting me? Is John blackmailing Bryson? Did Mike know all along that John was alive? I was so confused. So many unanswered questions swirling in my mind. That's what I get for just relying on the *Man* to take care of everything and not ask any questions. Maybe I didn't want to know at first. Now I need to know. But where do I start to get these unanswered questions answered? I first start with asking God to reveal those things that were right in front of me all along. Then, I need to "Quarterback" this with a Girls nite out. I'm going to text Tonya and Draya to meet me at Danny's Club tonight, we will troubleshoot this situation and get to the bottom of things. I don't want to see Bryson's ass right now so I'm going to skip the Lake house today. I told Draya not to mention anything to her father right now, so I know she'll play that part cool.

"Hey Mommy, give me some love." "Is Aunt Tonya on her way?" ask Draya. Yea, she called and said she was running a little late as always. "I'm hungry," said Draya. For once I'm not hungry Draya. But that Chef has some pretty good things on the menu here. I just want a drink right now. "So are you going to just ask Daddy why he was in the Hamptons with a Real estate agent and how the hell was John in the Hamptons?" ask Draya. I have so many questions Draya, I don't even know where to start. "Oh here comes Aunt Tonya, Mommy." "Hey Aunt Tonya, give me some love," said Draya. "Hey my favorite niece, what have you been up to since I last saw you?" ask Tonya. "Mike and I were in Atlantic City all week," said Draya. "You two love Atlantic City," said Tonya, "you mine as well buy a Condo there." "We are thinking about it," said Draya. I ordered a round of shots Tonya, this is a shot kind of situation. "You are right about that Sis, did you mention anything to Danny about it yet?" ask Tonya. No I didn't yet, I needed to talk to God first and calm myself down last night. I don't even know where to start Tonya. "You keep saying that Stace," said Tonya. "After we do a few of these shots and marinate on it, we will come up with something." Do you think that John was threatening to go to the police about me attacking him and Bryson is trying to protect me? "I'm not sure, Stace, but why didn't he let you know that John was at least alive and well," said Tonya. "Well Mommy, it all happened so fast, I don't really know what happened that evening myself, and on top of it I had been drinking wine," said Draya. "All that Mike told me about that day is that he and Daddy took John to the parking garage to put John in Daddys' SUV, and Mike didn't know whether John was dead or alive." "Mike said Daddy told him that he would take things from there once they got John in the car." "Daddy didn't want Mike to get any further involved and risk getting into some trouble, so Mike left it at that and never asked Daddy anything else about it," said Draya. So the only person who can really say what the hell is going on is Brysons' ass, and I guess John too… "Did you ever try calling Johns' cell phone after that day, Stace?" asked Tonya. No, as a matter of fact, I didn't, I just assumed he was gone. "Gone, meaning dead Stace?" ask Tonya. I guess that's what I kind of thought, I just didn't want to know, and Bryson kind of shielded me from knowing how he resolved it. But if John is alive, well, and hanging around the Hamptons, I need to see him and talk to him. "I'm curious to see if he has the same cell phone number, let me see your phone, Stace, let's try to call Johns' phone," said Tonya. The music is so loud that you won't be able to hear anything anyway. What are you going to say to him if he does answer the phone Tonya? I'm going to ask him where the fuck has he been and what's he up to," said Tonya. I think I need to have an in depth conversation with Bryson first, see what he has to say and then go from there, Tonya. Well I still think you need to tell Danny, Sis," said Tonya. "Yes, I agree with you on that Aunt Tonya, I'm not going to bother Danny with this tonight, but I will call him some time tomorrow and update him on what's new," said Draya. "Maybe you should hold off on talking to Daddy about what Ellen told you until we talk to Danny, Mommy," said Draya. Yea, I just want to have a lazy Sunday tomorrow anyway, rest my mind for what I know is going to be a full crazy week. "In the meantime, since we are here Sis and you called a girls nite out, let's try to have a good time," said Tonya.

"Wait a minute, is that the crazy Uncle Peter guy over there Mommy?" asked Draya. Yea, it's him, Draya. He must be here with that Tall girl and here comes Danny. Hey my nephew, I said with a smile in my heart, how's everything been going for you? "I'm good Auntie, everything is going pretty good and the wife and baby girl princess are doing well," said Danny. "Looks like yall are here ready to be bad," said Danny. "Nobody is going to be bad my Son," said Tonya. "You know we are too old to be acting up." "Besides that, I wouldn't want to mess things up for you." "How are yall going to be messing things up Ma, I'm glad y'all here, it's only 9 o'clock right now so it's a good laid back crowd for y'all right now." I have something else I want to tell you about, Danny. I will call you tomorrow some time. "Awrite Auntie, I'm here for you, you know that." Thanks Nephew, love you always. We need to let you get back to running your business. "Everything good, everybody knows what they are supposed to be doing, I got a good crew," said Danny. I'm going to tell the Chef you're here and to send yall out something special." You don't have to do that, I'm not hungry Danny. "Speak for yourself, Mommy.

Danny, please tell your Chef that your people are here and to hook us up with something good to soak up these shots my Mom got us doing," said Draya. "Mike is picking us up, I told him we would be ready by midnight," said Draya. "I have to eat something and make sure I have some food to go for Mike." "I'll send the Chef out," said Danny. Tonya looked at me with a sly eye, I tried not to even look her way, I didn't want Draya to feel any vibes on the Chef thing.

"Look Stace, I told you that looks like Ma's necklace!" said Tonya with the ghetto girl I'm about to slap somebody voice. "I'm going over there and introducing myself to her!" "Oh shit," said Draya, "please tell me we are not about to *set it off* in here." Look Tonya, behave yourself in here, I said looking over at the both of them with a sly eye. We just told your son that we were old and behaving ourselves, I said with a sarcastic undertone. "Who the hell is old!" said Tonya, "my ass is still good and ripe." "Actually, I'm still blossoming into a Phenomenal woman and my ass is still juicy!" "Haaaaa! That's my Aunty right there!" said Draya, cheering Tonya on. I know that's right, Sis, my ass is still ripe and juicy too! And thank God for the growth of our inner selves, and our mind and spirit too, the most important parts of this vessel. "Amen to that Sis," said Tonya. Well, with all this growth going on, I don't think you should confront that girl right now, especially after we have knocked a few shots back with attitudes going on, that might be a little dangerous, Tonya. "Well Mommy, if that looks that much like G-Ma's necklace, maybe you should let Aunt Tonya go do a mini investigation." "And if it's not G-Ma's necklace then she can put that out of her mind," reasoned Draya. Yea ok, I said sarcastically, I just know my Sister after a few drinks. And we already each had an attitude of our own about our own individual shit when we got here, I said with a reasoning of my own. "I'm going over there!" Tonya said as she stood up and started her sashay in the Tall girls' direction. Oh my God, I said to myself as I watched Tonya strut in that woman's direction. And just then I noticed the woman Tessa that was with the Chef that day in the DiBruno Brothers store heading towards the kitchen. My blood is starting to boil,... maybe it's the vodka, maybe it's not. Maybe it's that I have feelings deeper than I know for the Chef. Maybe I feel something about her being in the kitchen. The Chef and I had vibes from the beginning in that kitchen. It was our love for food and the art of food. We had a kitchen intimacy, just as intimate as when we were in that shower, but we had not done anything physical in that club kitchen. But still, it was just as intimate. But all I know right now is the moon must be full because there is a hell of a lot of energy in this space right now and it might be a little scary.

As Tonya is over there having a full fledged conversation with the Tall girl, I notice Danny walk past that Uncle Peter guy and give him a look, a look as if to say, what the fuck are you doing in here, and you need to roll rite now kind of look. Needless to say that Uncle Peter was up and out of there within the next couple of minutes. And then I saw Danny give the Tall girl a look as if to say, bitch you better get your ass ready to go on stage kind of look. And her ass was waving goodbye to Tonya as she quickly headed to the dressing room. A server brought out some appetizers, compliments of the Chef, it was a tray of Balls... Mac and Cheese balls, Crab balls and Gator balls, he sure got a lot of balls I thought to myself with an attitude. And I think that woman is still back in the kitchen with him. Fuck him, I'm a married woman, I need to focus on repairing my marriage anyway. I don't even know why I am worried about some bitch being in the kitchen with a Chef that I barely know in my nephew's new Club. This is crazy. "Stace!" Tonya said half drunk and loud, "that *is* Ma's necklace!" "I can tell from the designs of the Yellow diamonds in the middle!" "You remember Daddy had it set with three bigger yellow diamonds in the middle of the smaller white diamonds, one for both of us and him," said Tonya ready for a fight. "I don't want to cause a scene in here right now but we need to get that necklace from her right now!" "Absolutely!" added Draya to the mix. "I'm going to eat a few of these Balls," Draya said with a buzzed laugh, "and then we're going to grip Tall girl up in here tonight." I didn't get close enough to see the design Tonya, but maybe we should let Danny know and have him ask her to take it off and show him the back of it. You know Daddy had Ma's initials engraved on it. "Oh yeah, said Tonya like *Perry Masonary*. "Yeah, I almost forgot about that Stace, she said that it was a gift from a friend." "I wonder if that friend is that Uncle Peter guy," said Tonya. "I'm sorry to say Stace, but it has to be Bryson." "He is the only one other than you that has access to the box at the bank." "And I never took my key out of the lock box you gave me Mommy," said Draya. "You need to check that damn box first thing in the morning and check some other accounts while you're at it, Sis, but in the meantime, this bitch is not leaving this Club with Ma's necklace," said Tonya. "I'm right with you Auntie," said Draya. "Let's roll up on this bitch and take G-Ma's necklace back!" Look, *Set if off crew*, let's just calm down and mention it to Danny, I said trying to calm down Tonya's hype. In the meantime I'm going to try a Ball, I said…still pissed at that bitch back in the kitchen in my space.

"Hey Mommy," said Draya, "is that the Uncle Peter guy's wife that just walked in?" Oh yeah, that's her. She looks out of place and confused, I wonder if she's looking for him. "She probably is," said Draya. "Let's invite her over to our booth," said Tonya, "she might know a little something about what's going on." "Motion for her to come over Stace, she probably will remember you." And she might know something about what's going on with her husband and that Tall girl," said Tonya. Shit, what was her name again Draya? "I don't know Mommy, call Branson real quick, he probably knows, it's his friend's Aunt," replied Draya. Heyyyy! I said as I motioned and waved to Uncle Peter's wife. "I think she's coming over," said Draya. "She needs a makeover," said Tonya. Stop yall, she looks like she is looking for her husband and she didn't care what the hell she came out here looking like tonight. "Well, that might be why her husband is out here with a strip club bitch, she might want to spruce it up a little," said Tonya. Oh my God Tonya, give her a break. Just smile and be nice, she looks like she can use a little girl power right now, I said, be nice. "Hi, I'm Kathy, your neighbor Kenny's sister in law, I'm married to Peter, Kenny's brother." Hi, I remember seeing you around, I said, but I don't remember seeing you with them at our house the night of the 4th of July cookout. "I was at home alone," said Kathy. "Yes, I saw you around too, but we were never formally introduced," said Kathy Cooney. We were being somewhat bad tonight and taking a few shots, what do you drink? I asked. "I don't drink too much," said Kathy, "but I will have whatever you ladies are having tonight." "I heard that," said Tonya, "I'll flag down our Server."

"So, what brings you in here all by yourself tonight Kathy?" ask Tonya. "Well to tell you the truth, I was here trying to catch my husband red handed," replied Kathy bluntly. "Oh shute, you probably are going to need a double," said Tonya. Well, we don't want to get all in your business Kathy, but I understand if you need to vent. "It might help me if I do vent," said Kathy. "I really feel crazy and anxious, I just needed to get out and see things for myself," said Kathy. "Here is another round of drinks from Danny, and I also included your double shot Mam so you can kind of catch up to the other ladies," said the Server. "Would you like to see a menu?" "No thank you," said Kathy. "I'm too mad to eat right now." I know what you mean Kathy, that's exactly how I feel tonight, I said. But let's try and have a great time anyway, God will work it out, all things will work out for the better.

"Hey Aunt Tonya, Danny had new swings put in that VIP swing room, let's go up there and swing a minute," said Draya laughing. "I'm not swinging in any swing right now after drinking these shots Draya, what else is up there in that room?" asked Tonya. "There is a private bar and lounges." "It's nice up there, it's also some poles in private booths." said Draya with a devilish smile. Yea, I said, let's ask our Server if they can move us up there, there is a nice looking Bartender up there too Tonya. "Why did you say it like that, Stace?" "You say that as if I have a thing for Bartenders," said Tonya.

As we headed up the spiral glass staircase to the VIP swing room, the Server informed us that there were a few new Entertainers starting soon and they might be in that room practicing some routines. "That will be okay with us!" said Tonya being ornery. "I think I'll take another shot and some Cucumber mint water," said Draya. I think we all should have some of that Healing water, we are going to need it. Are you okay Kathy? I asked. "Yea, I'm good, thank you ladies for allowing me to join you tonight," said Kathy. "I feel better already." "You ladies really make me feel comfortable and welcomed, I appreciate that, it really feels sincere," said Kathy. I would appreciate the same thing Kathy, I said, my grandmother always told us to treat people the way you would want to be treated. And I can feel that you are good people. But don't get it twisted, everybody is not getting invited to the table, but I got a good vibe from you. "Thank you," Kathy said with a smile. "Now let me get this next round!" said Kathy warming up to let loose.

"Hello Ladies, I hope we are not going to be disturbing your private party up here," said some handsome, hot, actor looking kind of guys. "We are Adult Entertainers specializing in Drag, Little Dancers and special request Entertainers," said a Nice looking young man with beautiful teeth. "That's okay with us!" Kathy said with excitement. "Okay now Kathy!" said Draya. "That's right girl, enjoy yourself!" And next thing we knew, five Little People walked in with an attitude the size of Texas. The two men were twins with bow legs and big feet… The two women also looked like twins, and the third woman was a little taller than the other two but you couldn't help but notice they all had really big butts, even the guys.

We all started to loosen up and forget about all the other shit we each had going on. We really were enjoying ourselves, even Kathy. We were talking about goals and plans for ourselves, and all kind of things from recipes to health tips, to sex and men. We even had Kathy up and dancing, and we all were trying our own little moves on the pole. Before I knew it *Uncle Lukes*' "*Doo Doo Brown*" came on, and we were on the dance floor with the Little dancers smacking their butts while they were doing splits and twerking them little big butts up and down and all around that VIP Swing room. We were sure swinging alright, but not that crazy kind of swinging, just girls gone wild having a great time.

"Oh shute Mommy, Mike is on his way and we have officially turned into Pumpkins or Cinderella, or whoever, all I know is this party is over for the night," said Draya. Oh wow, we were having so much fun, but it's time to wrap this up, are you going to be okay to go home Kathy? I asked. I'm at my condo by myself tonight, the kids are downstairs with my neighbor Ellen's grandchildren. "I will pick the kids up tomorrow sometime Mommy," said Draya. "We mine as well go to your house for the night, Stace," said Tonya. "Let's stop

and get some cheesesteaks to soak up all this alcohol we had tonight."
Well, the Chef did send us that tray of balls, I said sarcastically.
"Mommy, you ate a few of the balls too, I thought they were good,"
said Draya. "Yes they were really good," said Kathy. "Yea, I liked the
balls of the Chef too," said Tonya looking at me with a side wink.
"But that was a few hours ago, we are going to need something with
bread since we had more drinks." "And since we're going to Stace's
place, we might want to keep a slight party going so we need to stop
and get some junk food," said Tonya. "The night is still young and
so are we," Tonya said with a cheery partygirl attitude. Okay Wild
Child, I said affectionately, we're not that young and neither is the
night, it's after midnight. "Stop Mommy," said Draya, "you know
that you can hang past midnight." "Kathy, are you going to need a
ride too?" asked Draya. "Well, I think I'm okay to drive home, I had
a really good time with you ladies tonight, I thank you for bringing
me out of my depressive state of mind I've been in lately." "This is
exactly what the Mental Health Doctor should've ordered. A good
time with people who share similar journeys, enjoying the present
moment, not necessarily worrying about the past or the future, just
the moment, my heart feels so much lighter," said Kathy. "I really
had a lot of fun and enlightenment." I'm glad you feel better Kathy,
I think we ALL made each other feel better. The power of girl power,
I said with a feeling of lightheartedness myself. But the invite still
stands to my home or our next girl outing, let's exchange contact
information and stay in touch. "I would love that," said Kathy. "Yes,"
said Tonya. "Let's all make it a point to get together at least a few
times a month and just do whatever." We can clear our minds and
have fun, I'm definitely with that," said Tonya. "Sounds good to me
too," said Draya. " I'm going outside to tell Mike to give us a few
minutes and we will be out."

We all needed to use the ladies room and get ourselves together. Thank goodness there was a private ladies room on the upper floor. It looked more like a dressing room than a restroom, but that's what I expected from my classy nephew. I decided to peek in the kitchen at the Chef while Draya went out to tell Mike our plans at stopping to get Cheesesteaks. Tonya and Kathy were still in the ladies room chatting. While I was trying to get a sneak peek at him, and to see if that woman Tessa was still around, Chef looked up and caught me peeking. He was back there alone and looked up and smiled. "Did you like the assortment of Balls I sent out?" Chef asked with a grin. Well, the food was good Chef, but the balls you had to have some woman in my space, to tell you the truth, no, I didn't like that at all. "Well, she is someone from my past, we are just kind of wrapping things up," said the Chef. Kind of wrapping things up? I kind of asked, allowing my jealousy to peek through. Anyway Gus, we are on our way home and I just wanted to say a little something to you tonight since we hadn't talked since that rainy day we had together. "Yes, there is a reason for that Stace and we will talk about that soon," said the Chef. "I heard you ladies had a great time up there in the new Swing room, and another one of your memorable events," laughed Gus. Yea, we needed that, we all had a lot on our minds and were feeling down. Needless to say we healed eachother's mood with our wild and crazy fun, but my son in law is out in the parking lot waiting on us, so I need to get going, but it's great seeing you again. "Great seeing you again too, Stace, can I hug you before you run out the door, Cinderella?" asked the Chef with puppy eyes. Of course, I said, melting into his chest. "The phone does work both ways, Stace," said the Chef. "You are a woman who knows what she wants and goes after it any other time." "The *Man* doesn't always have to be the one who makes the first move." I smiled, he got me on that one.

"Mommy come on, Mike and I have been sitting in this truck for darn near 20 minutes waiting on you guys, where is Aunt Tonya?" I thought she would have been out here by now Draya, I'll go back upstairs and see where they're at. "Okay, I'll come with you," said Draya. As we headed towards the ladies room, I could see a few dancers peeking in from the hallway. "What's going on in there?" asked Draya. I'm not sure Draya, excuse me ladies, I said as I was peeking in the ladies room to see if Tonya was still in there. Just then a few of the dancers went rushing in and all I could see was Tall girl bent down with her head in a grip by Kathy, Tonya somewhere in the middle doing what I wasn't sure and some dancers pulling on people, but who they were pulling on I wasn't sure either. But before I knew it, Draya and I were in the mix too, and I'm not sure who I was pulling or pushing, but all I knew is that nobody is going to be touching my sister. The next thing I know, Danny and a few Security guys were in the ladies room pulling all us ladies apart. What the hell just happened. I had no idea what happened and why, all I know is that our fun night just turned into chaos.

"What the hell is going on in here?" asked Danny looking confused and sweating. "I'm sorry Son," said Tonya. I was on my way out of the ladies room and the next thing I know I heard Kathy arguing with someone." "I went back inside just in time to see Kathy pull off Tall girl's wig and start hitting her with it." "I guess she must know who her husband is cheating with," said Tonya. "I'm worn the hell out." "I'm so sorry to all of you," said Kathy. "I didn't mean to ruin our great night we had." "Get your ass in my office," Danny said to the Tall girl. "Is everyone ok?" asked Danny. Yes, just a little pulling and grabbing Nephew, we're sorry, as soon as I saw my sister in something with other people's hands involved, it took me to that other level, you know I can still go there. "Yea Auntie, you have a lot of class, but can still whoop an ass if need be, you know I know that about you," said Danny, half laughing trying to catch his breath. "Yall wore me out in about forty five seconds," laughed Danny. "I better get my ass back in that gym on Monday, but yall worked me out for tonight." Kathy still had a strong grip on that wig, I carefully removed it from her hand as her hand was shaking. Hey Kathy, I said, I really would like if you came with us tonight to my house, we would like your company. "I don't want to put any further dampers on the good mood we had, " said Kathy. "Who said you put a damper on our good mood?" Tonya said. "That shit was fun and right on time, I wanted to punch that Tall bitch all night," laughed Tonya. "Give that bitch back her wig, stand tall, and let's get our composure and go." "You're coming with us and that's that," said Tonya. "Yes Kathy, you're one of us now," said Draya. "Oh shit, here comes Mike, let's go."

THE SLEEPOVER AFTER THE FACT

WE SURE NEEDED SOME heavy food after that Rumble in the Jungle. All Mike could say was Um, Um, Um and shake his head with a smirk. As we were standing in line waiting to order our Cheesesteaks, I felt something new. I couldn't quite put my finger on it, but I had a feeling that this crazy night was the start of a new feeling and a new life. The City looked sexy again. The night air felt still. We were still smiling, talking and laughing and the mood felt good. I was glad I had invited Kathy to come and stay with Tonya and I for the night. Although we had technically just met, you could feel she was a kind hearted person that wore her heart on her sleeves. And besides that, Kathy going home at that time could end up being a bad situation in one way or another. She needed an outlet and we were there to be able to offer some help. God put us all there for a reason, and I'm glad we were able to participate in his perfect plan. I'm also glad she was able to stand up to Tall Girl…

I always have new comfy clothes at home. Capris and T-shirts are my favorite and I have plenty of them to give out. We were all about average size so the tights could fit any of us. I gave them all the necessities and gave Tonya Braya's room to sleep in. She refused to sleep in the guest room where Draya sleeps, she said there was too much going on in that bed for her. Kathy said she was happy to take the sofa. Although I'm pretty sure we were going to be up on that rooftop for a while..

We felt comfy and free on that rooftop, the City sure is sexy from above. I had a few Lancaster Strawberry ale's in the fridge and they went perfect with the cheesesteaks and the decompression we all needed. Tonya also brought some weed with her, we were relaxing back and chilling in the lounge chairs. Nobody said anything for a few minutes, I guess we each were wherever we wanted to be at that moment, in our minds anyway. Although we each had situations with our husbands and significant others, we didn't talk about them too much, that is, not in detail anyway. But since we had Kathy here, we should see exactly what she knows if anything about the John situation.

Kathy started opening up about her husband having an affair and how it affected her already low self esteem. She says other than a few relatives she never really associates with anyone and never goes anywhere. And although she had goals in the past of starting a business, she had put her goals aside to help her husband with his Signage Detail Shop business. I could definitely relate to her feeling like she is giving up on her dreams and goals. And Tonya had similar dreams and goals and had kind of kept it to herself. Wow Ladies, maybe we should look into going into business together. "I love you Sis but I'm not sure it's a good idea to go into business with my family," Tonya laughed. "Besides, what type of business are you talking about?" Tonya asked. I'm not sure, Tonya, I laughed. "We had such a much needed good time at the club, maybe we should open a club of our own," said Kathy. Ha, Ha, girl, I couldn't be bothered with no club and people and drama, that would be too much for me. "But you are in the hospitality business Stace, and clubs are hospitality," laughed Tonya. Well, I *was* in the hospitality business Tonya, but I haven't had the passion for it in a while. And anyway, a full time club would be a whole lot and I'm not sure I have the strength for that right now. "Well it's food for thought," said Kathy. "I like you Kathy," said Tonya. "You think you have low self esteem, but you obviously still know you have that go getter attitude inside, ready to make moves, that's great." "I like being around people like that." "You still have a positive outlook even though you're going through some bullshit," said Tonya. "Yea, my Dad would always tell me to fight my way through it, and that's exactly what I try to do, just keep it moving," said Kathy. "We never had children, Peter didn't want any." "I always wanted kids but he didn't, and he was very adamant about that," said Kathy. "He wanted me to feel isolated and controlled and I allowed it, without even realizing it for years," said Kathy. "That's called Ambient abuse," said Tonya, to my suprise. I only recently heard of that on a talk show, I added in. "Well since I'm here I will tell you about how I put a camera in our house to see what Peter was up to while I was working at the Shop counter," said Kathy. "He knew I would be stuck at the reception area and would leave for hours at a time sometimes." He had the nerve to bring that Tall girl into our home on more than one occasion, but I didn't see her go upstairs or anything." "He just had her waiting downstairs as he got dressed, I guess they were going out somewhere," said Kathy. "I found out she was working at that club and that he sometimes picks her up from work." "So I decided to come and confront him about it while he was in action," said Kathy. "I also overheard him on a phone call bragging to someone about how he is blackmailing some guy over something he saw him do," said Kathy. "Do you know who the guy is that your husband is blackmailing?" asked Tonya. "Not really," said Kathy. "I just know he has to meet up with this person to get money from them in the Hamptons." "The Hamptons!?" Tonya and I said at the same time. Do you know what your husband saw the man do, Kathy? I asked. "No, not really, but I think he says he saw the guy carry out a body from some building. Peter does signage for a few of the businesses in that building," said Kathy. What's the name of the building? I asked. "Well it's actually a few of the buildings in this area," said Kathy. Well, Tonya and I looked at each other as if we were in a *whodunit* mystery movie. I know Bryson's ass is not being punked by somebody, and if so, why. And what the hell exactly is he being blackmailed for, I thought to myself, with the whole look of it expressed across my face.

We have to get to the bottom of this whole thing, I said to the both of them. But let's just marinate on this for a few days. I'm going to grab us another beer and light that joint back up Tonya.

GOTCHA!

THE LADIES AND I made a plan to go to the Hamptons in the middle of the week. We all fell asleep in the living room watching Cheaters, it comes on at 4am every Saturday morning. Sometimes *Cheaters* make me laugh when I need a laugh the most in the wee hours of the night and morning. Especially how Joey Greco says the craziest shit in a flat tone, unemotional voice and face. Hell, I've even learned a few things about relationships watching Cheaters. Well anyway, it always comes on Saturday at 4am, but they must have known we needed that type of entertainment right now, even though it was Sunday 4am and I'm usually deep in sleep at this time. I'm usually home way before midnight most Saturday nights, to tell the truth. Although I currently don't belong to any church home, I watch a few Ministers on TV and visit some favorite churches periodically. But I do have an ever growing relationship with the Lord Our God. But this Sunday, I just wanted to relax and plan the week out today. Tonya and Kathy just wanted coffee this morning, so they went downstairs together to get Starbucks. Braya and Branson came home by 9am and were waiting to be picked up by their parents. I had to have a talk with Draya and Mike about taking more of my time for myself. As much as I love my grandbabies, it's time for me to fall back somewhat and let their parents take more of the responsibilities. I know I like to be in control sometimes, of course, Mum Mom always know best, but I have to let them figure some things out for themselves. That's the only way they will learn and become self-sufficient. I am still learning about life myself.

As Branson was waiting for Draya and Mike, he sat on the couch next to me and snuggled up. He hasn't initiated a snuggle in a long time. He was getting so big so fast and it kind of made me sad in a way. But the kids are growing up like beautiful flowers. They are so smart and full of talent, it makes me learn more just by being around them. I wanted to wait until the right time to ask Branson to talk about what happened that night of his Piano recital. But in light of recent events, and the fact that I had so many unanswered questions, now has to be the time. What was John doing that day? Did John ever touch you in an inappropriate way? How did you feel about John? How do you feel about Mum mom's reaction to what I thought John did that day? What really happened in your eyes that day? Was John alive when they took him out wrapped in the rug? I wanted to know from Bryson what happened to John that night. How bad was he hurt, where did he go after that night? Where has John been since that night? Why didn't John try to contact me? If Bryson knows the whereabouts and howabouts of John, why has he not once communicated any of that to me? Is Bryson being black-mailed about that night? What exactly does somebody think they know? What the fuck, I probably have more questions than that. I think I'm going to lose it, I thought, shaking my head. But anyway, it's time for Branson and I to have that talk. And it's also time for Bryson and I to have that talk.

Hey my Little Big Man, I said affectionately to Branson. I wasn't sure when the right time was to bring up the night of your Piano recital. Everything happened so fast that night but you still managed to perform like a professional and I am so proud of you for just being you. No matter what you choose to do in life, I will always be there to support you and be there for you. I'm not going to push you to talk about that night if you are in any way uncomfortable. I just want you to know I am here ready to talk about it when you are. I know that I did not handle things the way I should have. Acting on emotions is never the right way to resolve any problems or issues. I was very wrong about what I did, but I'm not sure about what John did. Did John do or say something that you were uncomfortable with? "Well, first of all Mum mum, I know you were being protective over me as you always were since we were babies," said Branson. "I liked Uncle John, he did not do anything to me that made me feel uncomfortable. He was always nice to me and taught us a lot of things, not just about the Piano but about all kinds of things like the history of the City of Philadelphia. You overreacted Mum mom," said Branson with puppy eyes. Well, I thought John was doing something inappropriate to you, I said to Branson with my eyes starting to tear up. "No he wasn't," Branson replied. Well what was John doing the day when you were on the couch? "I didn't want to tell you, Mum mom. Uncle John said that it would really hurt you if I told you," said Branson. Tell me what Branson? "I saw John touching Pop pop in some kind of weird way," said Branson reluctantly. What do you mean weird, Branson? "See Mum mum, that's just why I didn't want to tell you." "I knew you would start questioning me, and I don't know anything about what they were doing," said Branson. "But I do know that Uncle John wasn't hurt all that bad because I looked out the window and saw Uncle John in the car with Pop pop. I also overheard them talking on the phone the next day," said Branson. Oh my God, Branson, so all this time I thought John had touched you inappropriately. That's what made me snap. And you mean all this time you were holding a secret about what you saw John and Bryson doing? The nerve of them to even put that on you. And Bryson has been allowing me to believe that John had done something inappropriate and all this time Bryson has been the one that has been inappropriate, to say the least! I don't even know what to say, Branson. All this time you have been carrying this weight around. Has Bryson ever had any kind of discussion about what you saw that day? "Not really Mum mum, all Pop pop said was, *'it wasn't what you thought it was and you didn't see anything anyway,'* said Branson. "Please don't mention this to Pop pop, I don't want him to be mad at me," begged Branson. I won't tell him that we had this discussion baby. I don't want you to have any more stress about this situation than you already have. Although it does make me feel much better knowing that Uncle John didn't do anything inappropriate to you. Are you okay Branson? " I'm good Mum mom." I'm glad you're good, Bran Man, that's what's most important to me, I love you my grandson. "I love you too Mum mom," said Branson with a light hearted smile. "But Mum mom, I really want to play the piano again." Okay good, Branson. I'm glad to hear that you haven't lost interest in playing. You have a God given talent you know. "Yes, I do know that, Mum mom." " Thank you for helping me to realize my gift and thank you for having Uncle John help me to bring out my talent," said Branson. "But now I want to take my Piano talent and my rapping talent and blend them together." "There is an Art school that takes gifted students and helps them to excel," said Branson. "Nolan's grandmother Miss Ellen was able to get him and Noel enrolled in the school. They will attend there in the second half of the school year, after the holiday break." "That's basically only a few months away." "Do you think you can get some information on the school, and see how we would go about getting me enrolled in that school, Mum mum?" asked Branson. Sure Branson, you know I would do anything to help you reach your God given potential.

"Mom is here," yelled Braya. "Good morning Mommy and my babies," said Draya. "How is everybody doing this morning?" "Good mommy," said Branson and Braya, as they both hugged and kissed their mom. "Does Aunt Tonya and our new found friend Kathy need a ride back to their cars?" ask Draya. Yea probably, I was going to take them to their cars but you can take them. They went downstairs for coffee. They've been down there a while, they must be bonding, I said laughing. "Yea, Aunt Tonya is probably trying to talk Kathy into a makeover," laughed Draya. "Well, are you guys ready to go?" Draya asked Branson and Braya. "Yes, I'm ready to go home," said Braya. "Is the pool done?" "Yea the pool is done, little Miss lady Braya, and so is the new inside kitchen, outside kitchen, and huge deck!" said Draya with excitement. "I can't wait to get in the new pool," said both Braya and Branson with their eyes lit up. "Your Dad and Uncle Danny are there doing some final touches with the outdoor furniture, I need to head back home now," said Draya. "Okay Mommy, you know what?" asked Braya to her mother, "I thought of some new flavored lip glosses and eye shadows." "We are going to get you a lab area in the house so we can work on those lip glosses and eyeshadows together, Braya," said Draya. Just then Tonya and Kathy came in the door laughing as if they were sisters, with their Starbucks in hand. It looks like they got a little chummy over our crazy girls nite out , I said to myself with a hint of jealousy.. I'm going to see everybody later, I'm just going to relax around the Condo today and make my plans for the week.

That was Ma's necklace after all like Tonya said. Danny took it from her after she told him it was given to her as a gift from that Uncle Peter guy. And I also found out that Bryson had a few other bank accounts that I didn't know about. Bryson was hiding things for a long time as I foolishly thought we were just fine. It hurt me a lot. And to top it off, he is in the Hamptons for what he said is a reunion with some of his old NFL team mates for the weekend. He said he was going a little earlier in the week to catch up with a few guys that were already there. Hum, I think I will call Tonya to see if she wants to go early too. Ellen has a home there and she said we can stay there this weekend. Although I'm sure she wouldn't mind if we go a little earlier. I invited Kathy to go with us. She was mad and bored being that her husband, Uncle Peter, hasn't been home since the weekend. I'm sure his mistress told him all about the situation in the club, and he was probably scared to go home and face his wife. Danny and his wife Michelle were actually planning a mini vacation being that she feels he works too much. Michelle is really excited about planning to travel and thinks she may be interested in becoming a Travel agent. I told her Tonya and I were going to the Hamptons and she wanted to ask Danny to drive there just for a few days in the middle of the week to take a break from the Club before the weekend crowd hits.

THE HAMPTONS

BEING IN THE HAMPTONS again after years bought back so many memories for me. After I think about it, I think it was something that happened here in the Hamptons that made me feel I wanted to leave the Party planning world behind. I was the best. The best Party and Event planner/Caterer in the Hamptons and beyond. I had some great times and met some very good people in the Hamptons, and of course, some very rich people. I did get a lot of my contacts and business referrals from a friend that I was very close with at the time. She was a fellow NFL player's wife. Her name is Pauletta and we haven't spoken since we had a blowout supposedly over a Birthday party we did together for a Celebrity. After I thought about it, I think it was more about a rumor that had surfaced about her husband having an affair, or let's just say a sexual encounter with another football player. What I heard is that years ago her husband was caught in the shower having some pretty thrusty sex with a fellow teammate and it was swept under the rug. She thought she overheard people gossiping about it at the party and thought I was the one who started the rumor.

That couldn't have been further from the truth. I heard about it and asked Bryson if he knew whether or not it was true. What I didn't know at the time is that maybe Bryson was dipping and dabbing in some things of his own. I thought it was time for Pauletta and I to talk, especially since I'm here in the Hamptons after five years. It has been five years off from my passion in life of making peoples special days fabulous. I'm going to give her a call to extend the olive branch, hopefully she takes it. Hopefully she even answers my call, what the hell I'm going to call her anyway.

Hey Pauletta, this is Stacia, I'm here in the Hamptons and wondered if you would be open to having lunch with me tomorrow. Give me a call back please when you get time, I'm here until Sunday. Thanks and I look forward to hearing from you soon. I left her a message,.. let's see if she calls me back. If not that's okay too, I just want to clear the air if nothing else. I adored Pauletta and miss her friendship dearly. I didn't realize how much until I came back to the Hamptons.

Tonya and Kathy were sure enjoying sight seeing in the Hamptons. They seem to be getting closer and are becoming real BFFs. I don't even think Kathy even gives a damn about that husband of hers right now. She has been seeing some eye candy of all sorts all around the Hamptons. And the rich lifestyle and mansions she sees is something she always envied. And that slimy Uncle Peter dude was sure not the one to give her that type of lifestyle that she deserves. I tried to call Bryson but I didn't get an answer. What a surprise. Bryson and I haven't been talking much lately. I think he senses that I know something. But I did tell Bryson that I would not be attending the NFL retired football players reunion with him because I didn't feel like being around some of the wives who were always gossiping and being judgemental about everything and everybody. Bryson knew of the tension between Pauletta and I, but he seemed to even fuel the tension at times. Now looking back, it seems like Bryson had a hand at creating and encouraging the tension. It was like he had a jealousy of our friendship, but I didn't realize that at the time. Anyway, the service is really bad in the Hamptons at certain places so maybe he just couldn't get service wherever he was...

To my surprise, I heard back from Pauletta by text. She wanted me to meet her at a small lunch cafe we both loved. Although I was happy to hear from her, I was a little nervous about seeing her again since the last time we saw each other it didn't end well. The client we were working for requested at the last minute that we use a certain wine he had in his wine cellar instead of the champagne he originally requested. He wanted the wine from the collection his father had saved for a special occasion in the wine cellar. This was a special occasion being that the client was going to propose to his girlfriend on his birthday and after she hopefully said yes, the fireworks would go off and the wine would be served. Pauletta had stormed out of the party before she bothered to tell me of the new wine pouring instructions. The client was upset but the champagne that we poured was one of the best champagnes. And anyway, no one really cares about the champagne, it's really just for toasting. Besides, most of the guests were already drunk way before the proposal. The girlfriend said yes, and none of the guests knew anything different about the wine, but the client and his father did. Oh well, he said they would use it at the wedding that he was going to use another Event Planner for. I haven't done another event since, I just didn't feel like it anymore.

Oh my God, Hey Pauletta, I said enthusiastically. "Hey Stacia," Pauletta said smiling as she reached out to give me a hug. Honestly, I think that was all we needed to put an end to whatever hurt emotions that we were feeling. We both picked up right where we left off. We were talking about old times and grandchildren and smiling at each other the whole time. Oh, and we were definitely enjoying our meal. That is until we bought up our husbands.

Our husbands, the men we thought we needed. Maybe we did need them at the time, but looking back they may have been what was in our way of reaching our true destiny at the time. But maybe it wasn't time... Only God knows the roads and road blocks you need to go through sometimes to get to the dream. Nothing good comes easy, that's for sure. There will be trials and tests along the way, but that fire ends up being the beauty of the dream.

"It was so good seeing you, Stacia," said Pauletta. "Let's stay in touch and get together again real soon." Definitely I said with a smile. "Some of the wives will be here this weekend for the reunion, I really don't feel like socializing too much with them," said Pauletta, "they are so phony." I know what you mean Pauletta. I spend more time with my grandchildren lately than with the adults. The kids are more genuine than most of these stuck up women. "Yea, you are so right about that," said Pauletta. "I have been seeing Bryson around here and there over the last couple of months, are you guys still thinking about buying a home here, like you said you were going to do years ago?" asked Pauletta. Well I'm not sure what Bryson has been doing here, but I know nothing about buying a home in the Hamptons at this time. I'm not sure where Bryson and I are headed right now Pauletta, we are not in a good place. "I know what you mean about being in a place with your husband. Brad and I are in a bad place too right now, and I'm not sure where we are headed either," said Pauletta. I'm sorry to hear that Pauletta, I never want to see couples break up after all these years. We all were once very happy and in love with our husbands. They were our best friends when the friends we thought we had were not there. Hopefully the friendship we have with our husbands will outweigh the fallen emotions we have for them at this time in our relationships. "By the way, I saw Bryson earlier, he said he is staying at the rental on Shore road," said Pauletta. Oh really, I said, I know where that is. "I thought that was being rented out to a college professor who recently moved out here and is great at playing the piano," said Pauletta.

I didn't know where Tonya and Kathy had drifted off to, but my heart was racing and I was determined to get to the bottom of things. I was headed to Shore road and I didn't care anything about what anyone else had going on.

As I headed up the walkway to the shore house, I got an eerie feeling that made the hair stand up on my arms and back. It felt like I was being shocked by static or something. I could hear the ocean crashing, like it was going to be a full moon and high tide. Maybe that is why I'm feeling crazy or something, like I'm going to go into a full blown anxiety attack at any moment. Even the seagulls were acting very erratically. I could hear them squawking and following me up the sandy wooden walkway as if they were talking to me and trying to tell me something. But in the midst of the ocean crashing and the seagulls squawking I could faintly hear a piano playing. As I got closer to the house I could hear it more and more. I knew that piano playing all too well, it had to be, no it couldn't be, but it had to be no other than...John. I felt as if I was going to faint.

Tears started to fill my eyes, I felt as if I could barely see. Who's house is this and should I knock on the door? I didn't have to, my body took over what my mind couldn't handle. I just walked right in that door... and there he was, John,... John who I loved and missed so dearly, John, who I was more angry at for a range of feelings and emotions and reasons, that at this time I couldn't describe. John, who deserted me and left a void in my life that only he could fill, John who I had once loved more than my husband, John…

John,…I said slowly and tearfully as he played the piano with great emotion almost like he knew I was his audience at the time. Just then John stopped playing and turned and looked at me with tears streaming down my face. "Hello Stacia," John said with an eerie look and voice, "it's good to see you." Good to see me John? I asked with a hurtful faint voice that could barely speak. Are you kidding me John? I said slowly with overwhelming emotion and pure shock. I didn't know if you were dead or alive, I said as I walked towards him, not knowing what I was capable of doing at the moment. As I walked towards John, he started to look deeper into my eyes and I could see the emotions that he too was feeling. "I missed you so much Stacia," John said with tears starting to fill his eyes. Just then, I heard a voice coming from somewhere in the home. As the voice got closer, I realized that the voice I am hearing is no other than my husband Brysons voice. "I got a little time before the award ceremony starts," said Bryson, as he came down the beautiful white spiral staircase of a home that should be mine. I watched Bryson come downstairs towards John, with a smile on his face and dick harder than I had seen in many years, with tears overflowing down my face. John looked at Bryson and then turned and looked at me with a look of inner pain from a two edged sword that was stabbing both he and I at the same time. "Oh shit Stacia!" Bryson said with enough shock to shribble that dick right back down to size, "what are you doing here?" Just then I went into shock and lost it. I could faintly hear Tonya's voice saying something as if I were in a dream or having an out of body experience. Suddenly there were more voices in the room and the voices started to get louder and louder. Before I knew what was happening I heard chairs being knocked over and voices screaming in the background, it felt like the whole room was being thrown around in a whirlwind, like in *the wizard of Oz*, the house was spinning and spinning. I felt myself starting to pass out. I woke up to blood everywhere,.... what just had happened?... I felt sick.

THE AFTERMATH

WAS THIS A DREAM? It seems like it was. I woke up to being in a club in the Hamptons with Tonya, Draya, Kathy and what, who, the Tall girl? You have to be kidding me. Just then Danny joins us in the booth. "Are you okay Aunt Stace," Danny says very delicately. I'm not sure my nephew, what happened and how did we get here? I said.

I must have blacked out. "Don't worry about nothing Auntie, just like I said, I will always have your back. I took care of everything."

What did he mean by he took care of everything? Where was Bryson? Where was John? What happened in that house? Whose blood had been all over me. All of us women looked at each other as if we had all just experienced *Hell.* I felt exhausted, we all had the ultimate look of exhaustion all over our faces. I'm sure in time, more than likely a short period of time, the tale of what happened from the Condo at The Phoenix building in Philadelphia to the Shore house in the Hamptons will reveal itself. Whatever happened will bond us for life in one way or the other and we are in for a rocky ride. I didn't need a drink, we were high off of what just happened. "What will you ladies and one gentleman be having tonight?" asked the Server. We all just looked at each other like we were in some strange universe. Danny looked at all of us as if to say, look, get it together, the show must go. "Bring us a bottle of your best champagne, we are celebrating the new life we are all about to experience," Danny said with a devilish smile...

THE END...

Menu from Piano Teacher

The first encounter of John and Stacia

- Filthy pepper filthy dirty martini
- The deviled egg trio
- Bloody mary Caviar deviled egg
- Smoked Seductive salmon deviled egg
- Crabby daddy deviled egg

Bransons' recietel

- Angelic froth espresso-tini w/orange marmalade glazed mint leaf
- Beef and blue meatballs
- Apple Butter Sage pretzel balls Stuffed w/ crab
- Bite size crepe stuffed w/glazed turkey bacon, spiced orange marmalade, mascarpone, chocolate shavings

John and bryson hangin in the city

- Bro man Philly cheese steak wraps
- Johnny walker black buffalo wings
- Dark and stormy Moscow mulls

Fourth of July at the lakehouse

- Roast pig trio
- Seafood pot
- Grilled salmon and garden veggies
- Grilled watermelon salad

- CARIBBEAN RICE AND BEANS W/
  SHRIMP,SAUSAGE,GRILLED CHX & PEPPERS
- GRILLED PARMESAN CORN ON COB
- RICHARDS HOMEMADE VANILLA ICE CREAM
- GMOMS RUTH APPLE PEACH COBBLER
- LIMONCELLO MARTINIS
- WATERMELON JELLO SHOTS
- GRANDMA STYER SWEET SUMMER TEA

MORNING AFTER FOURTH OF JULY COOKOUT

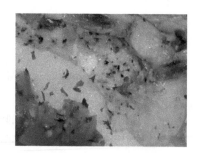

- COFFEE RUBBED RIBEYE W/SUNNY EGG
- FRIED DEVILED EGGS
- HOUSEMADE SALSA
- SHRIMP AND GRITS
- FRUIT SALAD W/CREAM
- CRAFT HOMEMADE BEER

WHAT'S UP WITH BRYSON LATELY

- CRAB CAKES
- CORN FRITTERS
- GMOM RUTH'S SLAW
- STUFFED FRIED SHRIMP
- COCKY COCKTAIL

Back to the City with Voodoo Vibes

- Gator sausage & pork bam burger w/creole mango mustard & trinity pepper slaw
- Voodoo vibe fries w/crawfish etouffee
- Jambalaya salad w/ creole mustard dressing
- French toast bread pudding w/whiskey glaze sauce
- Spicy sweet beignet w/whiskey coffee
- Lemon honey fresh mint w/spices refresher water

Back to Condo Life with Gossiping Ellen

- Taco lasaagna w/ lime crema sauce
- Key lime pie margaritas
- Key Lime Cheesecake w/kiwi, Strawberry & Chocolate

ABOUT THE AUTHOR

AUTHOR STEPHANIE JACKS WAS born and raised in Coatesville, a small City with big hearts in the western suburbs of Philadelphia. At a time when life was rich with character and generational families and family friends that are even more family today. She grew up in a household very similar to the movie Crooklyn, (which happens to be a family favorite) with Mom, Dad, 4 brothers, dogs, etc., so she had to be born 21. She spent a lot of childhood days playing double dutch, telling spooky stories in the grapevine huts that were in her childhood backyard and playing kickball in friends backyards.

Stephanie spent a lot of time growing up eating at restaurants and going to plays in Center City and a lot of Concerts including everybody from Prince to The Jackson's to Heavy D and Jay Z to Gerald Levert and Frankie Beverly... and can't forget how James Brown wore us out under the bridge at an all day concert, and he never seemed to get tired.

Stephanie spent the last 2 decades in Real Estate and Culinary Arts. She raised 3 great children as a single parent and has 14 beautiful grandchildren. Enjoys going to the Movies with the grandchildren and other fun things, as well as loving movies and TV shows at home, while cooking and eating everything. Stephanie also enjoys spending time and hanging out with family and lifelong girlfriends.

TABLE OF CONTENTS

Preface

Most men believe that accountability is the invincible weapon
for fighting lust, but many of us have found that this method falls
short. It helps for a while, granted, due to the repulsive power of
embarrassment. But what's next? We need something more potent
if we are to experience lasting victory.

Daryl Wingerd dug up and brushed off the Bible's core explosive
device for defeating habitual sexual sin. You won't find this concept
in most self-help books on the subject—even Christian ones. I'm
convinced you will discover here the volatile material able to finally
decimate lust as a pattern of life, in you and in those you help.
Like others, you may say, "I've not read a book quite like this for
clarifying the biblical way to succeed over this troubling issue."

The author writes in an easy style with short chapters, but handles
large and powerful biblical concepts. You won't be intimidated
by his words, but his words will intimidate your sin. Wingerd has
provided some questions at the end of each chapter for those who
wish to use the book for small group discussions, and for the man
who wants to reflect privately on what he has read. Due to the
brevity of the chapters, your small group may be able to cover more
than one chapter each time you meet. The book will be invaluable
to men in general—single and married, younger and older. Lust will
nip at us till the end if we don't deal with it biblically.

I'm often sobered by the idea that a sin neatly hidden in one man's
life is the same sin that entirely ruins another. Where one man will
find lust and satisfaction of that lust an intermittent problem at
worst, another man will say that what began as a private, occasional
sin proved catastrophic later. We're not dealing with trifling matters
when we talk about sexual sin. It has destroyed many men, torn up
many families, and blighted many histories.

Women may wish to read this book also. It will help them
understand what their husbands and sons may face. Though
writing from the man's perspective, the author is not unaware of
how lust can become a woman's problem as well. In fact, believers

in general may wish to read this book to discover how to overcome other habitual sins. The biblical principles will apply.

We rejoice at the wonderful liberty men are experiencing as they understand and apply these truths. Enjoy that liberty yourself.

Jim Elliff

President, Christian Communicators Worldwide

FACE REALITY

You probably experience pornographic temptation almost every day, and the Internet is not the only source. Try walking through a video store without being tempted to lust. Watch primetime TV without your conscience often telling you to look away. Find a grocery store where you can check out without standing next to a display of sexually provocative photographs.

The regrettable truth is, you live in a pornographic culture.

one

Two Men, a Park Bench, and a Confession

Two men sit together on a park bench, talking. Even from a distance it is obvious that one of them is troubled about something. His head hangs in discouragement as he speaks. The other man listens, but says nothing.

When a young couple walks by holding hands, the discouraged man stops talking and looks away, avoiding eye contact. The listener looks up at the couple and smiles politely.

Now we are closer and able to hear their conversation. The man who was listening begins to speak quietly, doing his best to preserve privacy. I'll call him Nick and the discouraged man John.

NICK. I can't believe you're looking at pornography again. I thought you gave that up when you became a Christian last year.

JOHN. I thought so too, but sometimes I just can't resist the temptation.

NICK, *sarcastically*. Can't? . . . or won't? I'm tempted too, but I seem to be able to resist.

JOHN, *sounding defeated*. OK, now I feel like scum.

NICK. Sorry, that's not the way I meant it. But looking at pornography isn't just a bad habit. It's a serious sin.

JOHN. I know it's serious, but there are worse things I could be doing. After all, it's not like I'm breaking the law.

NICK. Now wait a minute. Just because you can't get arrested for looking at pornography, what makes you think you're not breaking the law?

JOHN, *with a puzzled expression on his face*. What do you mean?

NICK. You call yourself a Christian, and Christians are people who obey Christ. So how can you say you're not breaking *His* law?

(*Long pause as John hangs his head again.*)

NICK, *exasperated*. Why don't you just quit? Just tell yourself you won't ever do it again.

JOHN. You're right. I should quit, and I want to quit, but . . .

(*Short pause. John sighs deeply.*)

NICK. But *what*?

JOHN. This may sound strange, but I've tried and tried to quit and I'm finally realizing that I don't know how.

Why do so many men who claim to be Christians fail in the area of sexual sin? One possible explanation is that some may not be true Christians. They have been deceived into thinking they can be saved while they go on loving and practicing their sin.[1] Despite this possibility, the "false convert" answer should not be our first response to confessions like the one Nick heard from John.

Real Christians are subject to temptation and may sin in many ways as long as they live. They are even encouraged to confess their sins to one another (as John did to Nick) so that other Christians can pray for them (James 5:16). Also, the church is given instructions concerning how to deal with true believers who are "caught in any trespass" (Gal. 6:1; cf. Matt. 18:15–17; Luke 17:3). If a man goes on cherishing his sin rather than forsaking it when confronted by other believers (in other words, if he does not repent), the church must consider him an unbeliever and remove him from their fellowship (Matt. 18:17; 1 Cor. 5). But we are never told to automatically conclude that a sinning brother is not a true Christian.

The Root of the Problem

Much of the difficulty among true Christians who feel powerless against sexual temptation stems from a lack of understanding (or even a complete *mis*understanding) of the fundamental spiritual difference between a Christian and a non-Christian. Christians are not merely people who have been forgiven of their sins through faith in Christ. They have also been radically re-created by the Spirit of God. The Bible calls this creative miracle "regeneration." I'll discuss regeneration in more detail later.

The lack of understanding about regeneration affects Christians who are sinning and those who try to help them. Much of what Nick said to John was true and necessary, but was his response a model you should emulate? Should he have been more understanding and encouraging? Should he have been even more severe in attempting to shame John into reforming himself? Most importantly, how should he respond to John's last statement? How would you respond? Is it enough to say, "Just quit"?

In this book you will discover the biblical response to a professing Christian who says, "I've tried and tried to stop looking at pornography, but I'm finally realizing that I don't know how."

---

1. Appendix A addresses the New Testament warnings about false assurance. Men who consider themselves to be Christians yet habitually view pornography or commit other sexual sins are encouraged to read this appendix thoughtfully.

Questions for Reflection or Discussion

1. What do you think are some of the factors contributing to the growing problem of pornography among professing Christians?

2. What would you have changed about Nick's response to John?

3. In what ways can you identify with either Nick or John?

two

The Significance of Desire

Moths are drawn to light. I don't know why, and I'm not sure the moths know either, but on warm summer evenings they fly away from dark places to flutter around whatever light they can find. Something in their nature makes them happy there.

Cockroaches, on the other hand, are repulsed by light. If you have ever lived in roach-infested quarters (like my apartment during college), you know that when you come home at night and turn on the lights, the roaches abandon the pizza crumbs and scatter for whatever dark place they can find. Light disturbs them. Something in their nature makes them happy only when they are cloaked in darkness.

Light and Darkness
In the Bible, the word "light" often depicts the nature and character of God—His holiness, righteousness, goodness, truth, and faithfulness. John wrote, "God is Light, and in Him there is no darkness at all" (1 John 1:5).

The attributes of God are summed up in Jesus Christ (Heb. 1:3), and Jesus described Himself this way: "I am the Light of the world; he who follows Me will not walk in the darkness, but will have the Light of life" (John 8:12).

Darkness, on the other hand, describes sin. The Apostle Paul warned Christians to stay clear of sinful practices by saying, "Do not participate in the unfruitful deeds of darkness" (Eph. 5:11). He also told us that "[God] has rescued us from the domain of darkness, and transferred us to the kingdom of His beloved Son" (Col. 1:13).

People naturally prefer moral darkness, even over Jesus. Notice how Christ described this preference:

> This is the judgment, that the Light has come into the world, and men loved the darkness rather than the Light, for their deeds were evil. For everyone who does evil hates the Light, and does not come to the Light for fear that his deeds will be exposed. (John 3:19–20)

Every Man Has a "Wanter"
Please forgive my non-technical language, but whether you typically respond like a moth or a cockroach when faced with a choice between Light and darkness depends on what your "wanter" wants. Your "wanter" is the deepest part of you—the part that produces and expresses your most meaningful desires. In the Bible it is called your heart. It is who you really are, the moral and spiritual center of your being.[2]

Getting a New "Wanter"
The man without Christ is self-willed, inclined toward disobedience. As Paul said, "the mind set on the flesh is hostile toward God; for it does not subject itself to the law of God, for it is not even able to do so, and those who are in the flesh cannot please God" (Rom. 8:7–8). Just as a pig could never fly unless God were to redesign it with wings and a lighter body, a man cannot love and obey God in a way that actually pleases Him unless God gives him a new heart.

When God gives a person a new heart, it is called "regeneration" (Titus 3:5) or being "born again" (John 3:3; 1 Pet. 1:3, 23). This New Testament language of new birth comes from God's Old Testament promise to His people:

---

2. See appendix B for more about the meaning of the word "heart" in the Bible.

> I will give you a new heart and put a new spirit within
> you; and I will remove the heart of stone from your flesh
> and give you a heart of flesh. I will put My Spirit within
> you and cause you to walk in My statutes, and you will be
> careful to observe My ordinances. (Ezek. 36:26–27)

Notice that God promised to "cause" them to walk in His statutes.
His miraculous work causes their obedience. Regenerate people
"*will* be careful to observe [His] ordinances." This promise applies
to every regenerate person, not just to those in the Old Testament.
Jesus was referring to this promise of a new heart when He spoke of
the new birth in John's Gospel.

> Truly, truly, I say to you, unless one is born again he
> cannot see the kingdom of God. (John 3:3)

If you are a true Christian (even if you cannot identify the precise
moment when you became one), God has removed your old heart
and has given you a completely new one—a heart that is inclined
toward believing in Christ and practicing righteous behavior.

Regeneration does not totally destroy a man's desire for sexual sin.
As long as the Christian lives in a mortal body, he will experience
desires for sin and for righteousness. John (the man in chapter 1)
obviously wants to stop looking at pornography. That is why he
confessed his sin to Nick and asked for help. At the same time,
his desire for sexual sin seems relentless. The purpose of the next
chapter is to help you understand and respond to both types of
desire you experience.

Questions for Reflection or Discussion

1. What would your closest friend say you desire more than anything else? What would lead him to this conclusion? Do you think his conclusion would accurately reflect your heart?

2. Read John 3:19–20 carefully and answer the following questions:

- What is "the Light"?

- Does *everyone* who loves the darkness hate the Light?

- According to Jesus' words, can a man love both the darkness and the Light? Explain your answer.

three

The Anatomy of Desire

John thought his desire for sexual sin would disappear now that he was a Christian. Instead the temptation was just as strong as ever. At times it seemed even stronger, which puzzled and troubled him greatly. He sometimes wondered if anything had really changed. Because John's struggle is common to many Christians, it will be helpful to understand the origin and anatomy of the often-confusing desires we experience.

The "Original Natural"

God created Adam and Eve with natural desires for food, for sleep, for companionship, and for sexual fulfillment. These desires (and others) may be thought of as "original natural" desires because they were part of God's original creation. They are inherently *good* desires. God was delighted with every aspect of His creation (Gen. 1:31), just as you would be pleased if you designed and created something special and it worked flawlessly. He was pleased when Adam and Eve walked and talked together, when they satisfied their hunger, when they slept, and yes, when they had sexual intercourse as husband and wife.

The "New Natural"

When Adam and Eve disobeyed God, He subjected their world to the curse of death and sin. Distorted and excessive desires erupted from within the now-corrupt hearts of men, including the desire to experience sexual pleasure outside of the union of a man and a woman in marriage. The Bible tells us that "God gave them over to degrading passions" as a judgment (Rom. 1:26).

Because of God's wrath following Adam's disobedience, there was a "new natural" in terms of human desire. Sin—the excessive and perverse expression of the good desires God implanted in mankind at creation—became the new ruling principle in every person from birth.

Something in a man changes when he becomes a Christian, but not everything. When a man is born again (John 3:3; 1 Pet. 1:3, 23) he is given spiritual life from God—a new heart and the life of God's Spirit dwelling in Him. This is what the Bible calls regeneration (Titus 3:5). But the spiritual difference resulting from regeneration is the only difference between the Christian man and his unregenerate neighbors, co-workers, and family members. Physically he is the same as he always was.

The butterfly is the same insect as the caterpillar it came from, but as long as it was a caterpillar, gravity bound it to the surface of the earth. Gravity still tugs downward, but the butterfly has the new ability to resist it and fly. Likewise, sin still tries to pull the believer downward, but he has the new ability to resist it and obey Christ. The butterfly's new ability came from a physical re-creation called metamorphosis. Its body became lighter and it grew wings. The Christian's new ability came from a spiritual re-creation called regeneration. He was given a new heart with a new nature, resulting in new desires.

The Two Sources of Desire

You might assume that your conflicting desires have the same source: the moral, spiritual center of your being, or what the Bible calls your heart. But you have only one heart as a Christian, and as we'll see later, it is new and good.[3] The desires that flow from your new heart (ultimately from God's Spirit) are righteous and pure. The deepest part of you agrees with God at every point. Your

---

3. More about this in chapter 8.

continuing opposition to God (that is, your continuing desire for sin) has a different source: the physical, mortal, unredeemed part of you—your body.

When I write about the Christian's body I mean his whole physical being: his brain, which receives and stores information and produces thoughts, desires, and emotions; the glands and organs that produce the chemicals and hormones that affect other parts of his body in various ways; his eyes, ears, nose, mouth, fingers, skin, nerves, and muscles, all of which detect, transmit, and/or respond to physical sensations that influence his decisions and behavior. The body is all of these things operating together, and all in imperfect ways as a result of Adam's sin.

The Bible sometimes refers to your physical body using the word "flesh."[4] The word is often used in a way that implies moral weakness or the tendency to sin.[5] In other places the writers of Scripture (particularly Paul) simply refer to the unredeemed part of you as "your mortal body," "your members," or "the members of your body."[6] As with the term "flesh," these straightforward references to the human body are often used in ways that imply moral weakness and the propensity toward sinning.[7] Your body itself is not evil, but as pastor and author Charles Leiter says, it is "the place where sin tries to reign or gain a foothold."[8]

The most important thing for you to understand at this point is that even though you have been born again, not every part of you has been made new. You are living your life as a Christian just like Paul lived his life—"in the flesh" (2 Cor. 10:3; Gal. 2:20; Phil. 1:24; 1 Pet. 4:2) with all of the bodily lusts for sin that are characteristic of

---

4. Rom. 7:18, 25; 2 Cor. 10:3; 12:7; Gal. 2:20; Eph. 2:3a; 5:28–29; Phil. 1:24; 1 Pet. 4:2; etc.

5. Rom. 7:18, 25; Eph. 2:3a; etc.

6. Rom. 6:12–13, 19; 7:5, 23; 8:10–11, 13, 23; 12:1; 1 Cor. 6:19 –20; 2 Cor. 5:10; etc.

7. Rom. 6:12; 7:5, 23; etc.

8. Charles Leiter, e-mail message to author, March 1, 2009, quoted by permission.

fallen humanity.[9] When you are tempted to view pornography or commit other sexual sins, your unrighteous desires are not coming from your new heart or your reborn spiritual nature. The sinful desires you experience as a Christian are due to your *physical* attraction to sin.

Because your righteous and unrighteous desires have different sources, they also have different qualities and characteristics. The next three short sections describe these important and encouraging differences.

1. Your righteous desires are spiritual rather than fleshly.
The unregenerate man wants what appeals to his flesh—his unredeemed physical body. Even if he appears religious or moral, it is for reasons of pride or fear. He possesses no genuine desire to please God (Rom. 8:5–8). On the other hand, the true Christian is characterized by spiritual desires—desires that come from the Holy Spirit. His body is unredeemed, so his fleshly desires for sin will always trouble him, but God has implanted new desires within him—desires for purity and righteousness.

Spiritual desires produce an ever-increasing degree of Spirit-led (i.e., godly) behavior in every true Christian. In fact, the characteristic of "being led [morally] by the Spirit of God" is one way in which the Bible *defines* the true Christian (Rom. 8:14).

2. Your righteous desires are overcoming rather than defeated.
Jesus Christ won the ultimate victory over sin when He died on the cross. The Bible tells us that God "condemned sin in the flesh" when He poured out His wrath on His beloved Son (Rom. 8:3). Christ's

---

9. An important note about the meaning of "in the flesh": Christians live in physical bodies—in other words, they live "in the flesh" (2 Cor. 10:3; Gal. 2:20; Phil. 1:24; 1 Pet. 4:2). But in Romans 7:5 and 8:8–9 we are told that Christians are no longer "in the flesh." This is not a contradiction or a different meaning of the word "flesh," but rather a different way of using the word "in." In Romans 7 and 8, "in the flesh" means "*under the control of* the flesh." Ephesians 2:3 expresses a similar idea: "We too all formerly lived *in the lusts of our flesh*, indulging the desires of the flesh and of the mind." As Douglas Moo puts it, to be "in the flesh" in this sense is to be "'enveloped in,' and hence controlled by, narrowly human, this-worldly principles and values" (Douglas Moo, "The Epistle to the Romans," *New International Commentary on the New Testament*, ed., Gordon D. Fee, [Grand Rapids: Eerdmans, 1996], 418).

victory over sin belongs to all who trust in Him. As Paul said, "The sting of death is sin, and the power of sin is the law, but thanks be to God, who gives us the victory through our Lord Jesus Christ" (1 Cor. 15:56–57).

Your desires for righteousness are overcoming desires. They are the fruit of Christ's death and resurrection. As Peter said, "He Himself bore our sins in His body on the cross, so that we might die to sin and live to righteousness" (1 Pet. 2:24; cf. Rom. 6:1–7; Titus 2:14). When you desire and practice righteousness, you are living out Christ's victory over sin. On the other hand, your continuing desires for sexual sin are defeated desires, tempting you to invest in a losing cause.

Everyone could understand a man buying stock in a small company with little chance of survival. The financial returns might be phenomenal if the company succeeds. But it would be irrational for a man to invest money in a business that has already failed and is in the economic grave. This, however, is the kind of investment you make when you give in to your defeated desires for sexual sin.

3. Your righteous desires are permanent rather than passing.
If you are a true Christian, you will live forever in "new heavens and a new earth, in which righteousness dwells" (2 Pet. 3:13). Your permanent, eternal desires are for righteousness. Your current desires for sexual sin may seem strong at times, but they are passing desires—only temporary.

Compare your eighty-five-year life on earth (or however many years the Lord gives you) with eternity. Even after fifty trillion years in heaven, it will not be true to say that "forever" is partly over. "Forever" has no parts. Since your experience in heaven will be one of everlasting righteousness with no hint of desire to do evil, why give your time or affection in this indescribably brief life to "the passing pleasures of sin" (Heb. 11:25)?

Questions for Reflection or Discussion

1. Read Proverbs 5:18–19. Suggest several words or short phrases to describe God's disposition toward your legitimate sexual desires.

2. Read Proverbs 7:6–23. List the numerous ways in which the immoral woman appeals to the young man's fleshly desires.

DESPISE DARKNESS

I recently attended a military graduation where a veteran officer read the text of a radio conversation between an Iranian radar operator and the pilot of an F/A-18 Hornet (the U.S. fighter jet flown by the Blue Angels demonstration team). The Iranian official thought the American jet had strayed into airspace controlled by Iran, so he ordered the American pilot to leave. The American pilot replied that he was over Iraq, not Iran. The Iranian, not convinced, warned that if the American warplane did not leave Iranian airspace immediately, Iranian fighter jets would intercept— to which the American pilot replied confidently, "Send 'em up. I'll wait."

This may have been a case of ill-advised showmanship, but it revealed the pilot's justifiable confidence in the dominance of the U.S. Air Force over every other air force in the world. I would not want you to become *over*confident—confident to the point of waiting around for temptation rather than running away from it (1 Cor. 6:18). But you *should* have confidence as you move forward from this point because the battle you are fighting has already been won by Jesus Christ. I will return to this encouraging truth later, but first I need to help you understand what pornography really is.

Imagine a juicy burger on your dinner plate. Now imagine that you know the meat is saturated with E. coli bacteria. Would you eat it anyway just because it looks good and would satisfy your hunger? Of course you wouldn't. Every rational person knows that having a full stomach isn't worth eighteen hours of vomiting and perhaps a trip to the emergency room. Instead you'll throw the whole thing in the trash and scour the plate with hot water and strong soap.

Pornography is E. coli for your soul.

The purpose of the next three chapters is to reveal the ugliness of sexual sin as one means of helping you hate and avoid it. (Only a fool would go on eating what he knows is making him sick.) Hatred of sin is not all there is to experiencing victory as a Christian, but it is an important part. When a man turns toward the beauty of Christ, he also turns away from the ugliness of sin. The Bible calls this turning around "repentance."

four

Irrationality 101

When Paul wrote, "No one ever hated his own flesh, but nourishes and cherishes it" (Eph. 5:29), he was reasoning on the basis of the fact that rational people seek their own good, not their own harm. Only those who are not thinking and behaving rationally practice self-destructive behavior.

If you continue in your habit of viewing pornography, you will be a case-study in irrational thought and behavior. You will be harming yourself in the following ways:

By viewing pornography in order to obtain sexual pleasure, you will rob yourself of sexual pleasure.
The common human experience is that focused, concentrated pleasure becomes less intense and less enjoyable when it is diluted through overexposure. The person who grazes throughout the day on snack foods obtains what he feels like he needs at any given moment, but all the while he is reducing the satisfaction he will experience when a proper meal is served. The same principle applies to the married man who grazes on sexual pleasure by viewing pornography (or even by allowing his eyes to wander lustfully in other ways throughout the day). He is robbing himself of the undiluted satisfaction he might otherwise experience with

his wife. Likewise, the teenage boy or unmarried man who views pornography and/or masturbates rather than waiting for God to bring him a wife is already working to dull the pleasure of marital sex.

Sexual sins will torment your conscience.

When a man's conscience is troubled by feelings of guilt related to sins he has committed, the experience can be so unpleasant that it can even cause physical distress. Consider King David's testimony following his sexual sin with Bathsheba:

> When I kept silent about my sin, my body wasted away
> Through my groaning all day long.
> For day and night Your hand was heavy upon me;
> My vitality was drained away as with the fever heat
> of summer. (Ps. 32:3–4)

> O Lord, rebuke me not in Your wrath,
> And chasten me not in Your burning anger.
> For Your arrows have sunk deep into me,
> And Your hand has pressed down on me.
> There is no soundness in my flesh because of
> Your indignation;
> There is no health in my bones because of my sin.
> For my iniquities are gone over my head;
> As a heavy burden they weigh too much for me.
> My wounds grow foul and fester
> Because of my folly.
> I am bent over and greatly bowed down;
> I go mourning all day long.
> For my loins are filled with burning,
> And there is no soundness in my flesh.
> I am benumbed and badly crushed;
> I groan because of the agitation of my heart.
> (Ps. 38:1–8)

David's oppressive conviction was God's way of drawing him to repentance. By the time God sent Nathan to rebuke David (2 Sam. 12:1–12), he was so broken in spirit because of the Lord's corrective discipline that he repented without hesitation (12:13). He simply could not bear any longer the feeling of being "pressed down" by the hand of God.

Feelings of guilt or conviction often lead to other harmful consequences. One man may withdraw into isolation and depression. Another may seek relief by focusing attention on the sins of people who are worse than him as he attempts to minimize the seriousness of his own sin. Yet another may become critical of the smallest faults in his wife and children as he attempts to divert his conscience away from his own sin. Sadly, feelings of guilt or conviction may even cause a man to neglect teaching his own children about the dangers of sexual sin. He would feel like a hypocrite, after all, warning them to stay away from the very sin he is practicing.

Viewing pornography today makes you more susceptible to sexual temptation in the months and years to come.
Pornographic images, once viewed, are permanently stored in your brain. Even if you completely stop viewing pornography at some point, images stored in your mind from previous acts of sexual sin will provide ready sources of temptation. These images can reappear in dreams, during times of depression, when you are angry with your wife, when you are tired, or when you are lonely. Even worse, they can reappear when there is no apparent reason at all. What you allow in will always threaten to come out. Therefore, as Paul instructed, "Make no provision for the flesh in regard to its lusts" (Rom. 13:14).

A so-called expert in human sexuality once claimed in my hearing that viewing pornography might have a positive social benefit. She claimed that it can prevent rape in some cases by gratifying a young man's lust in "harmless" ways. But viewing pornography only partially satisfies a man's sexual desire. Far from gratifying his lust in harmless ways, it actually makes him more dangerous. It feeds and strengthens sexual lust, creating an ever-growing inclination toward masturbation, premarital sex, adultery, homosexuality, or even criminal forms of sexual sin like rape, incest, child abuse, and bestiality. Almost every man who commits the worst forms of sexual sin began with something he thought of as less serious. The man who carefully avoids the sin of viewing pornography is far less likely to be "hardened by the deceitfulness of sin" (Heb. 3:13) to the point of engaging in these worse practices.

How deeply will *you* plunge into sexual sin if you start (or continue) down this immoral road? The fact is, you cannot know.

_____

Questions for Reflection or Discussion

1. What harmful effects of viewing pornography would you add to the ones listed in this chapter?

2. Given the irrationality of viewing pornography (and committing other sexual sins), why do you think it will continue to be a temptation for the Christian who has read this chapter?

3. Read Proverbs 7:21–23. Name the various word pictures the writer uses in verses 22–23 to describe a person giving in to sexual temptation. What is the common theme of these word pictures? How do these word pictures relate to the instructions given in verses 1–5 and verse 24?

five

Marriage Poison

Though they work at different speeds, termites and tornados both do serious damage to houses. Pornography has the same effect on marriage, whether suddenly or over the span of many years.

Below are a few reasons why pornography and marriage cannot coexist peacefully. The warnings in this chapter are also for the man who is not yet married but may be some day.

Viewing pornography is adultery.
Viewing pornography is not just a bad habit that can be tolerated in a marriage relationship. Marriage is defined by faithfulness and defiled by unfaithfulness. The married man who views pornography is cheating on his wife just as surely as if he were sleeping with another woman. As Jesus said, "Everyone who looks at a woman with lust for her has already committed adultery with her in his heart" (Matt. 5:28).[10]

---

10. There is a difference between the mental adultery described in Matthew 5:28 and the kind of adultery that involves sexual intercourse with another person. I would not want to be perceived as saying that both types of adultery are equally devastating to a marriage or equally defiling to the person who commits them. Nevertheless, since Jesus used the same word to describe both sins, we should never deny the seriousness of mental adultery.

Actually, a habit of viewing pornography is more like sleeping with *many* women. The married man who buys a pornographic magazine or logs onto a pornographic website is willing to commit adultery with whatever woman happens to be on the page. He doesn't even care to know her real name in order to have this imaginary relationship with her.

Jesus used the word "adultery" in Matthew 5:28 to refer to a married man's sin, but this doesn't mean single men are exempt. Don't believe the lie that says pornography and/or masturbation are not sinful for the teenage boy or the unmarried man. Paul encouraged singleness as a viable option for people who were otherwise permitted to marry, but he recognized the fact that singleness without self-control results in sexual sin. He therefore gave the following instruction: "But if they do not have self-control, let them marry; for it is better to marry than to burn with passion" (1 Cor. 7:9). Paul prescribed marriage, not masturbation, as the lawful remedy for sexual desire in single people. As the writer of Hebrews said, "Marriage is to be held in honor among all, and the marriage bed is to be undefiled; for fornicators and adulterers God will judge" (Heb. 13:5).

Viewing pornography is a degrading insult to your wife.
When a married man views pornography, he is saying by his actions that he finds his wife less appealing than the women he views in magazines, in movies, or on the Internet. He may not intend to say this. His wife may be exceedingly beautiful, and he may regularly tell her so. But his actions speak louder than his words.

Consider just how far the husband who views pornography falls from the biblical standard regarding how he should treat his wife:

> Husbands, love your wives, just as Christ also loved the church and gave Himself up for her. . . . So husbands ought also to love their own wives as their own bodies. He who loves his own wife loves himself; for no one ever hated his own flesh, but nourishes and cherishes it, just as Christ also does the church. (Eph. 5:25–29)

> You husbands in the same way, live with your wives in an
> understanding way . . . and show her honor as a fellow heir
> of the grace of life. (1 Peter 3:7)

Think deeply about the way your sinful habit contrasts with the
commands to "love," "nourish," "cherish," and "honor" your wife.
When you look at pornography you come far closer to slapping her
in the face and calling her ugly.

Nothing compares with the insult and emotional pain a wife feels
when she learns that her husband has been looking lustfully at
other women.[11] She once assumed that he found her more beautiful
and desirable than other women, but now she wonders if it was all
a lie. Most wives patiently tolerate many character flaws in their
husbands, but this defect they simply cannot bear without deep
pain. The Christian wife will forgive her repentant husband, but she
cannot erase the past from her memory. The pain of betrayal may
grow faint, but it will never disappear.

**Viewing pornography as a single man will make you more likely
to commit adultery as a married man.**
Many single men who have been overcome by sexual sin comfort
themselves by thinking, "At least this won't be a problem once I get
married." How wrong you are if you are thinking this way. Marriage
will not eliminate your fascination with sexual sin. By viewing
pornography, you are actually increasing your desire for sexual sin
while fostering a perverted concept of the frequency and nature of
sexual gratification.

Habitual premarital sexual immorality is also an indicator of a
heart that is unfaithful. Paul's prescription of marriage for the
Christian who was being tempted to fornicate (1 Cor. 7:8–9) does
not mean that the habitual fornicator is a true Christian. As Paul
said in chapter 6 of the same letter, fornicators will not inherit the
kingdom of God (1 Cor. 6:9–10).

Unmarried Christian ladies beware. If the man you intend to marry
professes to be a Christian but has shown a pattern of unwillingness

---

11. Please read my caution in appendix F before confessing sexual sins to your wife.

to wait for sexual fulfillment until marriage, it is unlikely that he is a true believer. Apart from the grace of God in regeneration, it is also unlikely that his heart will be faithfully yours throughout the marriage.

Questions for Reflection or Discussion

1. Read Hebrews 13:4 carefully. What does this verse tell us about God's disposition toward sexual intimacy in marriage? According to this verse, *why* is the marriage bed to be undefiled? What other words might you use in place of "undefiled"?

2. Read 1 Corinthians 6:9–10. Do you think the warning to fornicators and adulterers in this passage applies to the man who practices mental fornication or adultery (Mat. 5:28) but refrains from committing these sins physically? Explain your answer.

3. What are several benefits a single man can enjoy by staying away from pornography?

six

Fool's Vomit

I once heard about a man who spit himself to death. As the story goes, he died while competing in a distance-spitting contest on a bridge. Running toward the railing in order to build up speed, and being a bit drunk, he underestimated his forward momentum and overestimated the ability of the three-foot barrier to stop his six-foot, top-heavy frame. His foolishness was tragically rewarded when he hit the rocks below.

Another foolish fatality story (authentic or not, I don't know) involved a man who was showing his son the proper way to handle snakes. When the rattlesnake he was holding bit his hand, he angrily bit the snake back. Actually, he put the snake's head in his mouth and tried to bite it off, which explains how he died.

Even if these stories are untrue, senseless tragedies do occur. In a well-publicized incident, a man accidentally killed his wife when he shot a bullet through the wall of his own house. Why would he do something so foolish? Investigators determined that he used the gun to punch a hole in the wall for his satellite TV cable, but neglected to first account for the whereabouts of his wife, who was standing outside.

The Foolish Behavior Principle

Anyone can have an accident, but someone who acts foolishly is different in that he is certainly (or at least probably) headed for tragic consequences. Everyone should know better, but not everyone learns before it's too late.

In the Bible, the foolish behavior principle is repeatedly applied to sexual sin. Giving in to sexual temptation seems like a good idea at the time because it powerfully appeals to our fleshly desires. But later there are only negative consequences and regret. That's why the Bible warns us to flee from sexual immorality (1 Cor. 6:18) and calls people who engage in it "fools."

Proverbs 6:32 says, "The one who commits adultery with a woman is lacking sense; He who would destroy himself does it." In Proverbs 7, the man who commits sexual sin is once again described as "lacking sense" (7:7). He naively goes to the immoral woman "As an ox goes to the slaughter, or as one in fetters to the discipline of a fool" (7:22). "He does not know [even though he should] that it will cost him his life" (7:23). Proverbs 5 sums up the foolishness of sexual sin like this:

> For why should you, my son, be exhilarated with an
> adulteress
> And embrace the bosom of a foreigner?
> For the ways of a man are before the eyes of the Lord,
> And He watches all his paths.
> His own iniquities will capture the wicked,
> And he will be held with the cords of his sin.
> He will die for lack of instruction,
> And in the greatness of his folly he will go astray.
> (Prov. 5:20–23)

The New Testament continues this theme. Paul warned believers to stay away from fornication, among other sins (Eph. 5:5). He then wrote, "Therefore be careful how you walk, not as unwise men but as wise, making the most of your time, because the days are evil. So then do not be foolish, but understand what the will of the Lord is" (Eph. 5:15–17). In another place he wrote, "For we also once were foolish ourselves, disobedient, deceived, enslaved to various lusts and pleasures" (Titus 3:3).

The overarching biblical principle is this: "Like a dog that returns to its vomit is a fool who repeats his folly" (Prov. 26:11).

The Consequences of Playing the Fool
Our society would have you believe the exact opposite about sexual sin—that it is rewarding rather than risky, fulfilling rather than foolish. Mainstream media has dramatized, romanticized, and sanitized sexual sin for public consumption as a means to huge financial profits. Perverted sex plays a starring role in the movies and on TV. It sells music, magazines, make up, clothing, cars, cell phones, shampoo, diet plans, sporting goods, and just about any other product you can think of, to the tune of billions of dollars each year. Immorality is marketed so cleanly and professionally that most consumers have come to see it as normal, desirable, and without serious consequences. Even "decent" people who shake their fingers at prostitution and pornography go right on laughing and lusting at the parade of "respectable" immorality in the media.

Please don't play the fool yourself. It's all a huge lie. Sexual sin is not cool, funny, romantic, or profitable. It is grotesque in God's sight, and it leads to death just as surely as the hand of the butcher leads the ignorant ox to the slaughter. No one who views pornography can ever legitimately claim that he became a better person by checking out a pornographic website. In the end, no one will ever be glad he decided to spend all those hours looking at sexually explicit images. As mentally and physically gratifying as sexual sin seems at the time, the stimulation is temporary and unsatisfying in any meaningful or permanent way. The end result is always regret and remorse because of the bitter consequences in this life, the suffering of hell for eternity, or both.

Ask yourself what Paul asked the believers in Rome: "What benefit were you then deriving from the things of which you are now ashamed? For the outcome of those things is death" (Rom. 6:21). Sexual sin provides no benefit, only pain and sorrow.

Surely the fish frying in the skillet would have refused the bait had he known about the hook.

Questions for Reflection or Discussion

1. Why do you think the foolishness of sexual sin is emphasized so strongly in the Bible?

2. Read Proverbs 26:11 and then 2 Peter 2:20–22 (also see Heb. 3:12–14). Based on these passages, what is the greatest danger of returning to sexual sin after professing faith in Christ?

3. How might what you learned in this chapter help guide you as to what you should or should not watch on TV or in the movie theater?

ACKNOWLEDGE DELIVERANCE

Whether you have been a Christian for three months or thirty years, deliverance from sin is not something that is happening to you or might happen to you some day. It *has* happened to you. This deliverance is described in the Bible with two words: justification and regeneration.

Even if this is the first time you have heard the word "justification," you probably know what it means. It means that Jesus paid the penalty for your sin when He was crucified (1 Pet. 2:24). It means that when you first believed from a repentant heart, God applied Christ's payment for sin to your account, proving Himself to be "just [by punishing sin as sin deserves] and the justifier of the one who has faith in Jesus" (Rom. 3:26). It means that good behavior could never make you any more acceptable to God than you already are (Rom. 3:20; Gal. 2:16, 21). It means that through faith *alone* you are fully reconciled to God, standing rock solid in His grace (Rom. 5:1–2).

Justification delivered you from sin's penalty.

Regeneration delivered you from sin's power.

I said earlier that I would explain regeneration more fully, and we have arrived at that point. You once had a wicked heart and a corrupt nature, but God made you a new man—a righteous man with a pure heart and a good nature. You once were sin's slave because of your inner corruption and fleshly desires, but now, having been re-created by God, you are mastered by your love for Christ and your desire to do His will.

seven

New Creation

Getting the old you to look at pornography was as easy as getting a hungry dog to devour a juicy piece of meat.

Don't misunderstand—I'm sure you resisted sexual temptation sometimes (maybe even most of the time) because of social concerns or religious expectations. Perhaps you wanted to avoid offending your parents or your wife. Maybe you knew it would set a bad example for your children. You may have even restrained yourself because your conscience told you God was watching. This only proved that you were like a well-trained dog.

Dogs love bacon, but my dog has been trained to hold a piece of this savory meat between his front teeth and to wait until I say "OK" before eating it. The trick is obviously difficult. His strong desire for the meat makes him tremble with anticipation. Sometimes his tongue even begins to explore the bacon ahead of time. But he waits obediently, and as he grows more and more accustomed to performing as we expect, he is willing to wait longer and longer. "Good boy!" we always say. But even though he is well-trained, his desire for the meat is unchanged. He is only waiting for permission to do what his dog nature longs to do. When all external restraints are removed, his strongest desire determines his behavior and the meat disappears quickly.

Everyone knows that this is the way things are with dogs, but it is also the way things are with unregenerate people like the old you. When you restrained yourself from sinning, it was only because you lacked permission. Your response to external restraints may have made you look good on the outside, but the outward appearance of righteousness did nothing to please God or to solve your problem. As Paul said to the Colossians, external restraints "have, to be sure, the appearance of wisdom in self-made religion and self-abasement and severe treatment of the body, *but are of no value against fleshly indulgence*" (Col. 2:23).

The Old You Was Enslaved by Desire

As an unbeliever you gratified your desires for sexual sin whenever outside restraints were not strong enough to hold you back. Paul speaks about this in Romans 6, reminding Christians what they were before regeneration:

> But thanks be to God that though you were slaves of sin, you became obedient from the heart to that form of teaching to which you were committed, and having been freed from sin, you became slaves of righteousness. . . . For just as you presented your members as slaves to impurity and to lawlessness, resulting in further lawlessness, so now present your members as slaves to righteousness, resulting in sanctification. For when you were slaves of sin, you were free in regard to righteousness. (Rom. 6:17–20)

Slavery to sin was not just sometimes your condition as a non-Christian. You were always a slave of sin, even when your behavior appeared outwardly righteous. Romans 6 is not the only place where the Bible says so. Paul said this in his letter to Titus: "For we also once were foolish ourselves, disobedient, deceived, enslaved to various lusts and pleasures" (Titus 3:3). Paul didn't use the word "slavery" in Ephesians 2, but he described the same bondage:

> Among them we too all formerly lived in the lusts of our flesh, indulging the desires of the flesh and of the mind, and were by nature children of wrath, even as the rest. (Eph. 2:3)

The old you was a slave of sin, held captive by fleshly desires. The Bible could not have said this any more clearly.

But the Old You Is Dead

Now that you are a Christian you are no longer like a well-trained dog, refraining from sinning only because you lack permission. Your behavior has changed and is continuing to improve, but not solely because of external restraints. The pattern of your life is different because your desires are different, and your desires are different because *you* are different. You are not the same person you once were. That man ceased to exist the moment you became a Christian.[12] Pay attention to the death terminology in the following passages, and remember that what Paul says in each passage is true of you, the believer:

> For if we have become united with Him in the likeness of His death, certainly we shall also be in the likeness of His resurrection, knowing this, that our old self was crucified with Him, in order that our body of sin might be done away with, so that we would no longer be slaves to sin; for he who has died is freed from sin. (Rom. 6:5–7)

> For the love of Christ controls us, having concluded this, that one died for all, therefore all died; and He died for all, so that they who live might no longer live for themselves, but for Him who died and rose again on their behalf. (2 Cor. 5:14–15)

> I have been crucified with Christ; and it is no longer I who live, but Christ lives in me; and the life which I now live in the flesh I live by faith in the Son of God, who loved me and gave Himself up for me. (Gal. 2:20)

> Therefore if you have been raised up with Christ, keep seeking the things above, where Christ is, seated at the right hand of God. Set your mind on the things above, not on the things that are on earth. For you have died and your life is hidden with Christ in God. (Col. 3:1–3)

These are obviously not references to your physical death, because as you read this page your heart is still pumping blood through

---

12. See appendix E for further discussion of what the Bible says about your "old self."

your body and your lungs are still filling with air. But they do refer to a *real* death—the end of existence for one person and the beginning of existence for another.

You Are a New Creation

Even though you are the same as you always were physically, you have a completely new identity as a Christian, one that is defined on a spiritual level. You look like the person you once were, but you are not him. This is why Paul can say what he says in 2 Corinthians 5:

> Therefore from now on we recognize no one according to the flesh; even though we have known Christ according to the flesh, yet now we know Him in this way no longer. Therefore if anyone is in Christ, he is a new creature;[13] the old things passed away; behold, new things have come. (2 Cor. 5:16–17)

Your physical body is only a temporary dwelling place for the real, eternal, newly created you who will live forever in paradise with Christ. As Paul said, "while we are at home in the body we are absent from the Lord" (2 Cor. 5:6). His own preference was "to be absent from the body and to be at home with the Lord" (2 Cor. 5:8). Peter spoke of his own impending death as "the laying aside of my earthly dwelling" (2 Pet. 1:14). I will speak more in chapter 9 and appendix C about the relationship between you and the mortal body you temporarily inhabit, but it is important that you begin thinking of the real you—the person who will exist long after your mortal body is dead and in the grave.

You Are No Longer of This World

Christians live on earth physically, but spiritually they are citizens of heaven. As Paul said, God "raised us up with [Christ], and seated us with Him in the heavenly places" (Eph. 2:6). He "rescued us from the domain of darkness, and transferred us to the kingdom of His beloved Son" (Col. 1:13).

---

13. Or, "there is a new creation." It is possible that Paul is not focusing specifically on the individual Christian's new nature and identity, but on the fact that in Christ *all* things are made new. If this is correct, the "new creation" is not exclusively a reference to what the individual Christian *becomes*, but to what he becomes *a part of*. Even so, to be *part of* a new creation is to *be* a new creation.

It was this reality that enabled Paul to correct an error among the Colossians. He addressed them by asking why they were behaving "as if you were living in the world" (Col. 2:20). "*As if* you were living in the world"? What an amazing statement. Christians move among and interact with the people of this world (John 17:15). But as Jesus said of believers, "They are not of the world, even as I am not of the world" (John 17:16; cf. 15:19).

Imagine that you died and went to heaven, then later came back to the earth for a brief visit. Would you have any interest in trifling with pornography after experiencing the beauty and purity of heaven? Of course you wouldn't. Now stop imagining and start enjoying, because your new existence and citizenship *is* heavenly. As Paul said, "Set your mind on the things above, not on the things that are on earth. For you have died and your life is hidden with Christ in God" (Col. 3:2–3).

Always remember these four things about yourself:

- The old you was enslaved by desire.
- But the old you is dead.
- You are a new creation.
- You are no longer of this world.

Questions for Reflection or Discussion

1. Notice that I have not said, "If you do something your old self *will be* dead," but rather, "Your old self *is* dead." What is the difference between these two statements? What benefit does one have over the other?

2. Read Colossians 3:1–11. What facts are stated in this passage? What commands are given? What is the relationship between the facts and the commands?

eight

Obedient from the Heart

Just as children resemble their earthly fathers physically, Christians resemble their heavenly Father morally and spiritually. Paul described your new self as that which, "in the likeness of God has been created in righteousness and holiness of the truth" (Eph. 4:24). Peter described Christians as "a chosen race, a royal priesthood, a holy nation, a people for God's own possession" (1 Pet. 2:9). God's children "are His workmanship, created in Christ Jesus for good works" (Eph. 2:10).

Christians are not defined by a corrupt nature as they were before regeneration. They are now "partakers of the divine nature, having escaped the corruption that is in the world by lust" (2 Pet. 1:4). John described Christians as those who have been "born of God" and whose behavior imitates the character of their heavenly Father:

> No one who is born of God practices sin, because His seed abides in him; and he cannot sin [i.e., as a matter of practice] because he is born of God. By this the children of God and the children of the devil are obvious: anyone who does not practice righteousness is not of God, nor the one who does not love his brother. (1 John 3:9–10)

Your new identity as God's child is in one sense like adoption, but being God's child involves much more than a legal decree. You have been re-created in His likeness. You were born in the likeness of sinful Adam, but then you were born *again* in the likeness of our holy God.

You Have a Pure Heart

In regeneration you were given a heart that fits the psalmist's description of the man who may enter into God's presence:

> Who may ascend into the hill of the Lord?
> And who may stand in His holy place?
> He who has clean hands and a pure heart. . . . (Ps. 24:3–4)

Jesus said the same thing about those who will enter into God's presence: "Blessed are the pure in heart, for they shall see God" (Matt. 5:8). Like the psalmist, Jesus was describing the true believer—the regenerate man.

Good Fruit Comes from Good Trees

If you wanted to grow and harvest grapes, would you plant thorn bushes? You wouldn't make much money as a farmer if you did.

Each time Jesus used this illustration in His teaching (Matt. 7:15–20; 12:33–35; Luke 6:43–45), His point was to show the difference between the nature of the good man and the nature of the evil man. Just as grape vines produce grapes and thorn bushes produce thorns, the good man produces righteousness and the evil man produces sin. Following this illustration in Luke 6 He said, "The good man out of the good treasure of his heart brings forth what is good; and the evil man out of the evil treasure brings forth what is evil" (Luke 6:45).

From this we learn something important—something that might be different than what you have been taught before: not every person should be classified as "evil."[14] Some people are evil "by nature" while others are "good" by nature.

---

14. See appendix B for a discussion of Matthew 7:11 where Jesus refers to His listeners as "evil."

Jesus tells us who these good people are in Luke 8:15. They are true Christians—"the ones who have heard the word in an honest and good heart, and hold it fast, and bear fruit with perseverance." They were born the first time with the same corrupt human nature as every other person, but then they were "born again" (John 3:3; 1 Pet. 1:3, 23). They were given new hearts and good natures when God gave them spiritual life.

This is regeneration. God changes human "thorn bushes" into human "grape vines." Because of this work of God in transforming their nature, Christians no longer produce the "thorns" of sin like they did when they were unbelievers. Now they produce the "grapes" of righteousness—that is, they believe the truth, love Jesus Christ, and do God's will.[15]

You Have Been Delivered by Desire
Paul does not use the term "regeneration" in his letter to the Romans, but he clearly wants us to think of it in Romans 6:17–18:

> But thanks be to God that though you were slaves of sin, you became obedient from the heart to that form of teaching to which you were committed, and having been freed from sin, you became slaves of righteousness.

Believers "were slaves of sin," but they have "been freed from sin." More than that, they have become "slaves of righteousness." This leaves just one question: what causes a man to end his old devotion to sinning and establish a new devotion to practicing righteousness? The answer is found in the phrase Paul inserts between former slavery and present freedom: "You became obedient from the heart." God's creation of a new heart caused a change of desires, which in turn caused a change of masters.

Tom Schreiner, in his commentary on Romans, helpfully explains the meaning of this phrase, "you became obedient from the heart":

> People do not submit to sin against their will. Rather, they "freely" and spontaneously choose to sin. In other words,

---

15. See appendix D for further discussion about the relationship between nature and behavior.

unbelievers are slaves to sin in that they always desire to carry out the dictates of their master. This does not mean that those with addictions (e.g., to alcohol, pornography, or gambling) never wish to be freed. It means that the desire for these things is ultimately greater than the desire to be freed from them. Sinning is what they want to do. Only God, therefore, can release them from such subjection, for new desires are necessary to escape the bondage of sin. Of course, this is precisely what God has done. He has liberated them from the tyranny of sin so that they "have become obedient from the heart" to the gospel. He has planted new desires within them.[16]

People are enslaved by what they want most. What you formerly wanted most was sin, but now that God has changed you on the inside, what you want more than anything is to do His will. The good nature He has created in you is producing the good fruit of righteous behavior. It has happened to you just as God promised in the Old Testament:

> I will give you a new heart and put a new spirit within you; and I will remove the heart of stone from your flesh and give you a heart of flesh. I will put My Spirit within you and cause you to walk in My statutes, and you will be careful to observe My ordinances. (Ezek. 36:26–27)

As you know all too well, Christians can and do sin. But when sinful behavior erupts from a righteous man like you—a man who has become "obedient from the heart"—we must consider the source of that sin to be something other than his regenerate heart.[17]

The source of sin in a Christian—that is the subject of the next chapter.

---

16. Thomas R. Schreiner, "Romans," *Baker Exegetical Commentary on the New Testament*, ed., Moisés Silva (Grand Rapids: Baker Academic, 1998), 337.

17. See appendix B for a discussion of Jeremiah 17:9 and Mark 7:20–23 (with its parallel in Matthew 15:15–20), passages that are often thought to prove that the regenerate heart is a source of evil.

Questions for Reflection or Discussion

1. Read Luke 8:4–15 carefully and answer the following questions:

- In this parable what is the seed?

- What do the four kinds of soil represent?

- What word does Jesus use to describe the fourth kind of soil?

- When He explains the meaning of the parable in verses 11–15, what two words does He use to describe the heart of the person who is illustrated by the good soil?

- What does this parable tell us about the difference between the heart of a Christian and the heart of an unbeliever?

2. Read 1 John 3:7–10. Do you think other Christians would describe your practice of righteousness as "obvious"? How would the non-Christians you associate with describe your pattern of behavior?

nine

Body Language

In some ways the Christian is like the proverbial chicken with its head chopped off. Because of muscle and nerve memory, the bird's body continues flapping its wings and running around for some time even though detached from the control center that formerly commanded those movements. When I once cut the head off of a very large snake, the headless body continued moving like a snake. Even the detached head kept opening and closing its mouth as if it were trying to bite something.

Beheaded chickens and snakes are dead, but their bodies, which are accustomed to making certain movements, continue acting as though they were still alive. Likewise (though there is not an exact parallel), the old you has died, but because your unredeemed body is physically, mentally, and emotionally accustomed to sinning, you still have the desire to act like you did when the old you was alive.

One Christian writer described the corrupt pre-programming of his unredeemed body this way: "Countless automatic, chain reaction thought patterns have already been computerized away in my brain, ready for instant recall."[18] Whether these "chain-reaction thought patterns" draw you toward sexual sin, drunkenness, greed,

---

18. David Needham, *Birthright* (Portland: Multnomah Press, 1978), 126.

or selfishness, your regenerate heart is not the source of the sin. The culprit is your unredeemed body—your flesh.[19]

At this point I should remind you again that when I write about the Christian's body, I mean his whole physical being: his brain, which receives and stores information and produces thoughts, desires, and emotions; the glands and organs that produce the chemicals and hormones that affect other parts of his body in various ways; his eyes, ears, nose, mouth, fingers, skin, nerves, and muscles, all of which detect, transmit, and/or respond to physical sensations that influence decisions and behavior. The body is all of these things operating together as a unit, and all in imperfect ways as a result of Adam's sin. Your new heart is pure and inclined toward righteousness, but your body is still subject to the lure of sin. It is "the place where sin tries to reign or gain a foothold."[20]

You Are More Than a Body

The human body can be scientifically analyzed in an attempt to understand why people do what they do, but there is a spiritual aspect to the Christian that is beyond scientific examination. If you are a Christian, you are more than a body. God has created a completely new identity that cannot be seen or analyzed by scientific methods, and it is this new spiritual you that tells your brain how to think and how to direct the other members of your body to act. If this were not the case, you would still be a slave to your body's lusts, but the Bible assures us that you are no longer enslaved in this way. Physical corruption still influences you, but you have a new spiritual control center—a new heart—created, equipped, and directed by the Spirit of God.[21] Three passages in Romans 6 and 8 are particularly helpful in revealing your relationship to your unredeemed body with its lusts.

---

19. Despite the weakness of the flesh, it is never appropriate for a Christian to blame his body for the sins he commits while considering his new self exempt from responsibility. The Christian is one whole person with one will. For more on this see appendix C.

20. Charles Leiter, e-mail message to author, March 1, 2009, quoted by permission.

21. It is appropriate to describe the unregenerate heart as the "spiritual control center" of the non-Christian, but it is a spiritual part of him that is morally dead from birth as a descendant of Adam (Gen. 2:17; Rom. 5:12–21). As Paul said, all people are "dead in trespasses and sins" (Eph. 2:1; cf. Col. 2:13) until God makes them "alive together with Christ" (Eph. 2:5; cf. Col. 2:13).

Romans 6:12–13
Your body is your subject, not your master.
As an unbeliever you were given over to obey your body's sinful
passions (Rom. 1:26). You were "enslaved to various lusts and
pleasures" (Titus 3:3). You were living "in the lusts of [your] flesh,
indulging the desires of the flesh and of the mind" (Eph. 2:3).
You were voluntarily practicing "every kind of impurity with
greediness" (Eph. 4:19). But your body is no longer in control. *You*
are.[22]

Based on your spiritual connection with Jesus Christ in His death,
burial, and resurrection (Rom. 6:1–11), Paul gives you three
commands in Romans 6:12–13:

> 1. Do not let sin reign in your mortal body so that you
> obey its lusts.
>
> 2. Do not go on presenting the members of your body to
> sin as instruments of unrighteousness.
>
> 3. Present yourselves to God as those alive from the dead,
> and your members as instruments of righteousness to
> God.

Paul exhorted the Roman Christians like this because for them, the
power of sin had been broken. They had been given the ability and
authority to stop using their bodies as tools for sinning, and to start
using them as "instruments of righteousness" (6:13). As a man who
has been born again, you are like them. Because of your new desire
and ability to govern your body properly, you too can carry out
God's will.

Romans 8:12–13
You are putting to death the deeds of your body.
Christians are not playing tug-of-war with their sinful passions.
They are routing them out of their hiding places and killing them.

---

22. Just to be clear, your body does not have a separate identity or a will of its own.
When we speak as if the body has a separate will, we are simply illustrating the
source of the Christian's sinful desires, and we are following a biblical model. In
Romans 6:12 believers are told not to obey the body with its lusts for sin, and in 1
Corinthians 9:27 Paul speaks of disciplining his body and making it his slave.

Paul commands Christians to do this in Colossians 3:5:

> Put to death therefore what is earthly in you: sexual immorality, impurity, passion, evil desire, and covetousness, which is idolatry. (Col. 3:5, ESV)

In Romans 8:13 Paul uses similar "put to death" language, but this time he is describing the Christian rather than exhorting him:

> So then, brethren, we are under obligation, not to the flesh, to live according to the flesh—for if you are living according to the flesh, you must die; but if by the Spirit you are putting to death the deeds of the body, you will live. (Rom. 8:12–13)

Romans 8:1–14 is not a list of things Christians are supposed to do. It is a portrait of the Christian's new nature, and of the behavior that characterizes every true believer as a result of the Holy Spirit's presence and influence. In this passage Christians are described as follows:

- **They are regenerate.** That is, they "are according to the Spirit" rather than "according to the flesh" (Rom. 8:5).

- **They live by faith and desire righteousness.** That is, they set their minds on "the things of the Spirit" rather than on "the things of the flesh" (Rom. 8:5).

- **They are under the influence of God's Spirit rather than the influence of sin.** That is, they are people who "are being led [morally] by the Spirit of God" (Rom. 8:14) rather than "living according to the flesh" (Rom. 8:13).

- **They are killing sin.** That is, they are people who, "by the Spirit," are "putting to death the deeds of the body" (Rom. 8:13).

Romans 8:13 doesn't tell Christians to "put to death" the deeds of their body. Instead it informs them that true Christians are already doing so. If you are a true Christian, you are "putting to death the deeds of the body" by the power of God's Spirit.

Your relationship to sin is like the relationship you would have with a deposed dictator who has been overthrown, locked in prison, and condemned to death. He once ruled over you, but a new conquering authority has defeated him and has set you free. Likewise, "the law of the Spirit of life [i.e., the Holy Spirit] has set you free in Christ Jesus from the law of sin and death" (Rom. 8:2, ESV). Sin continues to exert its influence through your fleshly desires, but exerting influence is not the same as possessing authority. Sin has no more prospect of ultimate victory than a condemned man who struggles all the way to the gallows. He will bite you, stomp on your toes, and kick you in the shins on the way there, but he won't avoid his hanging.

Romans 8:23
You are anticipating the redemption of your body.
Paul encourages Christians later in Romans 8 by assuring them that the body they struggle with now will one day be radically transformed:

> And not only this, but also we ourselves, having the first fruits of the Spirit, even we ourselves groan within ourselves, waiting eagerly for our adoption as sons, the redemption of our body. (Rom. 8:23; cf. 1 Cor. 15:50–57)

The Spirit of God dwelling in us is a down payment on what we will be given later (cf. Eph. 1:13–14). Because of His presence and work we have a new heart with a new nature, and we are free from slavery to sin. The Spirit's presence also assures us that we are heirs of the kingdom of God. The one thing we lack is a body that *will not* be subject to the influence of sin and the temptations of the devil—a body that *will* be capable of enjoying the unimaginable pleasures of our future life.

Questions for Reflection or Discussion

1. In what specific ways does it encourage you to know that your body is the only part of you that remains unredeemed?

2. Read Galatians 5:24 and 6:14.

- What do you think Paul meant by "crucified the flesh" in Galatians 5:24?

- Would you say Paul gives the word "crucified" the same basic meaning in 5:24 and 6:14? Why or why not?

- Galatians 5:24 sometimes leads Christians to believe that it is abnormal for them to have sinful passions or desires. Do you think Paul intended for his readers to draw such a conclusion? Why or why not?

3. How might "automatic, chain-reaction thought patterns" tempt you to commit sexual sins? How about sins that are not sexually motivated?

ten

The High Calling of Being Yourself

You are not a spiritual schizophrenic. You don't have two hearts or a heart that is partially good and partially evil. You are no longer governed by a heart that is corrupt, or even partially corrupt. You are governed by an altogether new heart. The biblical foundation for saying this is the fact that your old heart has not merely been added to, modified, improved, or softened. It has been replaced. That was what God promised His people when He said, "I will give you a new heart and put a new spirit within you; and I will remove the heart of stone from your flesh and give you a heart of flesh" (Ezek. 36:26). Jesus Himself called the Christian's heart "pure" and "honest and good" (Matt. 5:8; Luke 8:15).

You also have just one nature, not two. Your battle against sexual sin is not a fight against a "sin nature" that dwells alongside your regenerate nature. It is a fight against your fleshly desires and against the tempter (Satan) who works in deceitful ways to entice you to give in to your fleshly desires. Because of regeneration you are a completely new creation with a completely new (and good) nature.

The Influence of Unflattering, Unbiblical Language

Charles Spurgeon was a pastor in London in the nineteenth century. His sermons, books, and devotional writings are still in print and are well worth reading. The following is Spurgeon's outstanding summary of what the Bible says about the Christian's nature.

> In the spirit of humility, we should recognize the true dignity of our reborn nature and then live up to it. What is a Christian? If you compare him with a king, he adds priestly sanctity to royal dignity. The king's royalty is often seen only in his crown. But with a Christian, it is infused into his inmost nature. He is as much above other men through his new birth as the man is above the beast. Surely he ought to conduct himself in all his dealings as one who is not of this world, but chosen and distinguished by sovereign grace. Therefore he cannot live in the same way as the world's citizens. Let the dignity of your nature and the brightness of your future constrain you to cling to holiness and to avoid every appearance of evil.[23]

In another place, however, Spurgeon spoke of the Christian's nature in a decidedly different way. Referring to himself as a Christian he wrote this:

> [I have] to wonder that I have any desire to be holy at all considering what a polluted, debased, depraved nature I find still within my soul, notwithstanding all that divine grace has done in me.[24]

Spurgeon's unflattering description of his own nature as a Christian was undoubtedly intended to reflect the reality that even as a

---

23. Charles Spurgeon, *Evening by Evening* (Springdale, PA: Whitaker House, 1984), 127.

24. Charles Spurgeon, "One Aspect of Christ's Death," Metropolitan Tabernacle Pulpit, Vol. 52, 1906, p. 293, found in The Ages Digital Library Sermons, Albany, OR, USA, 1997. Sermon #2986, preached on Oct. 14, 1875. http://media.sabda.org/alkitab-9/LIBRARY/SPR_SR52.PDF.

regenerate man he was troubled by fleshly desires.[25] His theological point was correct: because of the influence of their unredeemed bodies, Christians not only are capable of sinning, they do sin, sometimes in terrible ways. Nevertheless, he erred when he used unbiblical terms to describe this biblical reality. His "polluted, debased, depraved nature" language simply has no basis in Scripture with reference to the Christian.[26]

We should appreciate the overall contributions of many fine teachers like Charles Spurgeon—men who have described the believer's heart and nature in negative ways when wrestling with the reality that regenerate people sin. But we should also admit that these unbiblical descriptions of the believer's heart and nature, though well-intended, have often served to downplay the greatest spiritual difference between believers and unbelievers: believers have been born again, unbelievers have not.

The Christian Is a "Not Guilty New Creation"
I am not merely concerned about the technicality of using the right words. I am concerned about the influence of the words we use. By using degrading language to describe the Christian, many otherwise excellent teachers not only have strayed from the consistent emphasis of the New Testament, but have also persuaded regenerate people to think of themselves as nothing more than justified sinners—filthy by nature yet forgiven. How much more encouraged the Christian would be in his battle against sexual sin if he learned to think of himself as he really is:

- justified *and* regenerate or "born again" (John 3:3; 1 Pet. 1:3, 23)

- God's spiritual workmanship, "created in Christ Jesus for good works" (Eph. 2:10)

---

25. The author's opinion is that a person only has one nature, either good or evil (cf. Matt. 7:15–20; 12:33–35; Luke 6:43–45). Many teachers, however, define the Christian's flesh as his unredeemed human "nature" or "sin nature," while acknowledging the newness and goodness of the spiritual nature created by God in regeneration. In other words, they say the Christian has two natures, one evil and one good. See appendix D for more on the Christian's nature and the best terminology to use when describing it.

26. See appendix B for a discussion of Jeremiah 17:9 and Mark 7:21–23.

- "a new creature" (2 Cor. 5:17)

- a partaker of "the divine nature" (2 Pet. 1:4)

- created "in the likeness of God . . . in righteousness and holiness of the truth" (Eph. 4:24)

- a "saint" or "holy one" (Rom. 8:27; 1 Cor. 1:2; 6:1–2; 2 Cor. 1:1; Eph. 1:1; 2:19; Phil. 1:1; Col. 1:2, 26; Rev. 14:12; 19:8; etc.)

- "not of the world, even as [Christ is] not of the world" (John 17:16; cf. 15:19)

- "pure in heart" (Matt. 5:8)

- "obedient from the heart" (Rom. 6:17)

- an obedient child of God (1 Pet. 1:14; cf. 1 John 3:1–2, 9–10)

- "full of goodness" (Rom. 15:14)

- a "good man" (Matt. 12:35; Luke 6:45)

- a man with "an honest and good heart" (Luke 8:15)

Christians have been justified by God's grace through faith in Christ (Rom. 5:1) even though they have not completely been removed from sin's influence. These two factors (justification plus the continuing ability to sin) are what generate the common labels "justified sinners" and "sinners saved by grace." There is precious truth contained in these labels because no Christian is without sin and all are dependent upon God's grace in Christ. But to claim that either label fully describes the Christian is to overlook what God has done inside of the Christian. The Christian is more than just not guilty. He is a not guilty new creation.

What If I Told You to Harvest Grapes from a Thorn Bush?
If you are still corrupt by nature, as many well-meaning Christians say you are, then by encouraging you to stop viewing pornography

they are asking you to do something that is contrary to your nature. They are saying in effect, "Though you are polluted, debased, and depraved by nature, as a follower of Christ you must maintain a consistent pattern of sexual purity." In other words, "You must produce behavior that is uncharacteristic of what you really are." This not only sounds impossible, but also contradicts what Jesus said about grapes not coming from thorn bushes and figs not coming from thistles (Matt. 7:16). A bad tree cannot produce good fruit (Matt. 7:18).[27]

The reason for the unregenerate man's inability to obey God is the downward drag of his sinful heart and nature. He cannot elevate his desires above what he really is. If your heart is still corrupt even though you have been born again—if "bad" is what you are by nature—then why should you expect to produce a harvest of goodness? Why should you not instead expect yourself to go on sinning habitually? Consider an illustration from author Tom Wells on this point:

> Tell a healthy man that he is nearly dead. Then have someone else—a doctor, an expert on sickness—tell him the same thing. Have the diagnosis confirmed by a specialist. Would you be surprised if the man began to feel ill? Would you be amazed if he began to think that his prospects were not good? What else could he think? How else could he feel?[28]

The Christian can fall into a similar trap. Respected Christian leaders tell him that his heart is corrupt, or that he is still corrupt by nature. Because he often feels corrupt due to the influence of his flesh, he takes every sinful thought as fresh evidence that what he has been taught is true—that he is still characterized (at least in part) by a "sin nature." Naturally he begins to expect his behavior

---

27. Jesus used the "bad tree/good fruit" illustration to refer specifically to false prophets (Matt. 7:15–20), but the principle itself is universal, illustrating the difference between *all* unbelievers and *all* believers. In Luke 6:43–45 Jesus used the same illustration to refer to believers and unbelievers in general. See appendix D for more on the relationship between nature and behavior.

28. Tom Wells, *Christian Take Heart* (Carlisle: Banner of Truth Trust, 1987), 68.

to reflect this "sin nature," and since sinful behavior is what he expects, it is what he often settles for.[29]

Be Righteous by Being Yourself

Henrietta (Hetty) Green was one of the wealthiest women of the early twentieth century. She received an inheritance of $10 million, and by the time she died in 1916 she had grown her fortune to $100 million (somewhere around $1.5 billion in today's economy). Sadly, Hetty was also a miser. Though financially she was able to maintain a comfortable and generous lifestyle, she greedily clung to her money, consigning herself to a life of poverty and living in cheap boarding houses in New York City. When her son injured his leg, she chose to treat the wound herself rather than spend money for medical care. After two years, when the injury still had not healed, she sought free medical treatment, which the doctor refused when he learned who she was and knew she had the ability to pay. Eventually, because of her unwillingness to part with the paltry sum of money for his treatment, her son's leg had to be amputated.

Hetty Green somehow became convinced that hoarding money was better than spending it wisely. Her bizarre and tragic behavior resulted from this faulty perception of reality. You may not be a miser, but you will be like her in other ways if you go on ordering your life around a faulty or incomplete understanding of who you are in Christ.

Paul wrote, "Do not be conformed to this world, but be transformed by the renewing of your mind, so that you may prove what the will of God is, that which is good and acceptable and perfect" (Rom. 12:2). Eleven chapters of biblical instruction preceded this exhortation, and I would not want to oversimplify the connection of this verse with the rest of Romans. But whatever behavior Paul's statement refers to specifically, he was unarguably describing the relationship between thinking and behavior: by learning to think according to the truth, you will begin to act in ways that correspond to God's will. The truth is this:

---

29. Romans 7:14–25, when wrongly understood and/or applied, leads many professing Christians to accept patterns of habitual sin as part of the ordinary Christian experience. For more on the meaning and proper application of this passage see the author's article entitled "The Conviction of Fleshly Man: Why Romans 7:14–25 Cannot Describe the Christian Life," at www.CCWtoday.org.

- You have been delivered from sin's penalty *and* you have been delivered from slavery to your fleshly lusts.

- The old you no longer exists. You are a completely new person, created by God in righteousness and holiness.

- You live in an unredeemed body and often experience strong desires for sexual sin, but this does not prove that you are compelled to sin, or that you are evil, bad, or corrupt by nature.

The biblical realities summarized in this chapter are powerful spiritual weapons. In the mind of a regenerate man they represent an arsenal of encouraging ammunition, supplied by the Holy Spirit through the writers of the New Testament, for waging an effective battle against sexual sin. If by God's grace you use these truths to renew your mind, you will come to understand and enjoy your new identity in Christ, and you will begin to act consistently like the righteous man you really are. You will learn to be righteous by being yourself.

On the other hand, if you go on thinking of yourself as being forgiven but still filthy, pardoned but still governed by a corrupt heart or a "sin nature," you will be inclined to go on acting like the slave you are not.

Questions for Reflection or Discussion

1. Why do you think many teachers choose to describe the believer's heart as corrupt or deceitful? What benefit do you think they hope Christians will gain by thinking of themselves as having a "sin nature"?

2. How can a Christian maintain a proper sense of humility while at the same time acknowledging his deliverance from sin and the goodness of his regenerate heart and nature?

3. How does the message of this chapter differ from what psychologists and some religious teachers might call "the power of positive thinking"? (Consider this question in light of John 8:31–38.)

eleven

It Only Works by Faith

A race car engine is a well-machined but powerless piece of metal. It was designed to depend upon the explosive power of racing fuel and the skill of a trained driver for its proper functioning. Likewise, you have been re-created spiritually in the likeness of God, but you were designed to resist sexual temptation by depending on the power and wisdom of the One who created you.

Analyzing Peter's Moral Train Wreck

Peter voiced his confidence that he would follow Christ even to death if necessary (Mark 14:27–31). Later that night, when Peter had the opportunity to ask God for strength to resist the temptation to deny His Lord, he fell asleep. Jesus found him and said, "Simon [Peter], are you asleep? Could you not keep watch for one hour?" (Mark 14:37). Then Jesus said something that should have gotten Peter's attention: "Keep watching and praying that you may not come into temptation; the spirit is willing, but the flesh is weak" (Mark 14:38).

When Jesus said, "The spirit is willing," He was referring to Peter's willingness to obey—his good intentions. Even with good intentions and strong personal resolve, Peter was hampered by the weakness of his flesh. On his own, he could not and would not avoid his infamous denial of Christ.

You probably know what happened later that night: Peter was hauled away by four masked men armed with huge swords who threatened to chop off his head if he didn't renounce his loyalty to Christ. . . . OK, so that's not exactly the way it happened. Peter was confronted by a servant girl, twice, and then by a few bystanders who suspected that he had been with Jesus. No armed men, no threats of beheading, and yet Peter did exactly what Jesus said he would do, what he himself never thought possible: he denied Jesus three times in pathetic weakness. And then, when the rooster crowed, he wept (Mark 14:66–72).

Peter was overconfident and he lacked spiritual discernment. He thought he was strong enough and wise enough, but because he misunderstood his own weakness he was unprepared when the temptation came. Perhaps he would have stood firm if he had been approached by men armed with swords, so the devil sent a curious servant girl instead, along with a few nameless bystanders who were probably more interested in gossip than persecution. Faced with these "dangerous foes," Peter collapsed into sin.

The Schemes of the Devil

When you sin, you cannot blame another person, or God, or even the devil himself. You are to blame, and your physical body is the place in you where sin operates. But there is another influence—a spiritual enemy who draws believers toward sin. I am referring to Satan, who is also called the devil (Matt. 4:1; Eph. 6:11; 1 Pet. 5:8), the tempter (Matt. 4:3; 1 Thess. 3:5), and the adversary of believers (1 Pet. 5:8).

Satan rules over unbelievers. He has blinded them spiritually so that they cannot see the glory of Christ or believe the truth of the gospel (2 Cor. 4:4). He holds them captive to do his will (2 Tim. 2:26). They are slaves of their own fleshly lusts, and also of the devil who uses their lusts to hold them in bondage. Addictions to pornography, alcohol, or gambling may even be the result of demon possession in some unbelievers.

Satan possesses no authority over believers. The Holy Spirit now rules in their hearts, producing affection for Christ and the desire to obey Him. Even so, because of the Christian's bodily passions, the devil represents a dangerous influence. The following words were written to believers:

> Put on the full armor of God, so that you will be able to stand firm against the schemes of the devil. (Eph. 6:11)
>
> Be of sober spirit, be on the alert. Your adversary, the devil, prowls around like a roaring lion, seeking someone to devour. (1 Pet. 5:8)

World War II soldiers talked about fighting Hitler when they were actually describing their struggle against German soldiers under his command. Likewise, the writers of Scripture often spoke of the devil himself being the threat when the believer's usual contact is with one of the many demons under the devil's control. As Paul said, we struggle against "the rulers, against the powers, against the world forces of this darkness, against the spiritual forces of wickedness in the heavenly places" (Eph. 6:12).

It is probably impossible to pinpoint the devil's exact abilities and tactics, but he works in at least two ways to tempt believers to sin:

1. Satan tempts through false teaching.
False teachers are Satan's servants. Jesus called Satan "the father of lies" (John 8:44). Paul warned Timothy that "in later times some will fall away from the faith, paying attention to deceitful spirits and doctrines of demons" (1 Tim. 4:1).

Peter warns us to expect that false teachers will introduce "destructive heresies" (2 Pet. 2:1), going on to say that as a result of their teaching "many will follow their sensuality" (2:2). "Sensuality" may not refer exclusively to sexual sin, but it is clear that Peter was concerned about false doctrines that permitted or promoted fleshly living of some sort. These false teachers will "entice by fleshly desires, by sensuality, those who barely escape from the ones who live in error" (2:18).

The Bible rejects any doctrine that promotes or permits sexual sin, assuring us that "immorality or any impurity or greed must not even be named among you, as is proper among saints" (Eph. 5:3).

"Do not be deceived; neither fornicators, . . . nor adulterers, nor effeminate, nor homosexuals, . . . will inherit the kingdom of God" (1 Cor. 6:9–10).

Some of Satan's most energetic false teachers abuse the Bible in a different way. Rather than misinterpreting or glossing over individual passages that forbid sexual immorality, they strike directly at the root by tempting people to doubt the authority and accuracy of the Bible. A growing number of professing Christians are being told by these scholarly pawns of the devil that because of centuries of translation errors, scribal additions, and other factors, the Bible we now read is not a reliable or complete record of the words of God.[30] Then, once a person begins to *doubt* the Bible, it is much easier for him to *disobey* the Bible.

As with every other form of Satanic attack, your only sure defense against this onslaught is "the shield of faith with which you will be able to extinguish all the flaming arrows of the evil one" (Eph. 6:16).

2. Satan tempts believers by sending his captives to do his will. The Bible doesn't tell us explicitly that that the servant girl was sent by Satan to tempt Peter, but we do know that Satan has the ability to send people in this way. There is no doubt that Satan influenced Judas to betray Christ (Luke 22:3–4), and we know that many other people are held captive by him "to do his will" (2 Tim. 2:26).

Another glimpse into Satan's influence over humans is found in the book of Job. God permitted Satan to afflict Job when He said, "All that [Job] has is in your power" (Job 1:12). How did Satan choose to exercise the power God had given him? First he stirred up (or you might say he sent) the Sabeans to steal Job's oxen and donkeys and to murder his servants (1:13–15). Then he stirred up (or sent) the Chaldeans to steal his camels and murder more of his servants (Job 1:17). The Bible does not use the terms "stirred up" or "sent," but these evil people were not merely obeying their own impulses. They were doing Satan's bidding.

---

30. To learn more about the way false teachers misrepresent the facts in their attempts to cause people to doubt the Bible, see the author's review of Bart Ehrman's book, *Misquoting Jesus* (San Francisco: HarperSanFrancisco, 2005), at www.CCWtoday.org.

How did Satan stir up these evil people to do these evil deeds? Did he whisper in someone's ear? Did he implant evil thoughts into their minds? We are not told *how* he did it, just *that* he did it. And if he was able to send these people to do his will, why could he not send a servant girl to tempt Peter, or a seductress like the one described in Proverbs 7? Most importantly, why could he not send someone to lure you into sexual sin?

You won't see Satan opening a cage and sending a human captive on a mission. Most people who do his bidding aren't even aware that they are carrying out his will (just as the Sabeans and Chaldeans were ignorant of the fact that Satan was using them to afflict Job). But the reality is the same: Satan uses human pawns to tempt believers.

It Only Works by Faith
You are not strong enough to resist your fleshly sexual desires on your own, or wise enough to avoid Satan's schemes. As the psalmist said, "Unless the Lord guards the city, the watchman keeps awake in vain" (Ps. 127:1).

Given this unseen spiritual danger coupled with the weakness of your flesh, will you be self-dependent like Peter? Will you go to sleep tonight without asking God to guard you from Satan's devices and give you victory over your sinful passions? What about tomorrow morning before you go to work, and tomorrow evening before you go online to pay your bills, and the next day, and the next? Will you try to guard yourself against sexual sin by your own strength and wisdom, independent of God? If so, you will sin. The Christian life only works by faith.

The same Paul who spoke highly of the Christian's new self also spoke reverently of God's power and wisdom working in the Christian to bring about obedience to His will. God is the one "who is able to do far more abundantly beyond all that we ask or think, according to the power that works within us" (Eph. 3:20). "It is God who is at work in you, both to will and to work for His good pleasure" (Phil. 2:13). It is "by the Spirit" that you are "putting to death the deeds of the body" (Rom. 8:13).

Paul described his own conscious dependence upon God by saying, "the life which I now live in the flesh I live by faith in the Son of God, who loved me and gave Himself up for me" (Gal. 2:20). Later in the same letter when he said to the Galatians, "walk by the Spirit, and you will not carry out the desire of the flesh" (5:16), he meant essentially the same thing. To "walk by the Spirit" is to live in conscious dependence upon the Spirit. Since the Holy Spirit is "the Spirit of Christ" (Rom. 8:9), to "walk by the Spirit" is yet another way of saying "live by faith in Christ." If you will live in conscious dependence upon the Spirit of Christ rather than by mere effort, you will find yourself exercising the self-control that the Spirit produces in every Christian (Gal. 5:22), and "you will not carry out the desire of the flesh" (5:16).

If you hope to avoid committing a Peter-like blunder the next time you face sexual temptation, you would do well to meditate on what Jesus said to His disciples before entering the garden that night, just hours before Peter's infamous denial: "Apart from Me you can do nothing." (John 15:5).

Questions for Reflection or Discussion

1. Read 1 Corinthians 10:1–13. What lessons should we learn about dependence on God from verse 11? How would you summarize the point of verse 12? Verse 13 says God will always provide "the way of escape" from temptation. What ways of escape are implied in this passage?

2. Name at least three ways in which other Christians can help you depend on God.

3. How do you intend to begin demonstrating your dependence on God? Please be specific. It would be profitable for you to write out your intentions and commitments, or even to share them with another Christian who will hold you accountable.

EXPERIENCE FREEDOM

The Allied invasion of Europe began on June 6, 1944, and culminated in the defeat of Nazi Germany in May of 1945. The overall effort involved four basic and interrelated elements of military strategy:

- Sufficient troops, ships, planes, vehicles, guns, ammunition, fuel, food, and medicine to launch and sustain the invasion
- A reliable way of getting those resources to the front lines
- The effective deployment of resources at the point of attack
- The desire to win

Similarly, four interrelated elements of the Christian life, strategically combined and deployed by the Spirit of God who is at work in you, are facilitating your experience of deliverance from sexual sin:

- An arsenal of biblical truth
- A reliable way of getting those resources to the front lines of the battle in your mind
- The effective deployment of truth at the point of attack
- The desire to win

twelve

The Weapon That Works

We are back in the park now, listening to the continuing conversation between Nick and John. Here's where we left them earlier:

NICK, *exasperated*. Why don't you just quit? Just tell yourself you won't ever do it again.

JOHN. You're right. I should quit, and I want to quit, but . . .

(*Short pause. John sighs deeply.*)

NICK. But *what*?

JOHN. This may sound strange, but I've tried and tried to quit, and I'm finally realizing that I don't know how.

Nick's question, "Why don't you just quit?" didn't produce what he hoped it would. He wanted to challenge John to muscle up his personal resolve to resist sexual temptation, but he failed to consider that John had undoubtedly tried this on his own, perhaps many times. Having failed repeatedly, John finally asked for help. But instead of encouraging him, Nick's "motivating" question discouraged and humiliated him further. It implied that quitting should be a simple matter of making a decision.

Nevertheless, Nick's mistake accomplished something important. It exposed the real problem both men faced: ignorance. John was honest when he said he didn't know how to quit, and Nick discovered that he didn't know how to help him.

Now let's return to the same point in their conversation. This time Nick moves in a different direction, responding to John's confession with encouraging truth rather than mere motivation. He addresses John's plea for help by opening the door to an arsenal of biblical weapons against sexual sin.

NICK. Do you know why Jesus died for you?

JOHN. Yes, He died to pay for my sins and save me from going to hell. Why do you ask that?

NICK. Because His death accomplished more than just the forgiveness of your sins. He also saved you in another way.

JOHN. I'm not sure I understand.

NICK. The Bible tells us that Jesus came to "save His people from their sins,"[31] not only from sin's penalty, but also from its power. He died "to redeem us from every lawless deed," which means forgiveness, *and* He died "to purify for Himself a people for His own possession."[32] Do you believe Jesus accomplished both of these things when He died?

JOHN. Yes, I believe what the Bible says, but right now I don't feel purified.

NICK. I understand, but feelings are notoriously inaccurate. You won't make any real progress in your fight against sexual sin if you don't move forward on the basis of truth.

---

31. Matt. 1:21.
32. Titus 2:14.

JOHN. OK. What else can you tell me?

NICK. For starters, you are not the same person you were at this time last year, before you became a Christian. That man ceased to exist when you were born again, not merely in a manner of speaking, but *really*. The John who is sitting here talking to me today is not the same person as the John I knew then.[33]

JOHN. But I feel like the same person, I look like the same person, and in all too many ways, I act like the same person. What's different about me?

NICK. Last year God gave you a new heart—a good heart. He made you a new person with a completely new identity. That is what it means to be born again.[34] The old John was hostile toward God and habitually opposed to doing His will,[35] but the new John has been made in the likeness of God. The Bible says you have been re-created in righteousness and holiness.[36] You are a new creation,[37] God's workmanship, created in Christ Jesus for good works.[38] The real you is a partaker of the divine nature.[39]

JOHN. Then why am I still so rotten?

NICK. That's just my point. You aren't rotten. You're a child of God and a member of a royal priesthood.[40] As an unbeliever you were a slave of sinful passions,[41] but through Christ's victory over sin on the cross[42] and the Spirit's work of regeneration, you have become obedient from the heart to God.[43] The

---

33. Rom. 6:5–7; Col. 3:1–3.
34. John 3:3; 1 Pet. 1:3, 23.
35. Col. 1:21; Rom. 8:7–8.
36. Eph. 4:24.
37. 2 Cor. 5:17.
38. Eph. 2:10.
39. 2 Pet. 1:4.
40. 1 Pet. 2:9.
41. Titus 3:3.
42. 1 Cor. 15:56–57.
43. Rom. 6:17–18.

desires of your heart have changed from evil to righteous, and because of this change, you are no longer sin's slave.[44]

JOHN. I've read those things in the Bible, but I thought they were sort of like wishful thinking—what Christians will become someday instead of what they are right now. Isn't that true?

NICK. No, it isn't. They are true of every Christian right now.

JOHN. But it sounds like you're saying Christians are perfect, and if that's the case, I must not be a Christian.

NICK. I'm sure you've heard the saying, "Christians aren't perfect, just forgiven." That's true—Christians aren't perfect, and they are forgiven. But the words "*just* forgiven" give the impression that forgiveness is the only difference between a Christian and an unbeliever. As a Christian you are more than just forgiven. You are also a new creation.

JOHN. If I'm a new creation, then why do I still struggle in the area of sexual sin? That's not what a righteous life looks like, is it?

NICK. No, it isn't. People who claim to be Christians yet continue in patterns of sexual immorality may be deceived into thinking they are Christians when they have not truly been born again.[45] But the Bible also tells us that Christians can be temporarily overtaken by sin.[46]

JOHN. So how can I be sure that I'm a true Christian when I have this problem with viewing pornography?

NICK. Repentance will confirm your faith in Christ.

JOHN. Haven't I already done that by feeling sorry for my sin and by confessing it to you? Wasn't that repentance?

---

44. Rom. 6:16–22.
45. See appendix A.
46. Gal. 6:1.

NICK. No, not necessarily. There is more to genuine repentance than sorrow and confession. Anyone can feel sorry that he has sinned, but sorrow is often just regret for having been caught, the pain of a disturbed conscience, or sadness about the fact that it's impossible to hold onto sin and have eternal life. This is worldly sorrow, and the Bible tells us that it leads to death.[47] The kind of sorrow I'm hoping to see in you is the kind *without* regret—the kind that is glad the sin has been exposed, happy to be rid of it, and eager to do everything necessary to stay away from it in the future.[48]

JOHN. OK. I think I understand what you're saying, and it's encouraging to hear. But I'm still confused about one thing: if my heart is good, why do I even want to look at pornography?

NICK. Because part of you hasn't been redeemed.

JOHN. What part?

NICK. Your body—the mortal, physical, merely human part of you. The Bible calls it your flesh. Your new heart is pure, but your flesh still lusts after what God hates.

JOHN. Will I always desire sin because of the lusts of my flesh?

NICK. Yes, at least to some degree as long as you live. But your body is no longer in control. It is now your subject rather than your master. Through Christ you have been given the ability to please God by resisting your fleshly lusts.[49]

JOHN. Will my sinful desires always be as strong as they have seemed lately?

NICK. No . . . at least they don't have to be. As a Christian, you are "being led by the Spirit of God," and "by the Spirit you are

---

47. 2 Cor. 7:10.
48. 2 Cor. 7:9–11.
49. Rom. 6:8–13.

putting to death the deeds of the body."[50] Your fleshly desires once ruled over you like a dictator, but now they are like the leaves on a tree that was recently chopped down: even though they still have the appearance of being alive, they are beginning to wither.[51] Your sinful desires may seem to control you at times, but because Christ defeated sin on the cross[52] they have no real authority. They will weaken over time as you do what God instructs you to do in fighting against sin.

JOHN. What does He want me to do?

_____

Now that's a good question, one which we will answer in the following chapters. What John gained from this conversation was the awareness of an arsenal of truth in the Bible—weapons which he must now treasure in his mind if he is to replace his former unbiblical patterns of thinking. From these resources the Holy Spirit can keep him supplied to do effective battle against sexual sin every day.

_____

50. Rom. 8:13–14, quoted in reverse order (Note that these two verses are not commands, warnings, or exhortations, but rather descriptions of God's present and ongoing work in every true believer).

51. Charles Leiter, illustration given at a Christ Fellowship of Kansas City men's retreat, June 2009, Kirksville, MO.

52. Rom. 8:3; 1 Cor. 15:56–57.

Questions for Reflection or Discussion

1. At the end of the first chapter, I asked how you would have responded to John's confession differently than Nick did. How was Nick's response in this chapter similar to your answer to that question? How was it different?

2. Read 2 Corinthians 7:8–11. Based on this passage, what would you say are the marks of genuine repentance?

3. When David wrote Psalm 32, he had committed an awful sexual sin (you probably know the story, found in 2 Samuel 11). Read Psalm 32 looking for answers to these two questions: 1) How did David describe the feelings he had before openly admitting his sin? 2) What positive statements did David make about himself as a believer (and all believers), even though he had committed a terrible sin? Discuss your findings and the implications for your present situation.

thirteen

Be Battle Ready

The Allied troops who carried out the actual fighting that led to the liberation of Europe and the collapse of Nazi Germany played what we commonly think of as the heroic part in that great war. They dodged the bullets. They suffered the artillery blasts. They faced the tanks and flamethrowers. They suffered the cold and the hunger and the fear. They did the necessary killing, and the necessary dying. And, appropriately, they took home (or were buried with) the combat medals they earned.

Those soldiers were indeed heroes, but there is an aspect of war that is sometimes overlooked, and without which there would have been no victory in Europe. I am referring to something called "logistics"—the science and labor of supplying the battlefront. In every war, this massive effort is the Hercules behind the heroes.

This chapter is about being spiritually battle ready, something that cannot happen unless the weapons for doing battle against sexual sin are stored, organized, and consistently supplied to the front lines. This will take work on your part, but without it you will remain unprepared for battle.

In the last chapter John asked Nick what God wants him to do in order to resist the temptation to view pornography, and even to weaken his fleshly desire for sexual sin. Here is Nick's answer, and their continuing discussion:

NICK. He wants you to believe the truth.

JOHN. But I do believe the truth.

NICK. You believe the truth in a general sense, but you need to believe in a more active, effective way.

JOHN. What do you mean by that?

NICK. You hold a body of general biblical knowledge in your mind, and you believe all of it to be true. But truth stored in the back of your mind is like water in a well. It won't quench your thirst or clean your hands unless you draw it out and use it.

JOHN. I'm not sure I understand.

NICK. Do you know Jarrod, the police officer who goes to our church?

JOHN. Yes, I know him.

NICK. He's an award-winning marksman with his pistol. His shooting skill is obviously valuable in his line of work, but what would you say if you were to learn that he carried his pistol in the trunk of his police car while he was on duty?

JOHN. I'd say it wouldn't do him much good in the trunk.

NICK. Why not?

JOHN. Because he wouldn't have access to it when he needed it.

NICK. That's right. And that's why he carries it in a holster on his belt. I went on a ride-along with him a few months ago and I noticed something else. Several times he put his hand on the gun, wrapped his fingers around the grip, and unsnapped the holster even though there was nothing going on. I asked him why he did this, and he told me it was his way of keeping himself prepared to use the weapon instantly. Then he said something I'll always remember: "If I *stay* ready, I won't have to *get* ready."

JOHN. That's good, but I'm still not sure how it applies to me.

NICK. OK, here's my point: Truth is your weapon against sexual sin, but the truth you believe hasn't been helping you resist the temptation to view pornography. Why not? Because you have been keeping it in the trunk.

JOHN. You mean in the back of my mind, right?

NICK. Yes, rather than in the forefront of your thinking. You have been storing what you know in a place where truth is not immediately accessible—like water deep down in a well.

JOHN. What do I need to do differently?

NICK. You need to stay ready for sexual temptation by keeping the truth where it is instantly usable, and I'll tell you why: At the moment of temptation your mind quickly devises lies to persuade you to give in to your fleshly desires. You might think, "This is what I really need," or, "No one is watching," or, "I'm not hurting anyone." You might tell yourself lies about who you really are. "I'm still a sinner by nature, and God knows I can't help myself." You might use one sexual sin as a way of justifying another sexual sin. "I did the same thing yesterday, so one more sin won't hurt." You might even appeal to your pattern of failure as proof that sexual sin is irresistible. "I always give in sooner or later, so it might as well be now."

JOHN. I *have* had thoughts like those when I've been tempted to look at pornography. Have you thought that way too?

NICK. Yes, I have. In fact, I still hear the lies, and the temptation is still strong at times. Satan is hard at work through our corrupt culture, training our minds to lie continually about the supposed benefits of sexual sin. No Christian is immune to being tempted, and I wouldn't want you to think I'm sinless in terms of lust. But I learned very early in my Christian life how to resist sexual temptation consistently by overcoming the lie with the truth.

JOHN. What was the most important thing you learned?

NICK. Whether you sin or turn away from sin at the moment of temptation depends upon whether or not the truth is immediately accessible in the forefront of your thinking. In other words, what makes the difference is having the right *information* in the right *place* at the right *time*.

JOHN. That's easy to remember. When can I put it to use?

NICK. How about right now while we're sitting here?

JOHN. OK, I'm all ears. How do I do that?

NICK. Right now you have a strong conviction against viewing Internet pornography, but you have less resolve about lust in general.

JOHN. What makes you say that?

NICK. I've been noticing the movement of your eyes as attractive women have walked or jogged past us. Several times I watched your eyes move up and down as you examined their bodies.

JOHN, *obviously embarrassed.* You're right, and I'm sorry. It's just a bad habit.

NICK. I know, but it's more than a *bad* habit. It's a *sinful* habit. Jesus calls it adultery.[53]

(*John nods his head in agreement as Nick continues.*)

---

53. Matt. 5:28.

My point was not to embarrass you. I fight against the same temptation myself, as do most Christian men. But if you will reject the lie in preference for the truth, you will find yourself resisting that same temptation rather than giving in to it, even the very next time an attractive woman comes by.

JOHN. What lie?

NICK. The one that says, "Studying her body will be very satisfying." Or the one that says, "She'll be gone in a few seconds, and you'll regret it if you pass up this opportunity."

JOHN. So what truth will keep me from lusting?

NICK. How about the fact that no one is ever better by sinning or worse by obeying?[54] You have a fleshly desire to sin, but lusting will not produce the genuine satisfaction the lie claimed it would. Instead it will leave you feeling guilty, sorrowful, and more vulnerable when the next sexual temptation comes. Obedience, on the other hand, will bring you true happiness and genuine satisfaction because obeying God is what now defines you. It is what you want to do more than anything else.

Rather than remembering these things *after* you sin, keep the truth ready in your mind for unexpected temptations. Keep the right *information* ready in the right *place* for use at the right *time*.

If you *stay* ready, you won't have to *get* ready.

---

54. The statement "No one is ever better by sinning or worse by obeying" is from Jim Elliff, private conversation with the author, August 2009. Quoted by permission.

Questions for Reflection or Discussion

1. The Bible says Eve sinned because she was deceived (1 Tim. 2:14). Read Genesis 3:1–6 and name the lies Eve believed, leading to her disobedience. Name some of the lies that have persuaded you to give in to the temptation to view pornography. Take enough time to think about this carefully, and be specific in your answers.

2. What truth(s) from Scripture (either quoted or paraphrased) would have persuaded you to reject the lies at the moment of temptation? Again, think carefully and be specific.

fourteen

Prepare Your Mind for Action

Being battle ready takes work. If you want to experience victory at the moment of sexual temptation, you must work hard to keep your battlefront well-supplied. As Peter said, you must "prepare your [mind] for action"[55] (1 Pet. 1:13). Similarly, Paul wrote to Timothy, "Discipline yourself for the purpose of godliness" (1 Tim. 4:7). An unprepared or undisciplined mind is a vulnerable battlefront.

Nick went on to explain to John that making truth more and more usable in his battle against sexual sin would involve increasing his diligence in three spiritual disciplines: learning, memorizing, and meditating.

Learning Is Acquiring the Right Information
Learning is what you have been doing by understanding the message of the Bible so far as it has been represented in this book.

Learning is what you do when you listen to recordings of the Bible or hear biblically sound sermons. It is what happens when you engage in Bible study with biblically minded men or study the Bible

---

55. Lit. "gird up the loins of your mind," a spiritual illustration based on the practice of gathering or binding up loose clothing in preparation for running, travel, work, or battle (cf. Exod. 12:11; 1 Kings 18:46; Jer. 1:17–19; Luke 12:35).

on your own and understand its true meaning. Learning is simply acquiring the right information.

The righteous man is a learning man. He is never content with his current level of knowledge or satisfied with any ignorance of divine truth. "Teach a righteous man and he will increase his learning" (Prov. 9:9). "Wise men store up knowledge" (Prov. 10:14). Consider this passage from Paul's letter to the Colossians:

> For this reason also, since the day we heard of it [i.e., the Colossians' faith in Christ and love for each other], we have not ceased to pray for you and to ask that you may be filled with the knowledge of His will in all spiritual wisdom and understanding, so that you will walk in a manner worthy of the Lord, to please Him in all respects, bearing fruit in every good work and increasing in the knowledge of God. (Col. 1:9–10)

Paul was glad the Colossians understood the truth, but he wasn't content for them to rest in what they already knew. He wanted them to know more.

Christians are learners by divine design. Jesus explained to His disciples that it had been granted to them to "know the mysteries of the kingdom of heaven," but then He promised that "whoever has [such knowledge], to him more [knowledge] shall be given" (Matt. 13:11–12).

Memorizing Is Putting the Right Information in the Right Place
Memorizing is locking information in your mind in such a way that you can recall it accurately. All Christians do this to some extent already. To the degree to which you can formulate biblically accurate thoughts or statements even when you are not reading your Bible or some other biblical literature, you have memorized truth.

Memorizing Scripture is not difficult. How much effort would it take, for example, to memorize 1 Corinthians 6:18—"Flee immorality"? How long would it take you to memorize the words "Abstain from every form of evil" (1 Thess. 5:22) or "Abstain from fleshly lusts which wage war against the soul" (1 Pet. 2:11)?[56] These short biblical phrases are like hand grenades to blast away sexual temptation in the mind of the man who loves the truth and desires to live out the truth. You can do more of this than you have done to this point, and by starting small you will encourage yourself to memorize larger passages. Think of the value of memorizing a passage like Proverbs 7, in which a senseless young man is drawn away by sexual temptation. This would be an outstanding exercise for a young man who has entered puberty, perhaps followed by a special talk between the young man and his father or another Christian mentor.

The Holy Spirit purifies God's people by means of biblical truth. As the psalmist asked, "How can a young man keep his way pure? By keeping it according to Your word" (Ps. 119:9). But truth must be acquired and stored for it to be useful. The Spirit does not infuse truth into the mind apart from the believer's personal effort. "Your word I have treasured in my heart, that I may not sin against You" (Ps. 119:11).

Meditating Is Keeping the Right Information in the Right Place at the Right Time
Meditation is focusing your mind on the message of the Bible in such a way that truth is not merely learned and stored, but used. It is taking the truth down from the shelf and examining it carefully. It is enjoying the truth, appreciating the truth, talking to yourself about the truth, and asking yourself questions about the truth. It is having regular discussions with yourself about the truth—the way Nick discussed truth with John.

The man who is meditating is not sitting cross-legged on the floor with his eyes closed, his forearms resting on his knees, and his thumbs touching his index fingers. He is sitting comfortably on his couch holding a cup of coffee, or riding his bike for exercise, or driving to work, or standing in line at the grocery store, or lying in bed preparing to go to sleep, or trying to go back to sleep at 3:00 a.m. after being awakened by a barking dog.

---

56. See chapter 15 for more on abstaining from sexual sin and fleeing from sexual temptation.

Meditation is something that happens anywhere and everywhere, at anytime and every time during the day. As author Jim Elliff says, "You are always meditating on something. Why not make it the truth?"[57]

Bring the truth into any and every part of your daily life through meditation. In this way truth will be in the right place (i.e., the forefront of your thinking) at the time when it is actually needed— when lies begin to form in your mind in response to sexual temptation.

Questions for Reflection or Discussion

1. Name three times during your typical day when you could meditate on Scripture rather than on something else.

2. Name three times during your typical week when meditating on Scripture would help you resist sexual temptation.

3. I have heard men say, "I'm not much of a reader," when explaining why they don't know much about the Bible. What role would you say neglect, laziness, or distraction with other media has played in your own reluctance to study the Bible or read solid Christian literature? Name some of the spiritual advantages of developing good reading, listening, or comprehension skills. Name some of the spiritual disadvantages of having underdeveloped skills in these areas.

---

57. Jim Elliff, private conversation with the author, August, 2009, quoted by permission.

fifteen

Kill the Enemy

You are now familiar with the weapon that works against sexual sin (biblical truth), and you know how to supply truth to the front lines of the battle (learning, memory, and meditation). You also know that prayerful dependence upon God is critical. Now you need training in the practice of effective deployment. Holding a loaded rifle will do you no good when the enemy attacks unless you take aim and pull the trigger.

The Christian life is a dependent life, but not a passive life. Paul said Christians are putting to death the deeds of the body "by the Spirit" (Rom. 8:13), but the Spirit doesn't work apart from the believer's conscious involvement and effort. The Spirit is at work eradicating sin through your efforts to eradicate sin. If you wish to defeat the deeds of your body, you must actively engage them on the field of battle.

The Bible offers two primary principles for killing sexual sin. The first is abstinence, and the second is flight.

Abstinence: The "Never Again" Mindset
You might ask, "How do I put to death the deeds of my body, and how will I know when a particular deed of my body has been put to death?" Peter answers the first part of your question when he tells

Christians to "abstain from fleshly lusts which wage war against the soul" (1 Pet. 2:11). You kill sexual sin by abstaining from sexual sin.

Abstinence means none, not at all, never again. You cannot obey Peter's command by gradually weaning yourself from pornography, trying to cut back on viewing pornography, or viewing it only in moderation. You can only obey God by abstaining. "For this is the will of God, your sanctification; that is, that you abstain from sexual immorality" (1 Thess. 4:3).

Regarding the second part of your question, the more consistently you abstain from gratifying sexual lust, the closer it comes to death. Just as your craving for sugar feeds on sugar, your craving for sexual sin feeds on sexual sin. Abstaining from sugar will reduce your craving for sugar, and abstaining from sexual sin will reduce your craving for sexual sin. In this way you will (by the Spirit) progressively kill your lust and transform your behavior.

Please be careful here. The Bible tells us that if we resist the devil he will flee from us (James 4:7), but we also know that when Jesus resisted the devil, the devil "left Him until an opportune time" (Luke 4:13). In other words, he planned to come back and try again. Paul once wrote, "Let him who thinks he stands take heed that he does not fall" (1 Cor. 10:12). Don't be fooled into thinking you have put sexual lust to death the first time you resist the temptation to look at pornography or masturbate. You probably resisted these sins at times even as an unbeliever, and certainly you have resisted on most occasions as a Christian, but the lust has returned again and again to trouble you. Sin and Satan are tireless and deceitful enemies that will never stop seeking to control you.

Your fleshly desires for sin will harass you until you die even though they are defeated and passing. In some ways they are like the mythical multi-headed monster: chop off one head, and many others threaten. Heads that have been chopped off even seem to be able to grow back in the Christian who becomes careless or overconfident. For this reason you must remain vigilant and aggressive in recognizing and refusing to gratify your fleshly desires. Vigorously resist every hint of sexual temptation. Even the smallest crack in a dam may eventually lead to a catastrophic collapse. Likewise, even your smallest lapse into sexual fantasy may eventually lead to a disastrous moral failure.

Abstinence Requires Discretion
Discretion might be defined as knowing the weakness of the flesh, understanding the power of sexual temptation, and making every effort to see that the two are never unnecessarily brought close to each other.

The man who is trying to conquer drunkenness would be a fool to walk into a bar. Like a bed of dying coals that glows brightly and flames when oxygen is forced into it, his former patterns of thinking and acting like a drunkard would be stimulated by the familiar sights, sounds, and smells. The same is true for the man who is abstaining from sexual sin. He would be a fool to go on watching movies containing sensuality, thumbing through magazines that are likely to contain even mildly provocative images, watching late night cable TV, or surfing the Internet unnecessarily, especially when alone. As Paul said, "Make no provision for the flesh in regard to its lusts" (Rom. 13:14).

Flight: The Victory that Requires Retreat
Christian men are at war against sexual sin, but the biblical method for defeating sexual sin is not to charge toward the enemy, or even to stand and fight. The Bible yells, "Retreat!" "Flee immorality" (1 Cor. 6:18).

A handsome young Israelite named Joseph resisted and defeated sexual temptation by running away when his master's wife tried to seduce him. Day after day she flattered him with sexual advances. Then one day she brazenly took hold of his clothing and said, "Lie with me" (Gen. 39:12).

Joseph might have chosen to pull her hands away from his clothing and say like a conquering hero, "Not me babe. I'm saving myself for marriage." He might have tried to reason with her about the folly of her unfaithfulness—what I would call the evangelistic approach. Or he might have said politely and firmly, "Please leave me alone," and then gone back to his household work. These all would have been "charge" or "stand and fight" responses to sexual temptation, but none of them would have removed him from the presence of the enemy.

True resistance to sexual sin is running away—*fast*. Joseph knew his own weakness well enough to know that remaining near the source of this temptation would lead to disaster. "He left his garment in her hand and fled, and went outside" (Gen. 39:12).

Joseph is not the only man who has defeated sexual temptation by running away. A friend of mine once ran to his car and drove away when a seductively dressed woman approached him and attempted to engage him in friendly conversation. He didn't run away because she was repulsive or uninviting. He ran away because she was attractive and obviously available, and because he sensed his own physical attraction to her body. In obedience to Paul's command to flee immorality, he sounded the "Retreat!" alarm in his mind and quickly removed himself from the presence of the enemy.

Whenever Possible, Run Away Before You See the Enemy
Fleeing sexual immorality involves making decisions in advance of temptation. Remove yourself from the temptation to commit sexual sin by establishing certain non-negotiable standards concerning what you will, or will not, do.

Run away by deciding ahead of time not to watch a particular TV show or channel. Run away by agreeing with your wife that you will never use the Internet after she has gone to bed. Run away by pre-planning a route in the grocery store that doesn't take you down the magazine isle. In other words, run away by never getting close. Another friend of mine demonstrated this mindset when he turned down a much-needed job delivering bottled water. He did so because one of his regular stops would have been an adult bookstore, and he had already run away from sexual temptation by deciding that he would never enter such a place.

Run Away from Past Sexual Sins
Another way to "flee immorality" is to avoid dwelling on past sexual sins. Once you have acknowledged your sin to God, to your

wife (if necessary), [58] or to another Christian who is holding you accountable, don't make yourself pay for the sin by replaying it in your mind. Rather than making yourself hate the sin more, you make your problem worse by establishing the event more firmly in your memory.

As an illustration of the way this works, picture in your mind a purple gorilla seated in a fancy, white-tablecloth restaurant eating steak and lobster with a knife and fork. I'm serious. Imagine the image in detail. Can you see him? OK, now stop thinking about him. Put the image out of your mind. . . . You can see the problem, can't you? The image wasn't difficult to get into your mind, but it is very difficult to get out. Your mind absorbs easily yet expels reluctantly. The same is true of sexual images from past sins.

Instead of dwelling on your sinful failures, replace your self-debasing thoughts about your sin with thoughts about Christ. You cannot add any benefit to Christ's death by punishing yourself, so think of the complete forgiveness you enjoy because of His death on the cross. Think also about who you are in Christ—a new creation, a partaker of the divine nature, a child of God. Train your mind to think as Paul instructed the Philippians: "If there is any excellence and if anything worthy of praise, dwell on these things" (4:8).

Remorse is a natural response to a sinful failure, and in the true Christian it leads to repentance. But after this unavoidable experience of sorrow, there is no benefit in meditating on past sexual sins.

Not Running Away Is *Not* Smart

No sensible man would stand and fight if he suddenly came upon a swarm of angry hornets. The wise man would run away *fast* (or dive into a pond). Standing and fighting would only energize the enemy and result in many painful wounds. The same is true of sexual temptation. Whether you drive away, run away, walk away, look away, log off, or divert your thoughts, you are no coward when you obey God's command to flee immorality. Only a fool would stand and fight with such a deadly foe.

---

58. Please read my caution in appendix F before confessing sexual sins to your wife.

Questions for Reflection or Discussion

1. How would you respond if someone told you that the only way to know for sure that your will to obey God is getting stronger is to stand firm in the presence of sexual temptation *without* running away?

2. Name a few specific ways in which you could begin to exercise discretion as a way of avoiding sexual temptation.

3. Read Proverbs 7 again. Discuss the order of the poor choices that led the young man to commit sexual sin.

sixteen

Follow Your Love Drive

No one perseveres in a difficult pursuit apart from desire. The man climbing Mount Everest will endure the pain and brave the danger only if he has a strong desire to get to the top. Likewise, victory over sexual sin doesn't "just happen" to men who are apathetic or indifferent. The true Christian experiences victory because He has a God-given desire to win.

We have already dealt with the necessary weapon (truth), the supply mechanism (learning, memory, and meditation), and methods for effective deployment of these weapons at the front lines (abstinence and flight). Now we need to talk about motivation—not the "just quit" kind of motivation Nick tried with John at first, but the kind that "has been poured out within our hearts through the Holy Spirit who was given to us" (Rom. 5:5).

This chapter is about the love of God—not His love for us, but our love for Him. Our love for Him is never perfect, and many factors can cause it to decrease at times, but the believer's love for God is his most powerful incentive for pleasing God through sexual purity.

Here is John's next question, and the continuing discussion:

JOHN. I told you earlier that I didn't know how to stop viewing pornography, and you have helped me a lot already. But what is it that makes me *want* to quit?

NICK. Love.

JOHN. OK, . . . I was expecting a little more than that. I suppose this is a stupid question, but what difference does love make?"

NICK. Jesus once said to His disciples, "If you love Me, you will keep My commandments."[59]

JOHN. So does that mean that the person who doesn't obey Jesus doesn't really love Him?

NICK. Yes, that's one implication. In fact, just a few verses later Jesus said, "He who does not love Me does not keep My words."[60] The person whose life is characterized by sin rather than by obedience to Christ can't make a true claim of loving Him.

JOHN. That seems clear enough, but it doesn't really answer my question. What *difference* does loving Jesus make? Is it just another commandment on top of all the others, or is it related to obedience in some other way?

NICK. Love for God is what drives out sinful habits like viewing pornography. It's what produces obedience to Christ.

JOHN. How does that work?

NICK. When Jesus said what He said about obedience being connected with loving Him, do you think He was using a guilt tactic, like a spoiled child who tries to get his mother to buy him toys or candy by saying, "If you really loved me you would give me what I want"?

---

59. John 14:15.
60. John 14:24.

JOHN, *laughing.* No, not at all.

NICK. What about a wife who says to her husband, "If you love me you will give up your weekend softball tournaments"?

JOHN, *after a thoughtful pause.* That may be closer, but it's still basically the same thing—a guilt tactic intended to get someone to change his behavior. That's not what Jesus was saying.

NICK. So what was He saying?

JOHN. I think He was just stating a fact: the person who loves Him is the person who will obey His commandments.

NICK. And what does that say about the relationship between love and obedience?

JOHN. I suppose it implies that the main motivation for obedience to Christ is love, not guilt or obligation.

NICK. You're right. Christians do have an obligation to obey Christ. Obedience is even motivated by a healthy fear of God.[61] But neither obligation nor fear is the true Christian's ultimate motivation for obeying Jesus. Love is.

JOHN. But that brings us back to my question: *how* does love produce obedience?

NICK. A Scottish preacher named Thomas Chalmers once explained it in a sermon entitled "The Expulsive Power of a New Affection."[62] His Bible text for the sermon was 1 John 2:15—"Do not love the world nor the things in the world. If anyone loves the world, the love of the Father is not in him."

JOHN. Another fact about true Christians, like John 14:15, right?

---

61. Prov. 3:7; 8:13; 16:6; Eccl. 12:13; 2 Cor. 7:1; 1 Pet. 1:17.
62. Thomas Chalmers was a Scottish church reformer and theologian (1780–1847). The text of his sermon is available from a number of online sources.

NICK. That's right. 1 John 2:15 tells us what cannot be true of the person whose predominant affections are for worldly things. He cannot love God.

JOHN. What kinds of worldly things?

NICK. *All* kinds. "The world" is a general reference to the sinful, God-rejecting, evil-approving system that fallen humanity adheres to, and "the things in the world" are the various lusts and pleasures within that system—things like pride, sexual sin, hunger for power or fame, and cravings for money or material things, just to name a few categories of worldliness. The person whose strongest affections are for any of these things does not love God. The two loves are mutually exclusive.

JOHN. You don't mean that a man who often experiences tempting desires for sexual sin doesn't love God, do you?

NICK. No, a man's affections are revealed by how he characteristically *responds* to temptation, not by the mere *presence* of temptation. But the Christian is no longer enslaved to the dictates of his body or helpless in the face of temptation. He has a new authority and power governing his life, and new desires for something much better. He now wants what he never truly wanted before because he sees what he couldn't see before.

JOHN. What couldn't he see before?

NICK. The glory of God in the face of Christ.[63] The unregenerate man simply cannot see Jesus as He really is. Satan has blinded his mind so that worldly ideals and pleasures seem better than Christ.[64] The Christian's God-given ability to see and appreciate Christ sets him free from his former love for the world and its pleasures. Seeing Christ with the eyes of faith, he loves Him above all things, and his new affection

---

63. 2 Cor. 4:4–6; 1 Cor. 2:14.
64. 2 Cor. 4:3.

motivates him to obey Christ consistently. Chalmers demonstrates this point convincingly from 1 John 2:15.

JOHN. How?

NICK. First he explains that it is in the nature of every person to pursue what he deems most valuable. Some people call this the human quest for significance or meaning. For some unregenerate men it is the desire for money or material things; for others, power or fame. For many it is sexual gratification.

JOHN. So what happens when a man is born again?

NICK. It's simple, and the title of Chalmers' sermon explains it. For one affection to be expelled, a stronger affection must take its place. The old affection is literally pushed out.

JOHN. So when a person truly sees Christ and begins to love Him, his love for the world and the things in the world is pushed out?

NICK. Yes. And you already know this to be true. The expulsive power of a new affection is something everyone is familiar with. For example, how could I persuade my dog to give up the old dry bone he's been happily chewing on for days?

JOHN. That's easy: show him a juicy steak.

NICK. That's the point of 1 John 2:15. If a person's strongest affections are for sexual sin, he hasn't seen God. If he had seen Him, his old affection would have been displaced by a much stronger affection. As Jesus said, "No one can serve two masters; for either he will hate the one and love the other, or he will be devoted to one and despise the other."[65]

JOHN. Do all true Christians know the expulsive power of affection for Christ?

---

65. Matt. 6:24.

NICK. Yes. In one sense it is what defines them as Christians. They follow Jesus rather than obeying their fleshly lusts because they find the satisfaction of knowing Him to be better than the satisfaction they formerly gained from sinning. Even though they may not articulate it clearly, they know it by experience. Love for Jesus is the natural product of regeneration, and it *always* displaces the desire for sin as a man's strongest affection.

JOHN. You're talking about my deepest desires, right? This doesn't mean that a true Christian will never feel fleshly desires for sexual sin, does it?

NICK. No, it doesn't mean that. But your love for Christ is the desire that will affect your behavior the most. As Jesus said, "If you love Me, you will keep My commandments."

Let me put all of this in a simple way: if you love Christ at all, which every Christian does, then you can love Him more. And the more you love Him, the less you will desire sexual sin.

(*Short pause as John nods his head thoughtfully.*)

JOHN. Thanks for all your time today. I think it's starting to make sense. When can we get together again?

Questions for Reflection or Discussion

1. List a few reasons why a married man who doesn't love his wife might remain sexually faithful to her. List a few reasons why a man who doesn't love Jesus might maintain an outwardly moral life. Read Matthew 15:1–9. What does this passage tell us about the importance of right motives?

2. Besides the time when you became a Christian, describe a time in your life when a new affection changed your behavior. Did other people notice the change? How does this experience illustrate the principle you learned in this chapter?

3. Before you were born again, how was it evident that you loved the world and the things in the world? In what ways is it evident now that your affection for Christ is pushing out your old affection for the world?

seventeen

Fight **With** the Church and **For** the Church

The most important truths about experiencing freedom from
sexual sin have already been explained, so I won't retrace my steps
in this chapter. But there are two additional principles related to the
pursuit and importance of sexual purity:

- First, rather than fighting sexual sin alone, fight alongside
  others. You are not expected to do this all by yourself. God
  has given you the local church as a context for effective,
  sin-repelling fellowship.

- Second, rather than being self-focused in your battle
  against sexual sin, fight for a greater good. This isn't just
  about your own personal benefit. It's about establishing
  a legacy of freedom for those who will follow in your
  footsteps, and it's about the glory of Christ's kingdom until
  He returns.

Fight *With* the Church

There is something intangible about offending Jesus when you sin.
You know your sin grieves Him because the Bible tells you it does.

But because you cannot see Him with your eyes and you have no observable contact with His expressions of grief, you may not *feel* the seriousness of your sin. You also know that God doesn't hold your sins against you if you are a true believer (Rom. 4:7–8). But because you cannot actually see His outstretched arms of love, you may not always *feel* forgiven.

God has provided a way for you not only to *know*, but also to *feel* both the seriousness of sinning against Christ and the joy of being forgiven. In other words, He has provided a way for you to see and feel the gospel.

The Christian who privately confesses sexual sin to a few brothers in Christ will undoubtedly feel a measure of sadness and shame simply because of the nature of human relationships. No one enjoys admitting an embarrassing failure, and no one wants to disappoint his friends. But a change in behavior that is based solely on these factors has little more virtue in it than a dog's response to obedience training. The Christian has a stronger motivation: when he sees the responses of other Christians to his sin, he comes face to face with Christ's own response to his sin.

True Christians are genuinely grieved when a brother commits immorality, and in their sorrow, perhaps even in their tears, he can see Christ's sorrow and grief. When they labor with him in prayer for true repentance and check back regularly to be sure the sin hasn't been repeated, he can sense Christ's active concern as the "Shepherd and Guardian" of his soul (1 Pet. 2:25). Further, when they forgive and restore him following his genuine repentance (Luke 17:3; Gal. 6:1), they remind him of the gospel of God's grace—the unshakable acceptance and peace with God that is his despite his sin because of Christ's atoning sacrifice.

The Christian who has sinned and who experiences the gospel in these ways will turn away from sexual immorality the way one would turn away from a pool of vomit or a rotting corpse. He will eagerly return to the life of obedience—the only life that satisfies those who truly love Jesus.

Fight *For* the Church

There are many personal reasons for you to resist sexual temptation, but as a Christian you are fighting for a greater good than just your own personal benefit. You are one of many soldiers participating in a cosmic battle against evil—the struggle for the ultimate triumph of Christ's heavenly kingdom. The battle has already been decided, having been won by Christ on the cross, and He is seated on the throne of ultimate power and authority (Matt. 28:18; Eph. 1:19–23). But the Bible also tells us that He must reign "until He has put all His enemies under His feet" (1 Cor. 15:25)— until the last pocket of rebel resistance is destroyed.

Believers are not fighting alone. They are fighting shoulder-to-shoulder with other soldiers for the advance of Christ's glorious kingdom, clearing the spiritual battlefield for future waves of Christ-loving sin killers. Every generation will have difficulties to face, and all believers, whether famous or unknown, are called to participate in this ongoing mop-up operation. As it is in wars with bombs and bullets, so it is in this spiritual battle against the remnants of evil: what the individual soldier does (or fails to do) matters.

Paul described this ever-progressing and united effort in a different way. The church is not only a destroying army with Christ as its King and General, but also a growing and maturing body with Christ as its Head.

> Speaking the truth in love, we are to grow up in all aspects into Him who is the head, even Christ, from whom the whole body, being fitted and held together by what every joint supplies, according to the proper working of each individual part, causes the growth of the body for the building up of itself in love. (Eph. 4:15–16)

Because you are one of the "individual parts" of the body of Christ, your life has a dramatic effect on the other parts and on the whole. Just as your physical body needs every part to function properly, the body of Christ needs "what every joint supplies." It is "held together . . . according to the proper working of each individual part." There are no unnecessary parts. When any single part malfunctions, the whole body suffers. When a part works properly, the whole body prospers and grows.

Christians who are privately caught up in sexual sin are individual body parts that are *not* working properly. The man who is struggling with a habit of viewing pornography may maintain the outward appearance of spiritual health (through church attendance, public prayer, etc.), but his private sin has a deadening effect on his spiritual life. His malfunction may not be immediately noticed by others, but as he goes on gratifying the fleshly lusts that are waging war against his soul, he becomes weaker and weaker. Like a diseased organ in the human body that gradually surrenders its usefulness, the believer who is overcome by sexual sin loses his usefulness to the spiritual body called the church.

Consider the following ways in which your sexual sin will negatively affect other believers and the kingdom of Christ:

- The advance of Christ's kingdom requires prayer (Matt. 6:10), but you will likely enter less often into God's presence because of your disturbed conscience. Even when you do pray, you will be unbalanced in your focus, majoring on your own sin rather than the needs of others, the spread of the gospel, or the well-being of your local church.

- Christ's kingdom grows stronger through your growth in biblical knowledge, your ability to teach others, and your ability to refute false teaching (Eph. 4:11–15), but because every page in the Bible reminds you of your sin, you will likely read it less often.

- Christ's kingdom advances through fellowship and the strengthening of unity (John 17:20–21; Eph. 4:1–3), but you will likely fellowship with other believers less because in their presence you feel secretly ashamed.

- The kingdom of Christ requires perseverance and mutual encouragement (Heb. 3:12–14), but because you are privately discouraged you will encourage others less.

- The kingdom of Christ is a kingdom of purity. Individual Christians must be concerned not only for their own righteous behavior, but also for the godly conduct of other believers (Matt. 18:15–17; 1 Cor. 5). Because of your own sin you will be less eager to be involved in this way in the lives of others.

- The kingdom of Christ grows through evangelism—calling sinners to repentance. But since you need to repent of your sin, you will most likely be less effective in exhorting unbelievers to repent of their sins.

Like the soldier who goes into battle drunk or high on marijuana, you will be distracted from effective participation in the advance of Christ's kingdom. Because of your sinful weakness, others are more likely to suffer and grow weak. On the other hand, your personal spiritual advances will help others to advance spiritually, and will benefit the kingdom of Christ in noticeable ways.

- Your testimony of changed thinking and consistent purity will encourage other men who are now where you were before. Your persistent influence may even result in the salvation of a few unconverted members in your church.

- Your purity will strengthen your assurance of salvation (1 John 3:4–10), which will increase your joy and make you a more effective leader in your home and church. People follow joyful people, but they avoid (or at best, tolerate) those who live in a cloud of discouragement and negativity.

- With an undisturbed conscience you will pray more fervently and effectively, and as James tells us, "the effective prayer of a righteous man can accomplish much" (James 5:16).

- Your increased joy and enthusiasm for Christ will infect your children. Imagine what God might do in the future through one child who, through watching his dad serve Christ with joy, is gripped with a passionate desire to dedicate his life in energetic service to Christ.

- Your uninhibited eagerness to learn from God's word will encourage others to "[increase] in the knowledge of God" (Col. 1:10). In other words, your enthusiasm for truth will serve to make other Christians more battle ready.

- The man who has experienced the joy of freedom from sexual sin will be eager to invite others to enjoy the same freedom. Pornography is perhaps *the* most noteworthy slave-master for millions of unconverted men, but through the zealous efforts of redeemed instruments like you, God can set many of them free.

Wars are never won by individuals, but they are also never won apart from the individual efforts of many people serving faithfully side by side.

Great Britain was nearly overcome by Adolf Hitler's Germany near the beginning of World War II. The pilots of the Royal Air Force are often credited with saving their nation, and their heroic service should not go unnoticed, but it was the heroic service of the entire nation that led to victory. While the pilots fought bravely overhead, old men came out of retirement to work in factories, to fight fires, and to clear away debris. Women picked up hammers, drills, and rifles, and tended to the wounded and dying. Children collected scrap metal and donated metal toys to supply the factories producing bombs and bullets. Every man, woman, and child sacrificed, not only by working through the bombing raids and raging fires, but also by enduring the severe rationing of food, medicine, and other important commodities. Individual efforts varied, but every contribution was crucial to the overall war effort. *Together* they won the battle for their nation.

Your victory over sexual sin is a significant event. It may have generational effects by establishing a legacy of purity for your believing grandson—or perhaps for a great, great grandson whom you will never know. It could even affect the great, great grandson of another man in your church who today is feeling defeated by sexual sin.

Why are some families known for making a spiritual impact in this way, while others are not? At some point in their history, someone turned his back on sin and zealously followed Christ without compromise, and a pattern of faithfulness was established. One man's obedience makes the obedience of those who follow him a more reasonable expectation. You may not be able to look back on such a man in your own family's history, but you ought to be that man for your family's future.

_____

Questions for Reflection or Discussion

1. Have you ever belonged to a local church that was committed to the kind of fellowship described in this chapter? If so, how did that experience affect (or how is it still affecting) your ability to resist sexual temptation? If not, how do you think the lack of gospel fellowship is affecting your own sexual purity?

2. Read Hebrews 3:12–13 carefully. Based on this passage, what would you say to a professing Christian who says he wants to stop viewing pornography, but is unwilling to commit himself to the fellowship and accountability of a local church?

3. We began this book with a conversation between John and Nick. Please go back and re-read that conversation in chapter 1. Now that we have come to the end of the book, discuss how you are better prepared to respond to a man who says, "I've tried and tried to stop viewing pornography, and I'm finally realizing that I don't know how."

ADDITIONAL HELP

Please don't skip over the sections that follow just because they go by the name "appendix." They are not long or overly technical and I believe you will find them helpful. I have provided a brief summary of each one below. If you are doing a small group study, you may want to take additional time to study some (or all) of these together.

Appendix A, "**The Danger of Being Deceived**," is for the man who wonders if what he has read so far reveals that he may not be a true Christian.

Appendix B, "**Is the Regenerate Heart Deceitful and Desperately Sick?**" explains two different meanings of the word "heart" in the Bible, and deals with a few passages that some interpreters would say negate the main point of this book.

Appendix C, "**Abusing the Body Language of the New Testament**," answers a few questions about a Christian's relationship to his unredeemed body and the responsibility for the sins he commits.

Appendix D, "**The Relationship Between Nature and Behavior**," answers three important questions about how what we are by nature relates to what we do.

Appendix E, "**Have Christians Laid Aside the Old Self or Not?**" is a comparison of Paul's teaching on "the old self" and "the new self" in Colossians 3:9–10 and Ephesians 4:22–24.

Appendix F, "**Before Telling Your Wife**," is a caution to the married man. Please read this before confessing sexual sin to your wife.

Appendix G, "**My Personal Story**," is a brief testimony of the author's experience with sexual sin and deliverance.

Appendix A
The Danger of Being Deceived

I have used the term "true Christian" repeatedly in this book, and I have a good reason for doing so: true is the opposite of false, and not everyone who says he is a Christian really is one.

Are you a true Christian? Are you sure about that? If you are sure, are you sure you ought to be sure?

False professions of faith in Christ abound in our day, largely because of the widespread evangelistic practice of giving immediate assurance to new "converts" based solely on their physical, verbal, or emotional response when they hear the gospel. Many pastors and evangelists wrongly assume that converts can be known by their initial enthusiasm, their tears of apparent repentance, or the prayer they prayed to "ask Jesus into their hearts." Jesus, however, plainly taught that these initial *supposed* evidences of conversion are often nothing more than the stirred emotions or temporary zeal of the unregenerate heart, and that a person's conversion is only proved genuine through perseverance and fruitfulness (Matt. 13:3–9, 18–23; Mark 4:3–9, 13–20; Luke 8:4–15).

Assurance Is Ultimately Grounded in God, Not You

The assurance that you belong to Christ is not based on a special prayer or an emotional trip to the front of an auditorium, but it also is not based on perfect moral performance. If it were, then no man could ever be fully assured that he is a true Christian because no man will ever be perfect in this life. Every sin would lead to fear and doubt, and this should not be the case. True Christians should enjoy the strong confidence that they belong to Christ forever, despite the fact that they have fleshly desires and still find themselves sinning at times.

The confidence that you are a true Christian is based first and foremost on the promises of God and the redemptive work of Jesus Christ. His righteous life and sacrificial death fully accomplished the salvation of all who believe. Their sins are *all* forgiven, even the ones they commit as Christians (1 John 1:7, 9; 2:12). The salvation enjoyed by all true Christians is by God's grace through faith alone, not through works.

But Assurance Without Regeneration Is Deception

Despite the fact that God's promises are the ground of assurance, the New Testament is filled with warnings to those who practice unrighteousness yet are *sure* they are Christians.

> Do not be deceived; neither fornicators, . . . nor adulterers, . . . nor homosexuals, . . . will inherit the kingdom of God. (1 Cor. 6:9–10)

> Now the deeds of the flesh are evident, which are: immorality [fornication], impurity, sensuality, idolatry, . . . and things like these, of which I forewarn you, just as I have forewarned you, that those who practice such things will not inherit the kingdom of God. (Gal. 5:19–21)

> For this you know with certainty, that no immoral . . . person [fornicator] . . . has an inheritance in the kingdom of Christ and God. (Eph. 5:5)

> Fornicators and adulterers God will judge. (Heb. 13:4)

By this we know that we have come to know Him, if we keep His commandments. The one who says, "I have come to know Him," and does not keep His commandments, is a liar, and the truth is not in him. (1 John 2:3–4)

No one who is born of God practices sin, because His seed abides in him; and he cannot sin [i.e., as a matter of practice], because he is born of God. By this the children of God and the children of the devil are obvious: anyone who does not practice righteousness is not of God, nor the one who does not love his brother. (1 John 3:9–10)

These warnings inform us that repentance from sin and a pattern of righteous behavior serve as necessary supports for the assurance that you belong to Christ. The man who thinks of himself as forgiven must look for evidence that he has been born again. Because of the Spirit's transforming work (regeneration) in all those whom God forgives (justification), deliverance from the penalty for sin and from the power of sin are always found together. If you have not been set free from sin's power, you have not been saved from its penalty.

Paul wrote to the Corinthians, some of whom were still engaging in "impurity, immorality [fornication] and sensuality" (2 Cor. 12:21), "Test yourselves to see if you are in the faith; examine yourselves! Or do you not recognize this about yourselves, that Jesus Christ is in you—unless indeed you fail the test?" (2 Cor. 13:5). Clearly Paul thought that the Corinthians' habitual sin gave him sufficient grounds to ask whether or not these professing Christians were true Christians.

Take This Seriously: Deception Ends in Hell
Many professing Christians seem to have the idea that God's free grace permits them to live morally compromising lives. If they do not realize their error and repent, they will one day be reminded of Jesus' words in the Sermon on the Mount: "Not everyone who says to Me, 'Lord, Lord,' will enter the kingdom of heaven, but he who does the will of My Father who is in heaven will enter" (Matt. 7:21). Though they expected to be welcomed into heaven, Jesus will say to them, "I never knew you; depart from Me, you who practice lawlessness" (Matt. 7:23).

Unrepentant fornicators and adulterers will spend eternity in "the lake that burns with fire and brimstone, which is the second death" (Rev. 21:8). Many are already suffering in everlasting anguish. When you look at pornography, you are committing the very sin by which many of them were overcome—the sin they now wish they had never committed. Millions who were professing Christians are now suffering under the everlasting wrath of God. Will you continue practicing the same sexual sins that led them to hell, or will you seize the opportunity you now have to repent?

Do not be deceived; neither fornicators, nor idolaters, nor adulterers, nor effeminate, nor homosexuals, nor thieves, nor the covetous, nor drunkards, nor revilers, nor swindlers, will inherit the kingdom of God. (1 Cor. 6:9–10)[66]

---

66. *Wasted Faith* by Jim Elliff is an excellent tool for self-examination. This book (or audio book) may be ordered at www.CCWtoday.org. A helpful online study guide for *Wasted Faith* is also available at that address.

Appendix B

Is the Regenerate Heart Deceitful and Desperately Sick?

Once in the book of Jeremiah and again in Mark's gospel (with a parallel passage in Matthew), the human heart is described in negative terms. Many interpreters understand these passages to be descriptive of *every* human heart, including the regenerate heart of the Christian. I once held this understanding myself, but I am now convinced that only the natural (i.e., unregenerate) heart of man is in view in these places.

Before we discuss these passages, we should note that the word "heart" is used in at least two ways in the Bible.

In many places the word "heart" refers to a man's inner thoughts (or his mind) in contrast to his outward actions. When Jesus said that a man who lusts after a woman has already committed adultery with her "in his heart" (Matt. 5:28), He was simply saying that adultery can be committed secretly in the mind even when no physical contact occurs. When Mary heard the shepherds' account of the angels singing "Glory to God in the highest" (Luke 2:14), she pondered these things "in her heart" (Luke 2:19). This simply means she thought about what she had heard.

In other places, the word "heart" refers to man's spiritual control center—the part of him that governs his mind and directs his thoughts. I referred to it earlier as a man's "wanter." This is what the word "heart" means in the Bible whenever regeneration is the subject, or when the nature of a man's heart (whether good or evil) is being discussed.

> Moreover, I will give you a new heart and put a new spirit within you; and I will remove the heart of stone from your flesh and give you a heart of flesh. (Ezek. 36:26; cf. Deut. 30:6; Jer. 9:25–26; Rom. 2:28–29)

> Blessed are the pure in heart, for they shall see God. (Matt. 5:8)

> The good man out of the good treasure of his heart brings forth what is good; and the evil man out of the evil treasure brings forth what is evil. (Luke 6:45; cf. Matt. 12:34–35)

Now that we have seen how the Bible uses the word "heart," we are prepared to discuss the meaning of two passages that affect our understanding of the nature of the regenerate heart.

Jeremiah 17:9–10

> The heart is more deceitful than all else
> And is desperately sick;
> Who can understand it?
> I, the Lord, search the heart,
> I test the mind,
> Even to give to each man according to his ways,
> According to the results of his deeds. (Jer. 17:9–10)

It is one thing to admit that a man who is "pure in heart" (Matt. 5:8) might tell a lie in a moment of weakness. It is another thing altogether to say that his new heart is "deceitful." The spiritual center of a person's being cannot be "honest and good" (Luke 8:15) and "pure" (Matt. 5:8) and at the same time "more deceitful than all else" and "desperately sick" (Jer. 17:9). These terms contradict each other too strongly to be describing the same thing.

We should notice that Jeremiah 17:9 is found in a passage where a contrast has been drawn between the curses that will fall upon the man "whose heart turns away from the Lord" (i.e., the unbeliever; 17:5) and the blessing that comes to the man "whose trust is in the Lord" (i.e., the believer; 17:7). In other words, Jeremiah has described the heart of the unbeliever and that of the believer in opposing terms: the unbeliever's heart is oriented away from God, but the believer trusts in the Lord. Verse 9 logically follows this contrast only if Jeremiah was referring to the human heart in its natural condition (i.e., unregenerate) when he described it as "more deceitful than all else" and "desperately sick."

Jeremiah's main point in verses 9–10 is that only the Lord can see and accurately evaluate man's heart. Verse 10 even implies that He *will* see a difference between one person's heart and another, and will judge each person on the basis of the behavior that flows from the heart. But the need for God to see and judge in this way becomes irrelevant if every human heart conforms to the negative portrayal of verse 9. If all hearts are the same, all will be judged the same. Clearly not all human hearts are alike, however, as Jeremiah has already specified in verses 5–8. God recognizes this difference and judges men accordingly.

In this way Jeremiah 17:9–10 is similar to 1 Samuel 16:6–7, where Samuel is preparing to anoint a new king from among the sons of a man named Jesse. Samuel first notices the son named Eliab and thinks, "Surely the Lord's anointed is before Him" (16:6). Apparently Eliab was impressive in his outward appearance and had what it took to be king, or so Samuel thought.

> But the Lord said to Samuel, "Do not look at his appearance or at the height of his stature, because I have rejected him; for God sees not as man sees, for man looks at the outward appearance, but the Lord looks at the heart." (16:7)

The Lord directed Samuel to anoint David (16:12), Eliab's younger brother whom God Himself described elsewhere as "a man after My heart, who will do all My will" (Acts 13:22; cf. 1 Sam. 13:14).

God rejected Eliab and chose David on the basis of what He saw in their hearts. David's heart reflected the Lord's character and was inclined to obey Him, so it cannot be proper to describe his heart (or the heart of any true believer) as "more deceitful than all else" and "desperately sick."

Mark 7:20–23

> That which proceeds out of the man, that is what defiles the man. For from within, out of the heart of men, proceed the evil thoughts, fornications, thefts, murders, adulteries, deeds of coveting and wickedness, as well as deceit, sensuality, envy, slander, pride and foolishness. All these evil things proceed from within and defile the man. (Mark 7:20–23)

It is true that regenerate people are capable of committing any of these sins, but is the regenerate heart the source of sin in the believer just as the unregenerate heart is the source of sin in the unbeliever? In evaluating this question it will first be helpful to see the overall point Jesus was making.

Jesus' statement followed a question from some Pharisees and scribes who asked, "Why do Your disciples not walk according to the tradition of the elders, but eat their bread with impure hands?" (7:5). After rebuking the Pharisees for upholding their ritual purification traditions while disregarding God's commandments (7:6–13), Jesus explained to a crowd of listeners that "there is nothing outside the man which can defile him if it goes into him, but the things which proceed out of the man are what defile the man" (7:15). Later, in private with his disciples, He made the statement recorded in verses 20–23. His purpose wasn't to say all that can be said about the heart or nature of men. He was simply exposing the fallacy of the notion that ritual cleanliness equates with genuine purity. What a man eats has no moral consequence because it does not affect his heart. It simply passes through his digestive system and is expelled (7:19). A man is defiled by the things that proceed out of his heart.

In this context Jesus could have been using the term "heart" in one of three ways:

1. He could have been referring to a man's mind or inner thoughts (as "heart" is used in places like Matthew 5:28 and Luke 2:19).

2. He could have been describing *every* person's spiritual control center (i.e., the heart whether unregenerate or regenerate).

3. He could have been describing man's spiritual control center in its natural condition (i.e., the unregenerate heart).

If the first option is correct, then nothing Jesus said here would conflict with statements He made elsewhere about the goodness and purity of the regenerate heart. Even a man with a regenerate heart can think and behave sinfully at times.

The second option is how many interpreters understand this passage—as a generic reference to man's spiritual control center whether regenerate or unregenerate. As I will explain below, this interpretation fails to account for contextual factors in Mark 7, and it is inconsistent with the way Jesus' distinguishes between unregenerate and regenerate hearts elsewhere.

I lean toward the third option because Jesus' intent was to expose the hypocrisy of the unregenerate Jewish leaders. They were the ones whose hearts were far from God (7:6; cf. Jeremiah 17:5) and whose worship was in vain (7:7). Rather than making themselves pure through external morality and cleansing rituals, they were defiled by what their corrupt hearts were producing (7:20–23).

Jesus' portrayal of the Pharisees' hearts in Mark 7:20–23 is much like His description of the same group of men in Matthew 23:27:

> Woe to you, scribes, Pharisees, hypocrites! For you are like whitewashed tombs which on the outside appear beautiful, but inside they are full of dead men's bones and all uncleanness.

It would be an obvious interpretive mistake to liken the regenerate man to a whitewashed tomb—beautiful on the outside but corrupt on the inside. After all, Jesus' point in Matthew 23:27 was that the unregenerate Jews' outward display of morality was repulsive to God because it served as a mask to hide their inner corruption. As Jesus said to them elsewhere, "You are those who justify yourselves in the sight of men, but God knows your hearts" (Luke 16:15). Applying the "whitewashed tomb" metaphor or the words of Luke 16:15 to the regenerate man, however, would be no greater an error than including the regenerate heart in the meaning of Mark 7:20–23.

When Jesus said evil proceeds "out of the heart of men" (7:21), He was explaining the natural human condition by listing the natural product of the unregenerate heart. The Pharisees considered themselves better than all other men because of circumcision, possession of the Law of Moses, and ritual purity (Rom. 2:17–29; Luke 18:11–12). But because they were unregenerate, they were spiritually no different than the rest of fallen mankind as described in Genesis 6:5—"every intent of the thoughts of his heart was only evil continually." This ancient description of the natural man's heart is parallel with Jesus' description of what proceeds "out of the heart of men" (Mark 7:21). The point of both passages is to say that the natural human heart produces evil, not good.

We know that the regenerate man is not included in the otherwise universal description of mankind in Genesis 6:5 because a few verses later (6:9) Noah is described as "a righteous man, blameless in his time." Genesis 6:5 and 6:9 simply cannot describe the same man at the same time. In the same way, it is inconsistent with the rest of the New Testament to see Mark 7:20–23 (or the parallel passage in Matthew 15:18–20) as a description of the regenerate heart, which Jesus describes in positive terms elsewhere. A person's heart cannot be the source of "deceit" (Mark 7:22) while at the same time being "honest and good" (Luke 8:15). A man's heart cannot be the fountainhead of sins like adultery and murder (Mark 7:21) while at the same time being "pure" (Matt. 5:8). As James asks rhetorically, "Does a fountain send out from the same opening both fresh and bitter water?" (James 3:11). Even the simplest understanding of language tells us that two opposing descriptions of the human heart cannot describe the same person's heart. Take one last look at this important distinction in Jesus' teaching by directly comparing Mark 7:21–23 with Luke 6:45.

For from within, out of the heart of men, proceed the evil
thoughts, fornications, thefts, murders, adulteries, deeds
of coveting and wickedness, as well as deceit, sensuality,
envy, slander, pride and foolishness. All these evil things
proceed from within and defile the man. (Mark 7:21–23)

The good man out of the good treasure of his heart
brings forth what is good; and the evil man out of the evil
treasure [of his heart] brings forth what is evil. (Luke 6:45)

Mark 7:21–23 is obviously parallel with the second part of Luke
6:45, but it cannot describe the same "heart" that is described in the
first part of Luke 6:45. Jesus' whole point in the first part of Luke
6:45 is to say that good on the inside is the source of good, not evil,
on the outside.

But Didn't Jesus Call Christians "Evil"?

In Matthew 7:7–11 Jesus compares man's natural generosity with
God's divine goodness. He says to his listeners, "If you then, being
evil, know how to give good gifts to your children, how much
more will your Father who is in heaven give what is good to those
who ask Him?" (7:11). Because Jesus delivered this sermon to His
"disciples" (Matt. 5:1–2), some interpreters have concluded that
He was calling His own true followers "evil." Two considerations,
however, argue against this assumption:

1. Many (if not most) of the people to whom Jesus was
    speaking were "disciples" only in the broadest sense
    of the word: they were "learners" but not necessarily
    committed followers. Jesus' message in Matthew 5–7 is
    largely evangelistic. In 7:13–14, immediately following His
    comment about His listeners being "evil," Jesus exhorts the
    crowd to choose the narrow way that leads to life and shun
    the broad way that leads to destruction. In 7:21–23 He
    warns them that not everyone who calls Him "Lord" will
    enter the kingdom of heaven. In 7:24–27 He cautions His
    hearers not to hear only, but also to act upon His words in
    order to avoid destruction. When Jesus asks in Matthew
    7:9, "What man is there among you [who would not give
    his son good things]?" His point is that even a fallen man's

natural inclination is to give good things, not cruel things, when one of his children asks for a gift. When Jesus refers to His listeners as "evil" in verse 11, He is contrasting the natural human condition (i.e., unregenerate and therefore evil) with the good nature and character of God. But He never implies that the regenerate man remains "evil" by nature in the same way that unbelievers are "evil" by nature.

2.   In Matthew 12:34–35 Jesus addresses a group of Pharisees, and once again He calls His listeners "evil." But this time He makes it clear that He is referring to the unregenerate person by contrasting the evil man with the good man.

> You brood of vipers, how can you, being evil, speak what is good? For the mouth speaks out of that which fills the heart. The good man brings out of his good treasure what is good; and the evil man brings out of his evil treasure what is evil.

Just as there is a difference in nature between a good tree and a bad tree (Matt. 12:33; cf. 7:15–20; Luke 6:43–44), there is a difference in nature between a regenerate man and an unregenerate man (Matt. 12:34–35; Luke 6:45). Jesus only refers to one category of man as "evil," while the other He calls "good."

Appendix C

Abusing the Body Language of the New Testament

With what you now know about the sinful passions that remain in your unredeemed body, you might be tempted to conclude that your body is guilty of sinning while you remain blameless. Some have even drawn this conclusion from a faulty understanding of Romans 7:17—"So now, no longer am I the one doing it, but sin which dwells in me."

Your body is part of you. It is the physical instrument through which you experience everything you experience, and by which you do everything you do, whether good or evil. It is your point of contact with the physical world whether you are sinning or practicing righteousness.

It would be ridiculous for a man to say, "My body really enjoyed that meal," as though his body were somehow distinct from the rest of him. Instead he says, "I really enjoyed that meal." Likewise, there is no biblical basis for the Christian to say, "My body looked at pornography last night," as though his body were somehow guilty while he remained blameless. What he should say is, "I gave in to the passions of my body. I looked at pornography last night. I sinned."

Christians are "putting to death the deeds of the body," but the Bible never tells us that the body commits sin on its own, that it has a will of its own, or that it is inherently evil. You are tempted to sin because of the passions that remain in your unredeemed body (along with Satan's clever ways of appealing to your fleshly lusts). You commit sin by means of your body. But you are fully responsible for the sins you commit.

Here are four facts to remember about you, your body, and your sin:

1. You have a new heart that is pure and good—a new spiritual nature that is inclined toward righteousness rather than sin. This new creation is who you really are.

2. The sinful passions that remain in you are the passions and desires of your unredeemed body (i.e., your fleshly lusts). They do not find their source in your new heart.

3. Your heart loves righteousness and your body lusts for sin, but you are not a divided man. Your new heart and your unredeemed body are both parts of your one identity as a person.

4. Your unredeemed body is the source of your sinful desires, but you may not blame your body for your sin. You (as a whole person) sin when you fail to resist your fleshly lusts.

Appendix D

The Relationship Between Nature and Behavior

Three important questions often arise in discussions about the relationship between a person's nature and his behavior.

Question #1: Jesus said, "A good tree cannot produce bad fruit" (Matt. 7:18). If the "good tree" is the Christian, and the "bad fruit" is sin, why should we not conclude that Christians are incapable of sinning?

Answer: First we should note that Jesus used the "good tree/bad fruit" principle to refer specifically to false prophets (Matt. 7:15–20). But because the principle itself is unarguable and universal, it correctly illustrates the difference between *all* unbelievers and *all* believers. Jesus used the same illustration in Luke 6:43–45 without linking it specifically to false prophets.

Second, Jesus' illustration dealt with kind, not quality. He didn't contrast good grapes with bad grapes or good figs with bad figs. He contrasted grapes with thorns and figs with thistles—different kinds of fruit produced by different kinds of plants. As He explained in verses 16–17, "Grapes are not gathered from thorn bushes nor figs from thistles, are they? So every good tree bears good fruit [i.e., grapes or figs], but the bad tree bears bad fruit [i.e., thorns or thistles]." The point of the illustration is simple: people, like trees, produce what accords with their nature. "You will know them by their fruits" (7:16, 20).

Third (and most important), this was a whole-harvest illustration, not a small-sample illustration. Jesus was describing the harvest of a crop, not the inspection of an individual piece of fruit (note the word "gathered" in verse 16). The illustration describes the kind of crop a farmer should expect to gather when he goes into a particular field at the time of the harvest. When he goes into a vineyard, he rightly expects to gather grapes. If he goes into a briar patch, he should expect to find thorns. The illustration does not picture a farmer scouring his vineyard to see if he can find a single bad grape—or even a thorn—growing on one of his vines.

Another clue that this is a whole-harvest illustration and not a small-sample illustration is found in the passage that follows (7:21–23):

> Not everyone who says to Me, "Lord, Lord," will enter the kingdom of heaven, but he who does the will of My Father who is in heaven will enter. Many will say to Me on that day, "Lord, Lord, did we not prophesy in Your name, and in Your name cast out demons, and in Your name perform many miracles?" And then I will declare to them, "I never knew you; depart from Me, you who practice lawlessness."

Without explaining what "day" He is speaking of, Jesus says, "Many will say to Me on that day . . ." Given the harvest illustration that immediately precedes this passage, it is not difficult to discern that Jesus is speaking here about the final "harvest" of souls—the day of judgment. The clue that the overall passage was a whole-harvest illustration rather than a small-sample illustration appears when Jesus tells some to depart from Him because they "practice lawlessness" (i.e., sin as a matter of consistent practice). These are not righteous people whose behavior was imperfect. They are people who are known as sinners by the overall product of their lives.

To appeal to the good tree/bad fruit illustration as proof that a person with a good nature (i.e., a Christian) never sins would be stretching the illustration beyond its purpose. The simple point Jesus was making was that a person's nature can be known by the kind of behavior he typically exhibits—by the moral "harvest" of his life. The regenerate man may sin, but he will not be known for sinning. Instead, because he has a good nature he will be known for righteous living. This direct relationship between nature and patterns of behavior is spoken about elsewhere in the Bible:

> No one who is born of God practices sin, because His seed abides in him; and he cannot sin [i.e., sin habitually, or as a matter of practice], because he is born of God. By this the children of God and the children of the devil are obvious: anyone who does not practice righteousness is not of God, nor the one who does not love his brother. (1 John 3:9-10)

John clearly is not saying that a Christian *never* sins. We know this because earlier in the same letter he admitted that a Christian *can* sin:

> My little children, I am writing these things to you so that you may not sin. And if anyone [of you] sins, we have an Advocate with the Father, Jesus Christ the righteous; and He Himself is the propitiation for our sins. (1 John 2:1–2a)

The Christian certainly can sin, but it is not consistent with his new nature to sin any more than it is consistent with the nature of a grape vine to produce thorns. Even when the Christian does sin, he is forgiven because of Christ's sacrifice.

Question #2: Since Christians sometimes sin, and since a person's behavior is a reflection of his nature, why should we not conclude that the Christian's new nature is at least partially corrupt, or that he has two natures, one good and one evil?

Answer: Behavior doesn't always reflect nature perfectly. Genesis 1:31 tells us that all God created was "very good," but Adam still sinned. If behavior is always a perfect reflection of nature, we would be forced to conclude that the original creation was at least partially corrupt (which everyone should agree was not the case). We learn from Adam's example that evil can come from something that is "very good" by nature. We also read in the Bible that King Nebuchadnezzar acted like a cow for seven years (Dan. 4:33), but we would be wrong to conclude that he had the nature of a cow during that time period (or that he was part cow and part human). His example simply demonstrates that a human being is capable of acting like an animal—in other words, below his nature.

Pigs never fly because they cannot fly. Flying is not in their nature. Eagles, on the other hand, were designed to soar above the earth, and that is what they typically do. It would not be impossible for an eagle to wallow in a mud puddle like a pig, but if you were to see an eagle doing this you would be wrong to conclude that the eagle had the same nature as the pig (or that he was part eagle and part pig). Wallowing in the mud is within the eagle's capabilities, but it is not normal or natural behavior. It is below his nature.

Likewise, the Christian is able to sin because his new nature exists in an unredeemed body, but sin is not what he was re-created to do. It is not what he does "by nature." The fact that he sins doesn't prove that his nature is evil, or partly evil, or that he has two natures, one evil and one good. When a Christian sins he is acting in a way that is *below* his new nature, in a manner that is uncharacteristic of his new identity.

Many Christians have been taught to describe "the flesh" as the Christian's sinful nature or "sin nature." According to this teaching, the good nature created by God in regeneration exists in conjunction with a second "nature"—the believer's unredeemed mortal body with its fleshly inclinations. The word "flesh" does refer to the unredeemed human body, but it is not helpful to describe this physical (or fleshly) aspect of the Christian as his second nature or his "sin nature."

The Bible never explicitly uses two-nature terminology with respect to the Christian. Even though this two-nature description of the regenerate man is the logical result of combining biblical realities (i.e., the good heart and the flesh, both of which do exist in him), it is more biblical to speak of the believer as having only one *good* nature. In His good tree/bad tree illustrations (Matt. 7:15–20; 12:33–35; Luke 6:43–45), Jesus described men as either good by nature or evil by nature, never suggesting that the Christian possesses both natures at the same time.

I understand that there is a sense in which it is reasonable to describe the believer as having two natures. The debate as I have described it is over terminology more than theology. But as I said in chapter 10, terminology is important and influential. In the end, what better example could we look to when deciding what words to use to describe ourselves and other believers than the teaching of Christ Himself?

Question #3: If the regenerate person is capable of sinning even though his nature is good, doesn't that mean that the unregenerate person is capable of righteous behavior even though his nature is evil?

Answer: No, it doesn't mean that. When Jesus said, "The evil man brings out of his evil treasure what is evil" (Matt. 12:35; Luke 6:45), He was saying that *only* evil comes from the unregenerate heart. The regenerate man is good by nature but is sometimes dragged downward by the moral gravity of his fleshly lusts. The unregenerate man is evil by nature but he has nothing to pull him upward. Nothing within him can produce the ability to submit to God in obedience. Paul strongly affirmed this in Romans 8:7–8:

> The mind set on the flesh is hostile toward God; for it does not subject itself to the law of God, for it is not even able to do so, and those who are in the flesh [i.e., those who are unregenerate and under the control of their fleshly lusts] cannot please God.

Appendix E

Have Christians Laid Aside the Old Self or Not?

The "old self" (lit. "old man") is mentioned three times in the New Testament: Romans 6:6, Colossians 3:9, and Ephesians 4:22–24. Two of these passages are the subject of an in-house debate among Christians. The debate centers around this question: have Christians already laid aside the old self and put on the new self, or is laying aside the old self and putting on the new self something they still need to do?

First it will be helpful to compare these two references to the "old self" and "new self" in their contexts. I have italicized the pertinent words and phrases for easier comparison.

> So this I say, and affirm together with the Lord, that you walk no longer just as the Gentiles also walk, in the futility of their mind, being darkened in their understanding, excluded from the life of God because of the ignorance that is in them, because of the hardness of their heart; and they, having become callous, have given themselves over to sensuality for the practice of every kind of impurity with greediness. But you did not learn Christ in this way, if indeed you have heard Him and have been taught in Him,

just as truth is in Jesus, that, in reference to your former manner of life, you *lay aside the old self*, which is being corrupted in accordance with the lusts of deceit, and that you be renewed in the spirit of your mind, and *put on the new self*, which in the likeness of God has been created in righteousness and holiness of the truth. (Eph. 4:17–24)

Therefore consider the members of your earthly body as dead to immorality, impurity, passion, evil desire, and greed, which amounts to idolatry. For it is because of these things that the wrath of God will come upon the sons of disobedience, and in them you also once walked, when you were living in them. But now you also, put them all aside: anger, wrath, malice, slander, and abusive speech from your mouth. Do not lie to one another, since you *laid aside the old self* with its evil practices, and *have put on the new self* who is being renewed to a true knowledge according to the image of the One who created him. (Col. 3:5–10)

The Anatomy of the Disagreement

In Colossians 3:9 Paul describes laying aside the old self and putting on the new self as something Christians have already done. In Ephesians 4:22–24 he seems to instruct Christians to lay aside the old self and put on the new self as though both still need to be done. I believe Paul is saying the same thing in both places, using two different approaches to remind his readers of their conversion.

Why a Parallel Interpretation Makes More Sense

Paul begins both passages by reminding his believing readers that they should no longer live like unconverted people—like they lived before they became Christians (Eph. 4:17–19; Col. 3:5–9a). His basis for exhorting the Colossians in this way is the fact that they "laid aside the old self" and "have put on the new self."

Paul's exhortation in Ephesians depends upon the same fact, but rather than simply referring to his readers' conversion in the past tense (as he did in Colossians 3:9), he describes it from the perspective of a person who is being taught what it means to become a Christian in the first place. In other words, he reminds them that part of the body of introductory Christian doctrine is the exhortation to "lay aside the old self" and "put on the new self."

Contrasting the behavior he expects of Christians with the way unconverted people behave, Paul says, "But you did not learn Christ in this way" (4:20). His point is to say, "The basis I have for telling you not to go on living like unconverted people is the fact that you were taught differently from the very beginning. You did not 'learn Christ' in a manner that would permit you to go on living like the rest of the world."

In verses 22–24 (the controversial part of the passage), Paul switches from his negative expression about "learning Christ" (i.e., "you did not learn Christ" in a way that permits corrupt living) to a positive description of what they were actually taught:

> [At that time you were taught] that, in reference to your former manner of life, you lay aside the old self, which is being corrupted in accordance with the lusts of deceit, and that you be renewed in the spirit of your mind, and put on the new self, which in the likeness of God has been created in righteousness and holiness of the truth. (4:22–24)

The words I placed in brackets are not in the text, but they are implied, as the New English Translation's rendition of verses 20-24 indicates:

> But you did not learn about Christ like this, if indeed you heard about him and were taught in him, just as the truth is in Jesus. You were taught with reference to your former way of life to lay aside the old man who is being corrupted in accordance with deceitful desires, to be renewed in the spirit of your mind, and to put on the new man who has been created in God's image—in righteousness and holiness that comes from truth.[67]

As this translation reflects, Paul reminds his readers that *when they became Christians* they were taught to lay aside the old self and put

---

67. The NET Bible, New English Translation, 2nd Beta Edition (Biblical Studies Press, L.L.C., 1996-2003), 2147.

on the new self. Based on the implication that as true believers they had already done what they were taught to do, he exhorts them to continue behaving according to their new nature and identity.

Even if I am wrong—even if Paul was exhorting Christians to "lay aside the old self" and "put on the new self" in their present situation rather than reminding them that they did this when they became Christians—the Bible's basic instruction to the Christian remains the same: be who you really are (your new self), not who you were (your old self).

Your old self is not a part of your new person. He does not need to be resisted, restrained, renounced, or put to death, because he is already dead, having been crucified with Christ (Rom. 6:6; cf. 2 Cor. 5:14–15; Gal. 2:20; Col. 3:3). He no longer exists. To "lay aside the old self" is not to get rid of him, but rather to stop thinking and acting like he did when he was alive.

The flesh, on the other hand, will be an active presence in every Christian's life until "the redemption of our body" (Rom. 8:23). We know the flesh is active because the Bible tells us that it "sets its desire against the Spirit" and tempts believers to gratify its passions (Gal. 5:16–17; Rom. 8:11–12). It no longer enslaves us, but it still troubles us.[68]

A man might go by two different names, but he cannot be two different people at the same time. Because of the ongoing influence of your flesh you undoubtedly think and act like your old self at times, but it is no more possible for your old self to exist alongside your new self than it is for you to be unregenerate and regenerate at the same time.

---

68. When Paul said, "Those who belong to Christ Jesus have crucified the flesh with its passions and desires" (Gal. 5:24), he was not using the word "crucified" to signal the death of the flesh. He used "crucified" in Galatians 5:24 the way he used the same word in Galatians 6:14, to describe the severing of loyalty or allegiance.

Appendix F

Before Telling Your Wife

If you are married yet have been overcome by a habit of viewing pornography, it is possible that your wife knows little or nothing about your pattern of sexual sin. If this is the case, I would strongly suggest that you consult with a pastor before confessing your sin to her. A wise and experienced Christian can help you discern how best to address this matter with your wife, and in what degree of detail. It is usually best for confession in this area to be somewhat generalized, that is, you may wish to avoid many (if not most) of the details.

A truly repentant man will want to confess his sins, but he may cause further harm to his marriage by spewing out a detailed confession of his sordid behavior. Your wife may think she needs to know all of these details, but in the end she will not be helped by having a collage of images in her mind as a result of your vivid descriptions of repeated sinful acts. It is generally sufficient for her to know that you have sinned sexually, that you are repentant and seeking her forgiveness, that you are being held strictly accountable by godly men in your church, and that you have come to understand that sexual sin is inconsistent with who you really are in Christ.

A wise pastor will also be able to help your wife, through the counsel of a godly woman (or women) in the church, to deal with issues of forgiveness and reconciliation. You may be ashamed to know that other ladies in your church are aware of your sin, but your wife may not be able to bear this burden alone. Many wives need godly female companionship and counsel to help them through their pain.

If your sexual sin involved physical contact with another person, confession in greater detail is necessary. Your wife will likely request that you submit yourself to a medical examination to check for sexually transmitted diseases. Given all of the serious and even deadly diseases that are shared through illicit sex, you have a moral obligation to cooperate with this request—or better yet, to submit to an examination before she requests it.

Appendix G
My Personal Story

I know what it is like to be where many readers of this book are right now—practicing habitual sexual sin as an unbeliever or fighting a frustrating battle against the same enemy as a believer. But as a man who has been delivered by God's grace from slavery to sexual sin, I also know what it is like to walk in freedom.

I was exposed to pornographic magazines when I was twelve years old. In the heart of a boy who thought he was a Christian because of a prayer he had prayed, yet who knew nothing of the reality of regeneration or the power of love for Christ, the floodgates of sexual sin were flung wide open. For the next twenty-five years, through most of my career as a deputy sheriff and the first fourteen years of my marriage, I lived as an unconverted church member and a slave to sexual sin. I was thirty-five years old when God opened my eyes to the gospel and give me a heart of love for His Son.

I never returned to viewing pornography, but for several years after my conversion my struggle with sexual temptation was fierce and depressing. I knew I was in Christ, but since I didn't really know who I was in Christ or the complete story of what happened when I was born again, I relied more on personal resolve than on the Spirit of God or the encouraging truth about regeneration and deliverance. Because of my ignorance, I rarely experienced the joy that should accompany freedom from sin. Those were difficult years, and in some ways, wasted years.

I don't claim to be immune to sexual temptation even now. I still have to think through the lies and work hard to refute them with truth. I still have to run away from sexual temptation in my thoughts and in my day-to-day living in order to avoid sinning. I must still depend on God to protect me from Satan's schemes. If I fail to live thoughtfully and dependently in these ways, I can commit sexual sin just as readily as the next Christian.

My experience won't be exactly the same as yours, but I hope you will avoid a similar (or even worse) experience than mine by understanding these encouraging truths better than I did, sooner than I did. God was gracious to reveal them to me over the past few years as I studied and taught through Paul's letter to the Romans, and as I read a few excellent books.[69] Since understanding these things, I have become better equipped to help other men, not just to resist temptation dutifully, but to enjoy their freedom from sexual sin.

---

69. Most notably, *Justification and Regeneration*, by Charles Leiter (Hannibal: Granted Ministries Press, 2009), and *Christian Take Heart*, by Tom Wells (Carlisle: Banner of Truth Trust, 1987).

Please visit our web sites:

www.CCWtoday.org
This is our main site, with numerous articles, ministry tools, audio messages, and information about ordering our publications.

www.CCWblog.org
This blog showcases pertinent articles from all our sites on a weekly basis, and provides an opportunity for interaction with our writers.

www.BulletinInserts.org
This site provides timely and instructive bulletin inserts, handouts, and tracts. We offer free, downloadable inserts (also available in A4) for every Sunday of the year.

www.WaytoGod.org
This site contains articles and audio designed to guide interested people into a relationship with Jesus Christ. Here we also answer questions from inquirers.